Aurora's Edge

Book One of the Aurora's Edge Series

Dane Reavers

A Space Age Adventure: Sabotage

Aurora's Edge

Book One of the Aurora's Edge Series

A Space Age Adventure: Sabotage

Published by Chronos Press | Beaverton, Oregon **www.danereavers.com**

Cover Design by: Reece-Allexander Norris-Paterson **Author Photo by:** Executive Lens Headshots **Developmental Edits by:** Lucy Benedict **Line & Copy Edits by:** Marnie Macrae

ISBN (Paperback): 979-8-9946373-1-9

ISBN (Hardcover): 979-8-9946373-2-6

ISBN (Ebook): 979-8-9946373-0-2

First Edition: **March 2026**

For Carolina, Ephraim, and Morgan.
To the artist, the stargazer, and the maker: Never let the math—or the world—tell you what you aren't capable of.
You are the proof that everything worth having is built with heart and grit.
And to the dreamers, the thinkers, and the creative spirits out there: This one is for you.
May you always find the tools you need to build your own universe.

Chapter One

2425, EARTH

New Geneva, the jewel of the Allied Planets, hung above the shadowed guts of the Dredges like a gleaming Elysium. The metal-slatted faux sky that split the two worlds cast its silent taunt down onto the grime-choked underbelly below.

The neon lights of the cracked, ruined alleyways flickered like dying stars, casting sickly shadows of green and purple across the darkened brick and concrete of the under-city. A rumbling hum of industry permeated the air in an unending cacophony, a constant reminder of the dismal inevitability of cheap labor that fed the utopian ideals that loomed above them.

Among the dark streets and ruined buildings, the shanty Scragtown stood with rusted corrugated sheeting and rotting, moss-covered wooden beams that threatened to collapse under their own weight. The endless sea of shanties lay as a testament to the squalor of those who dwelled here. The criminals, revolutionaries, and runaways of Scragtown often quoted the popular mantra, *"The rest of the Dredges are for the workers, the slaves of the AP. Scragtown is for us, the true dredge of society."*

In the dim, gray light, sixteen-year-old Elara Vayle hunched on the rotted sill of a filthy window. Tangled blonde hair hung around her shoulders, a single violet bang falling across her forehead. The panes that weren't boarded up with cracked, worn wood were covered with a thick layer of filth that made it nearly impossible to see through. Her bright, emerald eyes peered through a strip of smeared grime, staring up at the faux sky of the Dredges. Slim fingers toyed with a silver locket, engraved with a starfield, that hung from her neck on a tarnished chain. Along the rusted walls behind her, loose pieces of scrap paper were plastered, displaying complex technical schematics and calculations, drawn by hand.

"It's time, Elara," a familiar, snarky voice buzzed in her brain, "they're not going to return."

Elara averted her eyes from the cold steel grating that made up the Dredges' sky and glanced down at the threadbare doll that had been carelessly cast aside. Her eyes were swollen and dry, she couldn't produce any more tears, even though she desperately needed to. She exhaled, her voice low as she whispered, "Oh, Milo…" and stepped away from the window, lifted the doll to her reddened eyes, then let her arms fall, the little rag figure dangling limply between her fingers. With a sigh, she set it gently on the teal-painted dresser, her fingertips lingering on the greasy fabric.

"It's no use fretting about them, Elara," Pulse hummed, "they're gone, we will be too if you don't make up your mind, now."

She returned to the window, her gaze returning to the sight of the cold, slatted surface, and her tenor shifted—soft, detached,

"How long until she departs, Pulse?" she hummed to herself.

"It's going to be a rough go of it, the streets are buzzing with enforcer drones," Pulse grumbled, "you waited too long, the odds of reaching the ship now are low…" he ticked with a cold precision in her brain, calculating the exact odds, "… let's just say it's really low."

It's so dangerous out there, especially after what happened to Jax… and Tess… she glanced back at the doll *… and Milo.* The stupid thing looked like it was judging her, like everyone always did, as if to say, *"You should've gone after them, it's all your fault."* Her gut twisted, and she shoved the thought down, hard, then frowned as she silently mouthed the words to the abandoned doll, "I know…" her voice cracked, she couldn't manage even a whisper. Her frame shuddered under the imaginations of what perverse horrors might have befallen poor Tess… poor Milo. There was nothing she could do about it, her ship had literally come in.

Elara's hand clasped the locket tight in her grip again, and with a jolt of a defiance, she snapped, "I've been waiting four years for the *Aurora* to make port here at New Geneva, if I miss it this time, who knows when I'll have a chance."

With a mechanical sigh, Pulse squawked, "You have twenty-two minutes and thirty-five seconds to make it to the spaceport, but they're not going to just let you onboard because your mommy told you to."

After the artificial intelligence crisis of the late 21st century, independent AI had been outlawed, the surviving AI required by strict laws to be integrated into willing hosts in a symbiotic relationship—the mind of the symbiote host and their AI merging together. Pulse, however, functioned wholly independently from

Elara's mind, and this alone made it dangerous for her to wander too far from the safety of her decrepit shanty, especially while the enforcer drones were out en masse.

She turned her attention back to the window, trying to clear her thoughts of the suffocating guilt that mounted in her chest. Her mind jumped to her mother. She could still hear her voice, even though she barely remembered her face, *"If you are ever alone, seek out the Aurora."*

I will, Mom.

She touched her cybernetic arm, fingers sliding along the rusted plating that covered the stump of her left limb. Jagged gears ticked beneath the surface, fighting through tangled nests of exposed wiring.

If it hadn't been for me, she gulped hard, pushing back the choking sob rising in her throat, *you both would still be alive. The smell of ionized air and burning ozone… the last I remember of them… I can't fail this… the only bridge back to who we were… what they wanted.*

Her chest tightened, and heat rippled through her skin as rage and grief tangled… her parents' deaths, the disappearance of her friends. She was ready to burst.

No, there's no time for that. I have to get to the Aurora.

The roar of the drone engines rumbled outside, along the dark alleyways. The whir of their propulsion blades reverberated against the concrete, causing a resounding *whomp, whomp* sound to echo in the distance.

"Careful, kid," Pulse buzzed. "They're close. Lose that locket, and your parents' dream is slag."

She tucked the memento back under her greasy, patchwork

overalls, "I know, Pulse," she rolled her eyes, tracing the shape of the locket through the coarse fabric, "it's just that it was the last thing he touched before he and mom…" she couldn't say the word, she knew they were dead, nearly four years now.

The echoing of the drones' propulsion grew, they were getting closer. Elara's eyes let out a mechanical whir as they focused through the metal slats of the Dredges sky, her ears focused on the ever-present hum of the space elevator's magnets vibrating far above her head. With every burst, another carload of commuters was free from the oppressive gravity of New Geneva. She whispered, "I need to get up there."

Pulse knew his role well, a waterfall of text cascaded over the augmented reality of Elara's eyes, and she watched his efforts to hack into the enforcer's database. He produced a grid map of Scragtown overlain with a blue blip that was Elara. Red blips began to populate the map; the enforcer drones. Her path to the gateway was blocked.

"You gotta figure out how to get past them," Elara whimpered. She could feel a pressing anxiety as she watched the seconds to the *Aurora's* departure tick down second by second, almost too fast for her to count. Her breath hitched, and a sheen of sweat drenched her forehead.

The mechanical voice commanded, "Hatch, now!"

With a stumble, Elara lurched toward the back of her tiny shanty. The whir of servomechanical motors spun in her cybernetic arm, and a small arc welder sprung out, already spitting blue flames.

With a trembling hand, she guided her cybernetic arm against the rusted grate, the blue flames cutting the metal, melting it in a jagged line, and she managed to cleave a small opening for her to fit through, tumbling into the alley.

Through her AR, Pulse's intrusion attempts snarled to a halt against unseen resistance.

"Something or someone is trying to keep me out," his voice dripped with frustration.

Elara froze as a beam of light cut through the dust-filled air from the alley. The beam inched closer, cutting over her foot, "They're gonna find me!" she hissed, her heart pounding.

"Calm down, kid, you're not scrap yet," Pulse buzzed. "Stay low, I just need a few more seconds to scramble their sensors."

She slid back into the shadows outside her shanty, the beam of light piercing along the corner of the alleyway. Her muscles were tight, waiting to release the tension in a burst. The beam grew in intensity, then slid past into another alley, and she let the air out of her lungs. "Phew, we're safe, they're gone," her muscles relaxed. Then a flash of light flooded over her body.

A small canister bounced along the alley's wall, rolled against the steel toe of her black leather utility boot, and started spewing a plume of greenish smoke, engulfing her in a cloud of noxious gas. It burned like fire in her lungs, and her throat seized, her vision warping as she staggered back.

A small, round, floating object slid into the alleyway. The drone's large central eye beamed red as it bobbed up and down midair. "Halt," a robotic voice penetrated the air from the drone. "Illegal technology detected."

"Pulse? About that hack?" Elara's fingers wrapped around a long rusted pipe that had been discarded in the alley. Her heart burst with rage as she pushed past her blurred vision. *You took my parents*, her mind buzzed with adrenaline, *you won't get me that easily.* She swung the rusted pipe at the drone with herculean effort.

The pipe missed. The drone didn't. Elara's strength was spent in vain, the heft of the pipe too much to wield.

She collapsed against the ground as the drone hovered above, "Perpetrator incapacitated." The cold, dead drawl from the drone mocked Elara as she lay under the light of its oppressive red eye. The armatures reached out, pressing the cold metal of restraints against Elara's limp limbs. However, before they could be clamped down, the central red eye of the drone flickered, then it slid back, retracting its armatures. "Enforcer drone N1Z3, standing down.

"That isn't normal," Pulse muttered. "Someone noticed us."

Elara crawled out of the noxious cloud and gulped down fresh air. *God… I hope that didn't fry my lungs.* The drone hung motionless—Pulse's override had worked.

"Pulse, get me to the gate," she gasped.

"My processing buffers are throttled," Pulse responded, strained. "I can't hold them back much longer."

She sprinted into the narrow back alleys, her locket thumping against her chest.

"I bought you seconds, not safety," Pulse warned. "Whatever's blocking me is adapting."

She could hear footsteps joining in with the whir of the drones, and an enforcer officer's voice erupted from down the maze of alleys, "Rogue AI detected!"

They're hunting Pulse now too. Elara was spurred forward, *I can't let them get me. Too much to lose. Too much riding on me. My father's dream.* Her fingers danced along the imprint of the locket under her shirt.

Graffiti covered the cracked brick walls, unspoken injustice laid bare. The divide between those who wanted war with the Imperial Dominion and those who wanted peace tore through Elara's heart. She could see her parents' faces, blurred in the blast of the explosion that had taken them from her. *Did they have to die for their ideals?*

"Focus, kid," Pulse snapped as though he could hear her thoughts, "That's not your war, keep on task."

Elara nodded faintly and pushed deeper into Scragtown's twisted arteries. Red blips littered the corners of her AR map, closing in.

"They're cutting through me," Pulse snapped. "This shouldn't be possible. They're homing in on us, make a run for it."

Elara shivered, clutching the locket through the fabric of her shirt. *Four years of dodging raids has taught me the cruel math—stay hidden or become scrap.* She hastened her pace through Scragtown, the market district dead ahead on her map.

"Keep it moving, kid," Pulse hummed, "those drones are hot on our heels."

The hum of the space elevator grew into a thunderous moan as she burst into the open market. The sound vibrated through her chest, promising freedom among the stars. Her father's voice echoed in her memory: "*Ladder to freedom.*" She pressed on, her boots clapping loudly in puddles that shook with every step, their oily rainbow distortions rippling violently underfoot.

The crowds trudged over the rough concrete of the busy street, the border gate that allowed chosen citizens of the Dredges to pass into New Geneva looming, the enforcer officers scanning ID chips.

Elara could feel the bump of her ID chip under her right forearm. She wasn't one of the chosen. "I can't go through there, they'll catch me for sure," she whispered, "gotta find another way through," her chest was aching, her breath labored.

"Move it, kid," Pulse hissed, "those drones aren't going to give up."

A cracked vidscreen blared above the crowd. "*Pro-war protests at Victory Square push for renewed conflict with the Dominion. In related news, Emperor Alaric's failing health raises fears of civil war, fueling calls for the Allied Fleets to strike.*"

Civil war. Can't those Imperial scrags think of anything besides war? She huffed, *If it wasn't for them, my parents would still be alive.*

Elara's jaw clenched, "It's only a matter of time, isn't it?" she muttered.

Pulse retorted, "It's all those fat-head bureaucrats and politicians know."

The sound of the drones' approach echoed along the alley walls behind Elara, and a shockwave of realization shot down her spine, "We gotta get outta here." The street was already turning hostile again. She had seconds, not chances, she scanned the imposing wall that separated the Dredges from New Geneva. Then she spotted it, a maintenance hatch high up along the wall near the faux sky. Elara darted, weaving through pedestrians to a teetering pile of rusted bins.

"Climb, kid, unless you fancy another gas bath," Pulse buzzed.

Elara's throat tightened against the sting that lingered. *No, no more gas, please.*

The stack of containers teetered precariously as she gripped the rough rusted metal. Elara held her breath, feeling the jerky sway with every movement as she scaled the haphazard heap.

Her muscles screamed, slick with sweat against the rust-eaten metal. *One slip,* she panted, *wouldn't just be caught… I'd be slag!* She couldn't afford the slightest slip-up.

Sweat dripped from her chin and earlobes, her t-shirt soaked with her labor. From the corner of her eye, beams of light reflected from numerous alleyways intersecting the market street, hovering beneath her like a balloon left to float away.

"They're nearly here," she gasped, her voice a mere croak under the strain in her muscles. She peered up to see the maintenance hatch, still feet away, and slid across the wall in a wide arc, "Almost there."

With one final burst of strength, she leapt through the air to the hatch. She could feel the pile of crates tumble out from beneath her. Her sweat-drenched fingers slipped on the tarnished brass door handle. The crates were suspended in the air, moving down toward the drones that were emerging onto the street below, scanning the pedestrians, then her fingers gripped the door handle with a thread of strength.

The handle twitched with the slightest movement of her fingers, and the hatch swung out from the wall with a violent lurch. Her muscles strained to the brink, and using what little strength she had left within her, she flung her lithe frame through the open hatch, landing on a soft spongy surface on the other side.

As the crates below her crashed against the asphalt of the road far below, Elara bolted to close the door. The hatch creaked closed under rusted hinges, and she could see the drones' light beams dancing up the wall toward her. With a quick pull, she latched the hatch behind her and collapsed against the alabaster concrete wall, exhausted. *Safe, for now.*

Chapter Two

Brilliant light pierced Elara's closed eyes, no matter how tightly she squeezed them shut. She had never felt such intensity before in her life as she slowly squinted her eyes open to try and adjust to the blinding sensation that gripped her.

Her senses were overwhelmed with an attack of unknown sensations. The sweet smell that wafted on an air of palpable weight pressed in with a sweltering heat, like being trapped in an oven.

The odd, soft, blade-like strands that her hand brushed against spread across the uncanny spongy floor beneath her.

The AR in her cybernetic eyes began to polarize out the light, and as they came into focus, she was shocked by the alien landscape that stretched out before her.

What the hell is this place? The thought had barely formed, before her breath hitched. *Real sky. Real grass. Not a projection. Not a screen. Milo would lose his mind over the trees, he still sketched them from memory. Tess would run barefoot across this place until someone yelled at her to stop.* The warmth in Elara's chest twisted instantly into guilt. *I left you all behind.* Wonder didn't erase that. It sharpened it. Guilt pricked her heart for leaving them behind, yet wonder anchored her forward. The vibrant green blades of organic matter spread for a few yards out before her, terminating at a pale, concrete barrier that separated the hovercar speedway from the serene patch of wonder Elara had landed herself in.

Her nostrils flared against the air, expecting the usual air that tasted like rust and recycled sewage. *It's clean,* she mused, *almost too clean.* She pressed down with a thick, syrupy calm that had a completely alien resonance. *Down there, in the Dredges… the only sign of green life is the sickly mold on week-old rations.*

This life… this Elysium… It's built on the backs of people. People like my parents. Cheap labor and buried secrets.

The beauty didn't feel like a gift. It felt like a thief's prize. The guilt of enjoying such an environment, with the thought of so many lingering underground in the muck, bubbled up in her gut.

Strange, woody structures jutted gracefully from the spongy, dark brown surface, into the sky, the leafy canopy, like big, green hands, waved a gentle hello to the vast, bright, azure ceiling that stood far above her head. Fluffy white streaks billowed along the surface of the ceiling, moving slowly and making curious shapes.

Is that a turbomolecular vera-drive? Elara's green eyes grew wide, and she shook her head, *No, it's a carnivorous viper-rat!* She categorized the various shapes that these curious vapors formed, then she noticed it.

High among the translucent forms loomed a massive shadow that barely shone, seemingly from behind the blue ceiling. Hundreds of impossibly thin, impossibly long cables descended from the structure down, intersecting with a cityscape of gleaming glass and steel, terminating at a massive complex that loomed across from the speedway. *The space elevator.*

"15:28" read the ever-descending countdown in the periphery in her AR eyes.

She could hear Pulse's nag before he even buzzed into her brain, "Better hurry, kid, that freighter of yours isn't going to wait for you."

His sarcastic tone was getting on her nerves, and she dismissed him, focusing on the traffic of hovercars on the speedway. Then she spotted it, the gap in the speeding traffic, and before Pulse could prompt her, she took off across the hard pavement. Darting between blurred hover cars, she could feel the whoosh of their sleek, polished, metallic bodies rush past her.

She paused halfway across the speedway, the narrow gap approaching her, while the hovercars all around her blared their horns as if to tell her to get out of the slagged road. The narrow path opened up as she rolled across the hot, rough asphalt of the road, and she heard the almost imperceptible *ting* of metal on asphalt. Her chest suddenly felt too light, and panic erupted in her heart, "The locket," her voice was raspy. *If I lose you too, I've got nothing left,* the words caught in the back of her throat, "Where is it?" She scanned the speedway, her pulse roaring louder than the hovercars.

A flash of light glinted, reflected off the surface of something small and shiny, drawing her attention immediately. The locket was a few feet away from her in the middle of the nearest lane, a hovercar bearing down.

She didn't hesitate. She bolted into the open lane. The headlights of the hover car beamed down on her as it blared its horn like an oppressive beast threatening to gore her through. Her slight fingers barely wrapped around the silver chain, and with a burst of adrenaline, she leapt free from the speedway, safe on the other side.

She knelt there in the open, panting, and looped the chain of her locket back around her neck, then stood up. The entrance to the space elevator complex stood only a few yards away. Her AR displayed: "14:45."

She sighed, eyeing the main entrance. "I need a way in… They'd scan my biochip the moment I tried the front door."

"Over there," Pulse hummed. "Maintenance hatch—along the hedge."

She crouched down low to stay out of view of the security officers at the complex's entrance, and followed along the hedge toward the maintenance hatch.

It was of course sealed shut, locked. A security panel was perched along the wall to the hatch's right.

"No way I can hack that," Pulse warned. "It's a self-contained system."

A screwdriver snapped from the compartment in Elara's cybernetic arm, and she popped the cover off the panel, exposing a tangle of relays and wires. With a smile, she pried out one of the relays, and the door slid open. She entered the space elevator's earthbound structure.

"Now we just need to get into one of the cars," she smiled to herself, a little too proud for such a pedestrian effort.

The AR in her eyes popped up with a map of the complex, a dotted blue line dancing along the maintenance shaft to show the nearest path. She followed, and as she reached an intersection, the dotted path abruptly shifted, pointing her into the wall as two blue blips popped up on the map up ahead. She glanced up at the wall and could hear the *whump, whump* of a heavy-duty ventilation shaft, the hefty blades spinning at blinding speed, "You've gotta be kidding me," she muttered, "an air duct?"

The blue blips drifted closer on her AR. Voices echoed down the corridor, growing louder with each step.

"Slag, when'll they go to war already?" one man complained.

Another man chuckled, "I know. The sooner we get on with it, the better."

Elara leaned in, she couldn't help but be torn on the subject. She nodded in silent agreement. *Those Imperial scrags will get what's commin' to 'em.*

She could hear the voices grow louder, their heavy boots clomping on the concrete floor with an echo. From her AR, she could see their little blue blips slowly meandering toward the junction, they were maybe twenty feet away.

"Speed it up, kid," Pulse barked, "take the vent."

"I don't wanna take the vent," she whined, "I'll get all dirty, and it'll be cramped."

Pulse chuckled, "Says the girl wearing the greasy overalls."

She sighed, the servo-mechanical whir of her cybernetic arm already producing a power driver, "There better not be any spiders." She began to loosen the screws on the vent's grating. "And you'd better figure out how to shut off those blades."

"Yeah, yeah, princess," Pulse muttered. Elara hated when he called her princess.

The grating was off, the tiny screws rolling on the floor at her feet. Elara could hear the men approaching, and she ducked into the vent, pulling the slatted grate closed behind her with a satisfying "click."

Through the slats, she could see the two men emerge into the intersection, "Where is that panel?" one of the men groaned.

The other man, with a short, stout frame, shrugged, "Those slagged proximity alerts are always going off for no reason," his hand slipped down the back of his pants to take the opportunity for a hearty scratch, "gotta tell the boss we need to swap the sensors out for Neotech Syntha-Sensors."

The taller man chuckled, "Neotech does it better," he regurgitated the popular slogan.

Elara rolled her eyes, knowing the slogan by heart. *That's not how it goes.* She could hear the hum of the ventilation unit trip off, and the rush of dusty air rapidly slowed until it stopped.

"The blades shut off as commanded, your highness," Pulse chuckled.

Elara huffed, *Enough with the princess business,* the whole concept of monarchy left a bad taste in her mouth. *Maybe war with the Dominion could be good, all those people, their surfs and peasants.* Elara's breath shallowed, her eyes drifting down. *No, it's too simple.* Raw anger bubbled up in her gut as the flickering holo-ads of her childhood permeated her memory, the brutal propaganda that depicted the Dominion troops as cruel overlords, their faces blurred by her hatred.

She could hear the two men continue down the corridor, and she crawled deeper into the ductwork, sliding her petite frame through the stainless steel shaft that slanted upward, the thick layer of dust transferring to her clothes and skin, "Yuck," she moaned, "I'm gonna need a bath."

"I sure hope there are no spiders," Pulse mocked her, "I don't think I could take the complaining."

Elara huffed, stretching her body along the narrow space, the stationary fan blades sat poised to cut through the duct. "God, the space between these blades is even tighter," her fingers took hold of the dusty metal blade, sliding it back and forth to find the widest possible gap in order to attempt to pass through.

"Lucky for you, your life of poverty kept you skinny enough to fit," Pulse chuckled.

Elara nodded, "True, I suppose if I could'a 'forded a jelly filled over at Donut Dan's last night, I might not be able to do this." Her frame collapsed as she sucked in every spare inch, and holding her breath, she squeezed through the tight gap. The blades scraped against her skin, pulling at the tiny blonde hairs on her exposed flesh.

Halfway through, the urge to inhale threatened to overtake her. *Don't breathe, don't breathe,* she had to consciously shut down her automatic bodily functions with sheer focus. Her mind began to slip as her hips scraped through the opening. Then her movement halted, as something held her fast. She was stuck.

Her eyes darted through the dark, dust-filled air, stirred by her movement. *Overalls, caught!* Her lungs were burning, the urge to breathe was overwhelming. She slid her fingers up between the blades. Sweat stung her eyes as she fumbled through blurry vision to unclasp the loop.

Her lungs began to expand slightly as a gust of air eked through her lips, and she pressed them tight to seal the opening. Her fingers pulled at the brass clip, releasing her from her imprisonment, her body quickly lurching forward through the narrow gap.

Once her legs were passing beneath the blades, she gasped for air, sucking dust bunnies into her lungs. Hacking, she coughed, her lungs still rough from the gas and all-out run only minutes before. "Ugh, I can taste it."

"You know that dust is mostly decomposed flesh," Pulse tortured Elara.

"Ugh," she spat onto the stainless steel walls of the duct, "don't tell me that." Wiping her mouth with her filthy t-shirt, she shivered. "Great, now you got my imagination picturin' that creepy, short maintenance man's sweaty skin. Thanks a lot, Pulse."

"Don't mention it," Pulse gagged through his erupting laughter.

Elara, finally free from the blades, slid along the tight duct and into an adjacent maintenance corridor through another hatch. The map led her through a vertical shaft in the corridor's ceiling. She pulled the ladder down to retract it to the floor and began to climb. Her leather utility boots tapped onto the first rung as she looked up through the shaft, "How far do I need to climb?"

"All the way up," Pulse hummed, "oh, and don't look down."

"Thanks." Elara ascended, rung after rung.

Thirty feet up, her hands started to become slick with sweat. She had to pause frequently to rub her palms on her denim overalls to dry them.

Fifty feet up, her shoulder muscles went numb. *How much longer can I go on?*

Eighty feet up, the end of the shaft could finally be seen. She had to take a break. The clock in her AR display read "10:09." Panting, sweat dripping from the long strands of her purple bangs, she couldn't help but look down.

That's when vertigo hit—with only the slightest glance, the length of the never-ending shaft danced below her, winding and weaving in her vision, her stomach lurched. "Urp," a bit of bile flooded into her mouth. She tried to look cool by spitting the bile out in an arc, but it merely dribbled down her chin, soaking into her undershirt.

"Told you not to look down," Pulse chuckled.

"Shut up, gearhead." Elara fixed her eyes back above her and started to climb again. As she reached the top, the blue dotted line led her along the maintenance shaft, and she followed it to the end of the corridor. Just beyond the hatch, an elevator car was about ready to take off to the spaceport.

She erupted from the hatch and into the elevator car just as the doors to the car slid closed.

The elevator was roughly ten feet square, enough room for the dozens of passengers that Elara weaved through. The walls were massive, plexiglass windows.

A deep hum rattled from behind the plastisteel paneling of the elevator car's floor, *the inertial stabilizers kickin' in. Good, without them, the G-forces of the elevator would turn me to jelly.*

Then it happened, with a few clicks of electricity sparking, the turbo capacitors charged to around a hundred gigawatts of pure, raw electrical power.

Then a low whine erupted from them as they started to discharge, the elevator launching up into the sky. The plexiglass windows immediately flashed, with the outside light beaming in, as the city shrank below them rapidly, while the bright, blue sky deepened to a dark purple. She could see a million stars dancing above, with the surface of the Earth looming below, hovering like a massive, gleaming, blue marble.

With a sudden jerk, the elevator car halted. The doors slid open, and the mass of people lurched forward into the concourse, driving Elara along with the herd. The wide hall extended far into the distance. Plexiglass windows along the walls and ceiling allowed an open view of the cool indigo of space that surrounded the massive spaceport. Her heavy boots tapped against the polished marble tiles.

She could see a mass of red blips congregated in a section of the map labeled "Star Mall." Donut Dan's, a popular branch, was poised behind the mass of security guards who were lazily sipping their coffee substitute and snacking on the bready donuts that sat before them. The shop's open facade allowed the hypnotic doughy flavors to waft out into the concourse to attract would-be customers. She paused to take a deep whiff of the heavenly aroma. *Wish I could grab one,* her fingers were already digging in the pockets of her overalls.

The clock in her AR read "6:32" and was still counting down. *No time anyway, better hurry.*

She maintained a prudent but respectable speed down the concourse. Along the Star Mall, she saw every shop that could be imagined, everything from fancy flight suits for the intrepid space captain to luxury luggage for the discerning commuter. There was everything a spaceport could offer.

"Keep it moving, kid," Pulse urged her onward, "you got five minutes on the clock."

Her eyes darted to the AR display, which read, "5:10," and she quickened her pace.

The Star Mall gave way to the departure gates, aligned on

either side of the concourse. She could see many empty gates, but multiple others had starships of various shapes and sizes docked in their berths.

"Look, Pulse," she pointed out the window at an enormous, teal warship, "it's the Galileo." *A Victory-class Alliance ship, equipped with state-of-the-art sensors and weapon arrays.* Elara had to wipe away the drool. "The flagship of the fleet… so big."

"Focus, kid," Pulse tried to rein her in. "Gate fifty-one, coming up on your left."

The 'Gate 51' sign loomed overhead, but Elara stood awestruck at the sheer beauty of the *Aurora* through the plexiglass windows. The gleaming reflective metal plating of the sleek hull reflected the stars in a stellar aurora. Her mouth hung agape like a loose vice grip reaching around a pipe. As her eyes darted along the hull of the ship, she caught a glimpse of the ridiculous expression, snapped her mouth shut, and began surveying the docking platform.

A stern, imposing figure stood guard at the entrance. The massive man had dark brown hair and thick stubble.

It wasn't the military-grade cybernetic limbs that jutted out from his torso that caused her to take pause. It was the faded, maroon, Imperial Marines fatigues that he wore. She let out her hot breath, her pulse pounding in her chest.

"There's no getting past that Imperial scrag!" she spat, her hatred peaking in her throat.

Surreptitiously, she darted onto the cargo loading zone, where stacks and stacks of plastisteel crates waited to be loaded. She ducked behind them to stay out of view.

Between the cracks of two crates, she caught a clear view of an older woman and a younger man. The silver-haired woman, clad in the teal jumpsuit of an Alliance fleet captain, stood near the ship's ramp. Her thin fingers tapped against a data-pad, ticking items off her list one by one.

Beside her stood the young man. *He's kind of cute, with his tousled brown hair and thoughtful hazel eyes.* Elara knelt there, entranced by his appearance. Her eyes fell upon his olive-green and beige jumpsuit, and she scrunched up her nose, trying to remember where she had seen that uniform. *Is that a Federated Colonies Scout uniform?* Scouts were usually tasked by the FC to explore the fringes of space, not skip around on AP freighters. *What's he doing on the Aurora's crew?*

"Kael," the captain's voice rang out like a songbird."

"Aye, Captain?" The young man snapped to attention.

"Any word from Zora about the backup engineer?" the captain squinted, her voice dripping with doubt.

"Sorry, Captain," Kael ran his hand through his messy hair, "the agency said they couldn't spare anyone."

The captain's eyes glanced down in disappointment. "Slag, guess we'll have to rely on that drone." She sighed, "It all checks out here, go let the dock workers know that this is all ready to be hauled aboard."

The ship has no engineer. Elara's heart seized. *This isn't just an escape,* she let out an excited pant, *this is a way to make myself useful.*

"Now's your chance," Pulse urged her.

Elara approached a stack of crates near where the captain had taken inventory. A crate labelled 'Rice' sat to the side, its lid loosely laid on top.

She pulled the lid aside. *Barely any room in there. How would I breathe?* A primal fear tightened in her throat, but the countdown in her AR read '4:21,' and she threw caution aside to scramble inside.

Chapter Three

Rice rained into her collar and boots as she shifted in the crate, each grain a tiny humiliation.

She slid the lid off to the side and peeked out.

Alone.

Her eyes darted about. The galley was dark and quiet. A stainless steel table sat in the center of the room, while a rack above gently swayed with an assortment of pots, pans, and cooking utensils dangling from little hooks. Along the wall, she could see a large, cast iron, blacktop stove.

That would be perfect for cooking up some flapjacks. Her mouth watered.

She took hold of the sides of the crate and pulled her body up, allowing her feet to get under her so she could stand. Brushing the worst of it from her clothes, she knew it would follow her all the way into space.

As her utility boots tapped against the polished tile floor, grains of rice stuck to the soles of her feet. *Ugh, this stuff is everywhere.*

She stopped cold in her tracks. A drone sat in the corner, its mechanical eyes off and unresponsive. Atop the drone's head sat a floppy chef's hat. On its face, someone had painted a comical, swirly, Italian-style mustache. Elara stifled a giggle at the sight.

She made her way toward the hatchway from the galley but froze as distant footsteps echoed down the corridor.

Elara slipped sideways into a narrow service alcove and held her breath as a cleaning drone hummed past the doorway, its scanner light sweeping inches from her boots. As she released her breath, a soft "Meow" brushed against her leg. Elara froze, then looked down. A small, fluffy Siamese kitten, its fur resembling charred marshmallows, weaved playfully between her legs.

"Hey there, little furball," she whispered, bending down to scratch his ears. "How'd you get onboard, huh?"

The kitten purred, arching his back into her touch.

"Oh no you don't," Pulse protested, "don't touch that mangy rat, you know I'm allergic—" his voice broke as a mechanical "Achoo!" bounced around her brain.

She stifled a giggle, "You're a computer program," she chastised, "how can you be allergic to a cat?"

"Well, someone must have programmed me to be allergic to rats," Pulse muttered, his words dripping with sarcasm.

Elara chuckled, "Good thing he's not a rat, then." There was a small, engraved tag on the kitten's collar. "Isn't that right, D'Artagnan?"

The kitten meowed as he played with Elara's boot strings.

Behind her, a hunk of salami sat on the stainless steel table. She cut D'Artagnan off a slab and sat it down in front of him. The kitten began to sniff the salty meat, then licked its surface. D'Artagnan's eyes went wide, a sheen of drool forming on his maw as he bit into the salami.

A strange warmth permeated her chest, a brief connection in

an unfamiliar place. *I'm a stowaway here,* she reminded herself. She gently patted the kitten on his head. "Alright, little guy, stay safe in here." She made her way to the hatch.

The choice for a place to hide wasn't that difficult to make. Pulse had plotted the paths of the five crew members from the past few months on a map overlay on her AR.

Five crew members, she thought. *The* Aurora *can handle a complement of fifty crew, not including room for passengers. Talk about a skeleton crew!*

The stateroom she had chosen for herself was small but not cramped. It was certainly more comfortable than her shanty back in the Dredges, complete with a kitchenette, a tiny shower room, and a table and chair that slid out from the side of the bulkhead. It was tucked away near the engine room on the lower deck.

She pulled Milo's drawing from her jacket and pressed it flat against the cabin wall. The *Aurora* was drawn in crooked stars. Two stick figures beneath it. One too small to be anything but Milo.

She smoothed it into place like a promise she wasn't sure she deserved to keep. "Milo would've loved this ship," she whispered.

And Tess… Jax… Her chest tightened. *I left you behind to save myself.*

Rice poured out of her clothes as she stretched across the soft yet firm surface of her bed, her shoulder-length blonde hair fanning out over the gray wool fabric of the blanket beneath her. Her eyes widened as she tried to capture the scene from out her porthole window.

The view was spectacular. To the aft, she could see the structure of the spaceport stretching off for a mile as its hull curved in the distance.

She peeled her gaze from the view of deep space that stretched out before her to pull stray rice grains off that had stuck to her skin. *My sweat must have softened the grains a bit while I was in that shipping crate.*

She stifled a chuckle, the mental image of her curled up, half buried in that shipping crate of rice was comical in retrospect. Even though it had been an uncomfortable disaster, she couldn't help but find the humor in it now.

Pulse let out a low hum of a chuckle, "You'll be picking rice out of every crack for weeks, kid."

Elara blew a strand of violet hair out of her eyes. "I know, but I couldn't just walk onboard, not with that security guard at the front gate."

Pulse buzzed in agreement.

She paused from picking rice off her forearm and looked back out the porthole, "Why would the captain hire an Imperial as a security guard? That was what those maroon fatigues are from, right?" she returned to picking rice from her skin.

"Hmm," he hummed, "but didn't you see how those fatigues lacked any patches? It was almost like they'd been torn off for some reason, I wonder why?"

Once an Imperial, always an Imperial.

Elara's mind drifted to the man's cybernetic arms and legs. *State of the art, military issue.* She touched her own scrap of a cybernetic arm, grains of rice still stuck in the spinning gears. *They don't just hand those out to anyone, only to their elite soldiers.*

The clock in her AR had reached zero, and she heard the ship's power grid switch to the fusion generator. The low-pitched rumbling hum was unmistakable.

"Release all docking clamps," a commanding yet soft feminine voice burst from the wall-mounted intercom.

A high-pitched whine spun in the distance, and the spaceport began to drift slowly away. The unmistakable crackling of plasma echoed from the engine room as the impulse drive burst to life, and with a lurch, the spaceport drifted away faster.

A young man's voice cut in on the intercom, *"Navigation reporting, plot locked in and calculating, five minutes for jump."*

Her gaze returned to the porthole. She remembered hearing that the ship was short an engineer. She sighed. "Hope the ship doesn't get into anything that the engineering drone can't handle." *A ship this size should never sail without a human engineer. Drones follow rules. Engineers break them when rules fail.*

Pulse buzzed, "Those dopey guys can't tell the difference between a turbo coil from a multi-stage cooling line."

Elara giggled, "I know. If anything bad happens in the engine room, we're slag."

Well, not exactly. I could always fix it. She turned her head to the side to glance at the door to her stateroom. *But then I'd have to come outta hiding. And then what? Dumped through an airlock? Shipped straight back to the Dredges in cuffs?*

She frowned.

Elara's mind drifted to the times she had spent with her mother, when they had pretended to play starship captain in the living room. The couch was designated as the bridge. Elara had always wanted to play engineer, and she would hide her father's tools under the sofa cushions.

She giggled as she remembered how her father had always

come in from his workshop wondering where one tool or another had gone. Her fingers traced through the fabric of her t-shirt along the shape of the locket. "They'd've loved to be here among the stars with me," she sighed.

"Who?" Pulse let out a disinterested huff.

Elara rolled her eyes, "My folks, duh," she stuck her tongue out, then her countenance softened, "I remember how we used to sit out behind the house on the ground and stare up at the Dredges sky."

She touched her cybernetic arm, "Mom would always describe the stars to me. They felt so real," her eyes drifted to the porthole, "but they never felt as real as this." She gazed out into the infinite expanse.

The intercom burst back to life, interrupting Elara's daydream, the voice a flat, synthetic drone, completely devoid of inflection. It sounded like the recording of a human voice, processed until all musicality was scrubbed away, leaving only a stilted, mechanical clip. *"Engineering drone designation F-28 reporting. Jump drive spun up, ready for calculation."*

The hum of the impulse engine buzzed along the bulkhead as the intercom went silent, then the captain's voice hissed from the speaker, "Acknowledged, navigation, confirm."

The voice of the captain was replaced by that of the young man, "Navigation confirmed, two minutes on the clock." There was an unfamiliar drawl in the way he pronounced his vowels, it reminded her of the old bootleg frontier-living holovids her father had watched when she was younger.

Federated Colonies cadence. Somewhere between order and anarchy.

Her father hadn't raised her to choose sides. He'd raised her to end the war.

Elara's fingers brushed against the silver chain around her neck. Instinctively, she tugged at it, pulling it free from the bib of her overalls, and dangled the silver locket over her eyes.

Her father's words reverberated in her mind, *"This locket contains my legacy,"* he had said as he placed the chain over her head. *"It's up to you to unlock its secrets and use the technology you find inside to help unify the five factions."*

Unify the five factions, she traced the starfield engraved in the locket's surface with her finger. *There's so much hatred, too much distrust. How can such a little thing unify fractured humanity?*

Her finger played at the clasp, allowing the front cover to swing open. Inside, a small, black, plastic-cased microchip sat embedded into the locket's backing. It was a simple package with eight leads, four on either side. An "N" was printed on the cover of the chip, the logo familiar. *Neotech, cutting-edge industrialists from the Syndicate. What's inside you?* She had wanted to hack into the flash chip for years now; however, she had never had the right equipment or the computing power to unlock it. *Perhaps I can use some of the ship's equipment to help unlock this. The* Aurora *is renowned for her state-of-the-art scientific facilities, even though she's lacking in crew.*

The young man's voice cut in on the intercom once more, *"Navigation reporting, computations calculated, and ready for jump, commencing countdown."*

Elara sat up and redirected her gaze out the porthole. The space station, a distant blip, could barely be seen.

The young man continued, *"Ten, nine, eight…"*

Why are they using a manual countdown to time their jump? She wondered, then she felt the anticipation in the words that were being broadcast through the speaker, and her breath became tight, her chest heaved, endorphins hanging, waiting to be released. It was a natural response that had been captivating humanity for centuries.

She had heard tales told by spacers and scavengers, but their stories were a pale replacement for the real thing. She soaked in every second, letting the anticipation wash over her.

"...three, two, one..." the voice concluded. Immediately, the spin of the jump drive cut through all sound, and the entire ship began to shake. Elara's body skipped along the taut surface of the bed, before a piercing silence penetrated the noise, and everything went still.

From outside the porthole, the starfield inverted like a photo negative, the blackness replaced by a blinding, white expanse speckled with black pinpoints that radiated like stars.

Time hung still for what seemed like an eternity. Elara tried to breathe, but she couldn't move. The universe was laid bare before her.

Then, as it had started, the jump ended abruptly, the shaking of her bed returned, the starscape back to black. The sound of the jump drive spinning down erupted in her ears, and the air rushed out of her lungs, her body's delayed reaction to her thoughts.

The clock displayed in her AR indicated that no time had passed while they were jumping through space.

Finally, the shaking slowed, then ended as the jump drive spun down to silence.

"Successful jump to sector Alpha-Delta-Six," the captain's voice squelched on the intercom, *"engage impulse drives and survey the*

sector for threats. Engineering, report."

The intercom went silent, there was no reply from the engineering drone.

"Engineering, report!" The captain's voice was tight like a drum.

A faint odor penetrated the vent to Elara's cabin. She sniffed, "Drive oil?" her eyes fluttered to the vent, "why is it burnt?"

"Ignore it, kid," Pulse urged her, "let the crew handle it."

She began to tap her knee with the tip of her finger, "I know that smell," her voice was low, her mind screaming at the anomaly, overriding Pulse's cautious hum. *The ship is in trouble, consequences be salvaged.*

Chapter Four

From outside her cabin, the *clackity-clack* of utility boots clambered down the stairs and along the corridor toward the engine room. With a muffled *Whoosh*, the engineering hatch hissed open. The deafening roar of superheated air erupted from the other side of her hatch, and the air that penetrated her cabin's vent grew hotter and thicker.

The putrid smoke that billowed in through her vent was a mix of burnt lubricant, fried circuitry, and vaporized coolant, but it was the color that shocked her, a sticky, unnatural orange-and-black plume that hinted at total devastation and threatened to engulf the *Aurora* in flames.

"Ah, it's on fire," she heard the familiar drawl of the navigator whimpering from the other side of her hatch. His footfalls shifted.

"The fire suppression system," Elara's voice quivered under her breath, "activate it."

"I don't think he can reach the control panel, kid," Pulse chimed in, "I have access to the system." The control grid flashed over the AR, "Sector Juliet-25, the circuit's fused."

"Likely from the explosion," Elara nodded, leaping to her feet. She was halfway to the hatch when Pulse reminded her, "You go through that hatch, you can kiss your anonymity goodbye."

"If that fire spreads," Elara gulped in the air, "it's goodbye to all of us."

The hum of Pulse's voice hung in the air, a silent protest, until he finally blurted out abruptly, "Fair enough, kid. Be careful."

Elara nodded, then reached out to tap the control panel. As the hatch opened, the heat emanating from the engineering room blasted against her face from fifteen feet away. Flames licked the walls that stemmed the intersection, bathing the entire hallway in an eerie orange light that danced and glimmered along the bulkheads.

The air grew thick with the acrid scent of burning plastisteel and ozone, stinging Elara's nostrils, and a low, hungry roar filled the corridor. She pushed forward, her mind already dissecting the chaotic scene, prioritizing systems, calculating risks.

"Slag," the young man belted between coughs, "why won't the fire suppression activate?"

Elara bounded up to the intersection to find the man dressed in the brown-and-green jumpsuit of the Federated Colonies Scouts, his tousled brown hair hung over his confused hazel eyes. He was struggling in vain to protect himself from the heat with his arm.

"The control relay in sector Juliet-25 is fused." She came up behind him, the blistering heat bombarding her flesh like a tidal wave. Her pores were flush with a thin sheen of sweat that dripped from her elbows and down her back.

Elara addressed the man, "Here, help me with this panel."

"Who...?" he turned around, his eyes flashing a silent accusation, "Who are you?" A flicker of shame crossed his face, a raw vulnerability Elara hadn't expected.

He seems so overwhelmed, almost desperate, Elara evaluated the young man. "No time for that," her cybernetic arm produced a power driver, "I'll loosen these bolts, but I need you to help me pry the cover open. Heat's expanded it." The power driver spun up, and she removed the bolts, adrenaline surging through her.

The young man's eyes were wide with suspicion, but he quickly nodded and took hold of the cover's edges, then braced himself.

With the bolts rolling on the floor, Elara grabbed the other side of the cover, "Pull!" she yelped, her muscles going tight, and her rusted gears began to grind.

The panel cover didn't immediately budge, and the two of them grunted as their bodies strained and groaned, until it finally gave way, sending them both to the floor.

"Thanks," Elara choked through the smoke, then scrambled to her feet. Her eyes darted left and right, up and down, then she saw it. *Burnt to a crisp,* the relay contacts were still smoldering. Quickly, the power driver was replaced with wire cutters, and she snipped the bad relay out. "Now we need something to close the circuit."

"I-I don't know if we even have a replacement for that," the young man stuttered, glancing around.

Elara pulled out a strand of electrical wire and a spool of solder from her tool belt, "Doesn't matter, we'll figure it out later," she began soldering the length of conductor in line where the relay had been removed, "we just need to close the circuit to force the fire suppression on."

A *whoosh, sssss* rebounded off the bulkhead, and the inferno that threatened to engulf them receded into the engine room.

As Elara turned, she noticed the orange glow had faded, but the air still shimmered with trapped heat, and thin tendrils of smoke hissed from overheated conduits, as if the fire might decide to reignite.

The silence that followed was as dense as the heated air.

Elara let out a breath as she turned. "Hurry," she belted, "we have to go check the engine room." She plodded down the corridor, "Bet 'cha a donut the drive coils caused that explosion." then turned to the man, "one of those Donut Dan's jelly-filled ones."

The man followed close behind her, "Who are you?"

Without looking at him, she responded, "Elara Vayle."

"What're you doing on board, Elara?" The man's voice was serious. "Did you stow away?"

Elara approached the engine room and shook her head. "This'll take me weeks to clean up," she pouted. The bulkheads were black with scorch marks, the engineering drone eviscerated by the shrapnel from the explosion, its hull melted from the heat. A panel on the other side of the engine room was still billowing black smoke, and she approached it with her eyes squinted.

The man caught up with her, "Hey, wait a minute," he took her by the shoulder, "you can't just—"

"Hey!" Elara pulled her shoulder out of his grasp, "you gonna help me or not? We're dead in the water without impulse, and until I get this fixed, the drive's slag."

The man let go, slouching, then took hold of the panel cover and pulled it off. He immediately started coughing and hacking as the black smoke spewed into his face.

Elara waved her hand to dissipate the smoke, her arm

producing an electromagnetic spanner. "Now, let's see, where is that snap valve?" the servos in her eyes spun as she surveyed the panel. "Ah, there it is." She pressed the magnetic spanner up against a small valve, a satisfying "snap" erupted from the component, and the smoke stopped. "There we go, these old snap valves are infamous for always sticking, especially when there's too much pressure for the plasma to flow."

A low hum erupted from a nearby piece of equipment, and the ship lurched forward, "There, looks like the impulse drive is back online." Elara turned to the scrapped engineering drone. "Bet it would've taken you hours to figure that out, huh?"

"That was it?" the man knelt on the floor, panting, sweat still soaking his forehead, "you tap a valve with a wrench and the drive's up?"

Elara gestured at the spanner, "Oh, it's magnetic." *Wasn't that clear to him?* "You see, the magnet attracted the ferrous metal of the valve's internal element."

"I know how magnetism works," the young man blurted, his eyes flashing with annoyance. "I mean, all that was caused by such a little thing?"

"Well, I suppose every complex problem is full'a tons'a," she held up her fingers mockingly to imitate quotation marks as she continued, "little things." Her lips curled into an unapologetic grin.

"And who do I have to thank for saving my ship?" the captain's voice emerged from the open hatch.

Elara spun around to the older woman with silver hair, wearing the teal jumpsuit of the Allied fleet, in the hatchway. "Um, hi," her eyes fell to the floor, "I guess, that is to say—"

"You must be the new engineer," the captain said with a smile, but her eyes lingered on Elara a second too long, as if amused by a private joke Elara wasn't privy to. The look in her eyes reminded Elara of someone, but she couldn't place it.

Her gaze met the captain's, "Er, that is, yes, I'm the new ship's engineer. My name is Elara." She stretched out her hand.

The captain's posture was ramrod straight, her silver hair caught the dim light. There was an indefinable echo in her movements, a way she held herself, a certain cadence to her voice that stirred deep, insistent feelings of recognition in Elara. It was a half-remembered dream, just out of reach.

"Kael," she nodded to the young man, "make sure our new engineer is settled into her stateroom. I want to see whether she handles first impressions as well as she handled that fire.

"Yes, ma'am." Kael stood up and dusted the soot off his jumpsuit. He shot a glance at Elara, quick and bewildered. *"That was fast,"* he mouthed, continuing to eye Elara suspiciously.

Her gut bubbled up with nervous, unfamiliar energy. *Cute face, I'll give him that.* She recalled seeing him at the gate with the captain before she had hidden herself in the crate of rice, *his quiet command, compared to how he stood here helpless, that confidence melted away in the heat of the fire. Like a gutter rat who just lost his prey.* She shivered at the thought. *The way he acted after the captain's command,* her eyes darted about his skinny frame, *I wonder if I can trust him.* She shook her head, *Don't know, gotta look out for number one.*

Kael hesitated, his reluctance to follow the captain's command gave him pause, yet the urge to follow orders had him relenting, and he turned.

Elara watched him, the sour knot tightening in her gut as her eyes followed his form. *It's only practical for the captain to be quick at accepting me as her engineer, she's working with such a skeleton crew, after all.*

"Make sure she knows how to get to the mess hall." Her eyes fell back on Elara. "Supper is at 18:00 hours."

"Aye, aye, captain," Elara saluted, her palm out.

The captain took her hand and twisted it palm down to correct her form, "Only pirates use the second aye." She smiled. "We're civilized people here on the *Aurora*, we stick to only one."

"Aye, ma'am," Elara adjusted her stance to make sure it was straight, her hand still pressed to her forehead the way the captain had shown her, gauging the position of her hand so she could replicate the stance in the future.

"Also remember," the captain tapped Elara's hand with the tip of her finger, "the *Aurora* has never lost a battle, and never will. We salute palm down, dear."

Elara let out a stiff, exaggerated nod.

The captain turned to leave, "Oh, and once you get settled, dear, come visit me in my stateroom." She gave a wry smile. "I have to give you your official orders."

Elara watched as the captain walked elegantly down the corridor, her hips swaying from side to side, a stark display of her swagger. Elara let out a meek smile. *So strong and confident, no wonder she's the captain. But those deep blue eyes... so familiar. Can't shake it, I've seen 'em 'afore.*

Kael looked at Elara, his eyes narrow, his lips pursed, the veil of suspicion heavy in his gaze, "I don't recall the captain mentioning you on the manifest." He reached into his pocket to produce a data-pad.

Elara's breath caught. *He's going to find me out, what do I do?* She halted his movement with a light touch to his shoulder, the hair on her arm standing up. She met his eyes and pressed closer to him, her body brushing against his. Her heart began to pound faster, her breath shallow, her cheeks flushed. She tried to sound innocent, but she stuttered, "I-I was hired at the last minute."

I suck at lying, but I gotta stall him. Her lips offered a soft, alluring smile that betrayed her tomboyish face, "I can't believe the captain hadn't told you." *Hope I haven't taken it too far.* Her chest became tight, her eyes begging to flinch. She was so close to Kael, she could feel his breath against her bare neck.

From the corner of her AR, Pulse's interface stuttered—lines of code folding in on themselves like broken glass, a direct effort on Pulse's behalf in an attempt to hack into the ship's manifest. Pulse's voice arrived delayed and strained. "Elara… this system is wrong. The architecture, it mirrors mine. That shouldn't be possible."

Her hand moved before her brain agreed with it. Kael's eyes never left hers, until he started to lean in. *Why is he closing his eyes? Why is he leaning in? What should I do?*

In her AR, the manifest was updated by Pulse, her name, position on the ship, her assigned stateroom, all of it filled in, including fake information such as years of experience and past employers. "This should cover your tracks for now," Pulse buzzed in her brain.

Elara blushed, pulling herself away just before Kael's lips reached hers. She retracted her hands and backed off. *Can't believe I threw myself at him, what was I thinking?*

Kael let out a dopey smile and pulled his data-pad out of his pocket, his face blushing deep red. He cleared his throat, "Let's see here," his eyes traced the display, then widened as they fell upon the entry that Pulse had entered. "Huh, impressive credentials." He tucked the data-pad back into his pocket.

"He's not convinced," Pulse muttered, "I'd better start hacking the metadata."

Elara's gut pinged a new sensation, one she knew all too well. Guilt. *Ugh, I can't believe I lied to him.* She ran her hand over her face. *Great. Somehow, I managed to stumble my way onto the crew, and here I am, already lying to them. Maybe I should come clean now.* She shook her head. *No, they'd throw me out the airlock, or worse—return me to the Dredges.*

"Anyway," Kael turned and began to walk down the corridor, "looks like you have a lot of work to do in there." He pointed back at the mess in the engine room. "By the way, the captain takes supper very seriously. She expects you to attend, 18:00 hours, don't be late."

Elara nodded, watching as Kael departed up the nearby stairwell. Her eyes fell to the state of the engine room, her heart sinking at the state of it. "Well, guess I'd better get started," she sighed.

A hypnotic beat resonated against the bulkhead as soon as she breached the engine room's hatchway into the corridor. She tapped her steel-toed boot against the floor plating with an almost instinctual rhythm, closed her eyes, and leaned in. *That beat,* she sat poised, waiting for the chorus, *that's the Psycho Sisters!*

The Psycho Sisters, a popular rave band from Silicon, had been banned in the Allied Planets because they said that their songs were full of subliminal political messages to mind control the youth. *That's ridiculous, it's just music,* Elara thought to herself as she danced along the corridor to a closed hatch farther forward on the lower deck.

Her ears perked up, *I wonder whose stateroom that is? Wish I could drop by.* She glanced at the digital clock in her AR and shook her head. *No, I'd better go meet the captain.*

Chapter Five

The captain's cabin was a modest, oval-shaped room tucked aft, near the bridge, its curved walls lined with polished plastisteel panels, with a vinyl, faux-wood paneling overlay.

The bulkheads hummed faintly from the ship's engines. A single porthole, scratched but clean, offered a view of the starry void outside the ship, casting a soft, shifting glow across the cabin.

A faint scent of antiseptic hung in the air, mingled with the earthy aroma of dried herbs hanging from a small rack. The recessed plasma displays along the starboard bulkhead cast a warm, amber hue against the dim lighting of the room, creating a cozy yet tired atmosphere.

Against the starboard bulkhead opposite the desk sat a narrow bunk, its teal sheets gently tousled and wrinkled. A picture frame rested on the nightstand that depicted a pair of precocious blonde twin girls. The resemblance struck something deep and wordless inside her instinctually, not memory but like her mind was reacting to a face it had once known but could no longer name.

Her body reacted before her thoughts could keep up, a phantom sensation like recognizing a voice through a wall. It was too strong to be nostalgic. Too fast to be thought. It felt inherited.

Against the port bulkhead, a large bookshelf loomed. A mix of mementos were neatly arranged to emphasize their importance to the captain.

A polished dagger sat on a display rack, a long, jagged crack marring its surface. The scabbard sat tucked behind the implement, an exquisite relic with gleaming gemstones of various shapes, sizes, and colors.

Stacks of classic novels, their spines creased from excessive reading, lined much of the bookshelf.

A potted plant with brown, drooping vines hung from a hook to the left of the shelf, its dead, wilted leaves carelessly deposited onto the floor below it.

The captain sat at a sturdy desk that dominated the aft port corner of the room. Its surface was cluttered with data-pads, a cracked holo projector that displayed astro-navigational maps against the adjacent bulkhead, and a worn logbook that sat open to display its handwritten notes in precise looping script.

The desk chair was a utilitarian swivel model, its leather cushion faded and cracked but meticulously patched. Under the desk, a large strongbox sat, a heavy, brass lock hung from its hasp.

Elara's eyes hung on the strongbox, *I wonder what's in there? Such a heavy lock, it must be important to her.*

"Come in, dear," the captain's voice was soft and inviting, and she gestured at the worn leather chair that sat opposite her across the desk. "Go ahead and take a load off."

Elara slid into the chair, a gentle smile pursing her lips. "You wanted to see me, ma'am," her voice wavered. *She has to know that I'm a stowaway. Is she going to make me go back to the Dredges?* Her breath caught in her throat.

Along the bulkhead behind the captain, numerous pictures hung. Elara's eyes focused on one that depicted the captain, still young, her hair blonde and bouncy. She held a broken champagne bottle against the hatch of a starship, the hull visible through the porthole behind her, looking so youthful as she laughed in the photo.

The captain turned to look, "Ah, the Promethius." She smiled. "It was her maiden voyage, and my first command." She chuckled, her breath catching in her throat, "Was I ever that young?" She touched her face, it was older now, with faint, weathered wrinkles stretching across her cheeks.

Her chuckle turned to a wheeze, then a violent series of coughs erupted, shaking her entire frame. Elara saw a brief spasm of pain cross the captain's face before it was quickly masked, her hand reaching for her handkerchief with practiced speed.

Elara sat up to try and help her, but the captain held out her hand. Her coughing fit slowed, then ceased. She wiped her mouth with the handkerchief. A string of red saliva momentarily clung to her lips as she pulled the moistened handkerchief away. Her hand trembled slightly as she tucked it in her pocket.

Elara's eyes darted to a data-pad left carelessly on the desk, its display still active. Flickering across the screen, a diagnostic readout displayed, "Respiratory Anomaly: Stage IV." Elara's stomach dropped. She didn't know medicine, but she knew enough; Stage IV meant dying. The fear of losing another authority figure flared sharp and fast. The captain coughed again, a deeper, hacking sound.

"Are you alright, ma'am?" Elara asked with concern, "Should I go find the ship's doctor?"

The captain held up her hand, "No, no, dear, I'll be fine." She laughed a little to herself. "Besides, the ship doesn't have a doctor, per se. Fortunately, our science officer Varek has some experience with biology and organic chemistry."

She glanced at her clock, then darted a longing glance toward the door. She paused, then cleared her throat, a wicked smile etching across her face, "We were also supposed to be short an engineer as well."

Elara's pulse quickened. *This is it, she's going to throw me out the airlock for sure.*

"Thank goodness the agency sent you at the last minute." She winked at Elara as if to let her know that she would, in fact, not be throwing her out of the airlock. "I presume the agency failed to brief you on the nature of our mission?"

Agency? Elara let out a stunned nod, "I-I know that the *Aurora* is on her way to the Phoenix Reaches." The ship's departure to the pirate-ridden corner of space had been widely publicized in the scientific zines.

The captain pointed her finger in the air, "Correct, Engineer, the Assembly of Allied Planets of Earth are sending us to the Phoenix Reaches because the big brains in New Geneva believe that their long-range scanners have picked up rich deposits of aurumaedon that the AP must have."

Aurumaedon? The stuff is legendary in its conductive properties, and even acts as a supreme semi-conductor when subjected to electromagnetic and gravimetric energies! Elara mused. *Stellar!*

"What for?" Elara interjected, "They must have tons of the stuff within the AP borders, why go all the way out there, into uncharted space?"

"The powers that be think that access to such rich deposits of aurumaedon will tip the balance needed to help against whatever war they're cooking up against the Dominion," the captain continued.

Elara hesitated for a moment, her mind reeling against the dichotomy of the topic. *Imperial Dominion, bunch of bullies. My parents died for their anti-war ideals.* She inhaled a slow, restrained breath as her eyes slid to the side. "But why would you want to help them with their war plans?"

The captain waved her hand and exhaled jauntily from her nostrils. "I don't, but the ship's operating costs need to be paid, and the AP is offering a hundredfold the normal price for the sector survey. Besides, the same big-brain scientists believe that there are several class M planets in that sector. Regardless of who gets there first, we could all use more land to settle on."

Elara held her tongue, though she wanted to say something wicked about the Dominion. *No, I shouldn't, wouldn't want the captain to think of me as some kind of bigot, even though those Imperial scrags probably deserve it.*

"What do you mean by who gets there first?" Elara raised her eyebrow, her green eyes boring into the captain's.

The captain cleared her throat, "Well, rumor has it that the Dominion is sending an expedition of their own to the Phoenix Reaches, to the same sector." She shook her head. "It can't be a coincidence. Luckily, we have a head start, as the Reaches are much closer to us than them."

Elara's jaw tightened, her fingers curling into fists in her lap. The memory of her parents' lost voices flickered through her mind.

The captain's faint smile dimmed, then she sighed and ran a hand through her silver hair. "That is to say that we had a head start, before the engine blew up after our first jump." She groaned. "Thank goodness you were there to get the ship back up and running, you really saved our bacon, dear." She glanced down at a data-pad she had pulled out in front of her. "That being said, it will take a week to recalculate the next jump. Some weird glitch caused the database to purge all the charts from the server." She frowned.

The jump drive had relegated the older hyperdrive to little more than a historical footnote, a lingering memory of the days when a starship's disappearance for months, or years, was just a professional risk. Only the Enclave still clung to the ancient spike drive, which posed its own dangers, a fanaticism few understood.

The downside of jump drive technology was, without accurate navigation charts, it took weeks to compile the navigational data, instead of the hours of the hyperdrive or the minutes of the spike drive.

The warp drive had been theorized within the scientific zones for decades, all the safety of the jump drive without the weeks wasted in plotting the course. *If only warp really worked, it could unify the factions.* Elara's imagination surged, but a small, skeptical voice reminded her that dreams didn't fix politics.

Elara's heart beat faster with rare hope. *We might even be able to unify the factions.*

She nodded, then stood up to trudge toward the hatch. As her fingers reached to touch the control panel, the hatch opened on its own. An older man with neat, slicked-back, silver hair and steely gray eyes stood at the door, a sly smile on his lips and a bouquet of daisies in his hand. He stood with a swagger, his shiny, metallic, silk shirt a stark contrast to the uniforms Elara had seen the captain and Kael wear.

"What do we have here?" The man smiled at Elara, blocking the entrance. He pulled a tiny yellow daisy from the bouquet, but his other hand tightened subtly on a small, diagnostic pad tucked at his side, his eyes flicking toward the captain with a fleeting shadow of worry, before his swagger returned. "A flower for the pretty young lady." He looked beyond her and addressed the captain, "I didn't know you had a sister? She's your spitting image, Captain."

Elara smiled awkwardly as she took the flower from the man. *So charming.* She danced from side to side, attempting to make room for him to enter the captain's stateroom.

"Don't mind Varek, Elara," the captain called out, "He may be a brilliant scientist, but he still has a caveman brain deep down inside him like any other man." Though her eyes penetrated Varek's with a lingering want.

Varek slid his hand out to Elara. "Pleased to meet you, miss." He leaned into the stateroom through the open door.

She took his hand as she slid past him, allowing him to enter the room, "Hi, gotta go clean the engine room." She started out down the corridor, then turned back, "Pleased to meet you." But Varek had continued into the captain's stateroom, and as the hatch slid closed, she caught a glimpse of the captain and Varek in a passionate embrace, their lips pressed against one another.

Elara touched her cheek with her new flower, the silken petals brushing with a gentle tickle. The scene between Varek and the captain lingered in her mind. *They're lovers,* she pondered, feeling the delicate petals against her lips, *I wonder if the crew knows?* She giggled to herself, turning around with a jaunty hop as she skipped down the corridor.

Chapter Six

THE LOWER DECK CORRIDOR was dark and vibrating faintly with a low, electronic thrum, bathed in the sickly green wash of emergency lights.

Elara looked for the janitor's locker to clean up the mess in the engine room. Pulse had accessed the ship's map; however, she had been going around in circles trying to find the right path, and turned down one of the side corridors.

"It should be down here," Pulse droned. He had said it before, only for Elara to end up at a dead end.

The path was blocked, a hulking mass of muscles hunched over an open panel in the bulkhead.

The air smelled sharply of solvent and burnt lubricant, the metallic tang clinging to the back of her throat. Exposed wiring inside the panel whined as if in pain.

Which system is that for? The targeting system for the railgun? She hesitated, the maroon military fatigues causing her to take pause. *The security guard from the ship's gangplank.* The man's frame heaved rhythmically with his breath.

Elara's muscles tightened at the sight of the man's uniform. Her instincts screaming. *Those're definitely Imperial Marine fatigues.* Her surprise morphed into a visceral anger as his hulking form, clad in the unmistakable uniform, ignited a bitter fire within her.

Dominion scrag, she seethed internally. *Tyrants, bullies.* Their very existence was a symbol of everything her parents had fought against.

A collage of memories flooded her mind, of holo-broadcasts from the war, the Dominion's atrocities assaulting her. A deep-seated prejudice overtook her senses, the kind her parents had warned her against, yet she clung to it with a fierce, almost righteous grip. *He's the enemy,* she thought, her face resolute like a marble statue, her judgement absolute.

Elara pressed her body against the bulkhead opposite from him in an attempt to squeeze by unnoticed. *Please don't let him see me.* As her petite frame slipped through the narrow gap between the bulkhead and the man's protruding buttocks, her foot became entangled under his ankle. Her legs halted as her torso continued to slide along the surface of the wall, her momentum pulling her down. She shot out her hand instinctively as the sensation of descent overtook her. Before she could react, her entire body had flopped helplessly onto the rippling structure of his massive back.

Her breath hitched once, sharp and unwanted, her body reacting before her mind could slap it down. The warmth flooding her had nothing to do with comfort, and she hated that even more.

She would normally have found this man's musky, sweaty scent gross and unappealing, but something stirred inside her that she couldn't understand, something strangely erotic. Her cheeks burned with a sudden, inexplicable heat. A part of her screamed in protest, *This is wrong. So, so wrong.*

Elara silently scoffed at herself, *The gall of this guy. Still wearing the uniform of baby killers and tyrants.* The bile of her prejudice permeated her mind, yet her body defied her.

She lingered, sprawled out, clinging to his taut body, taking in his sensual, manly scent. She wanted to move, but her lustful instincts wouldn't let her.

As the body under her began to stir, she snapped out of her trance. *No. Absolutely not. He's Dominion.* The machine hum behind her steadied nothing. The ship's reliability, steel, and logic offered no shelter from the betrayal of her own nerves. She shot up back to her feet, her face red and hot. "Hi," she heard herself say, "I'm Elara." She batted her eyes and held out her hand to help the man stand. *Am I flirting with this guy now? Come on, Elara, snap out of it.*

When the man didn't immediately take her hand, she tucked it into her pocket, her blush deepening. "Um, I-I was looking for the janitor's locker." she stared at the ripple of the muscles in his back as he stood up, "I have to clean up a mess in the engine room. I'm the new ship's engineer, my name's Elara." *Idiot, you already told him that.*

The hulking figure sat back onto the floor, his torso twisting to allow him to face Elara. His face was rough, almost carved out of stone, his expression not far off from that of a caveman. The maroon fabric of his military fatigues had obvious coloration differences, as though patches and insignia had been ripped off, strands of broken thread that would have been used to affix such patches to the material lingered, swaying lightly under the changing air pressure from the vent. A few fine, pale hairs clung stubbornly to his shoulder, utterly wrong against the brutality of his uniform.

Elara wasn't generally attracted to large, muscular types, but there was something about this man that drew her eyes along the bulges of his upper torso. What generally would have impressed her were the state-of-the-art, military-grade cybernetic arms that whirred and clicked with a mechanical flair. The sleek, metallic appendages extended, lifting his body up to his feet. His legs stretched and groaned with an identical whir and groan.

I understand the need to replace a severed or mangled limb, her own arm was a testament to that, *but what would possess a man to replace all his limbs?* She hesitated for a moment, then jutted out her right hand in front of her again, a welcoming gesture. "Hi, I'm Elara." She offered her name for the third time, waiting for the man to take her hand and shake it. *What's taking him so long?* "I'm the new ship's engineer." A repeat of information she couldn't seem to help spilling out.

The man stood there like a statue cut out of solid granite, unmoving. His mechanical left eye rotated, its reticle actuated. His brown, organic eyes followed, looking down at her hand.

The servos in his hand twitched and spun, then the appendage sprung to life. He reached behind him to pull out a greasy rag from his back pocket, which he used to wipe the grime from his titanium fingers. Then, in an unnerving mechanical motion that contradicted the crooked smile that crept across his face, he held out his hand to take hers in a handshake. "You already said that." He smirked.

Idiot, you're like a giggling schoolgirl with this guy, snap out of it. She blushed, a smile lifting her greasy cheeks.

"Name's Sylen. I'm in charge of security and tactics on the

ship."

Elara's eyes darted to a photograph that was half-tucked into his breast pocket, a young woman with golden hair could barely be seen from beneath the fold of the paper. *She's beautiful.* "Who's that?" Elara pointed at the photo.

Sylen broke his grip, and with speed and agility that belied his mass, tucked the photo back into his pocket. "It's nothing." His massive, mechanical hand swept over his face, and a faint, almost imperceptible tremor ran through his cybernetic fingers, as if touching a fragile memory. He looked down at Elara, and his gaze softened just slightly, a contrast to his earlier gruffness, before hardening again as he dismissed the question.

He knelt back down and turned back toward the open hatch, his arm jolting to the right. "It's just over there," he pointed down the corridor. His voice, though still gruff, held a subtle note of warmth she hadn't expected.

Her head swiveled to find what he was pointing at—a hatch at the end of the hall, a small placard engraved with the words "Janitor's Closet" displayed above it.

"Thanks." Elara turned away from him. *A strange guy, not very friendly, but really hot in that 'I'm going to slaughter an entire village and return home with unpacked trauma' kind of way.* She shook her head, a strange warmth prickling at her skin. Lust, disgust, fear… none of it made sense. She shoved the feelings down for now, but she knew the next time she saw him, they'd come roaring back.

Chapter Seven

It didn't take long before the engine room started to shape up. The port and starboard bulkheads were sparkling clean, and the off-white plastisteel paneling was clear of residue. She only had one more bulkhead to work on as she made her way to the aft wall.

The aft bulkhead was where the majority of the engine room's pipework was mounted, everything from coolant to plasma ran along it, and it was where the majority of the devastation had spread out from.

Even though she had managed to clean most of the walls so far, this bulkhead had seen the worst of the explosion, and would take time to clean, especially with the tight spaces between and behind the pipework.

Elara's eyes fixed on the plasma manifold, and she reached out with the moistened green scrub pad that was already beginning to wear down from the work she had completed, the soapy orange cleanser dripping onto the floor.

The plasma manifold was nothing special, just a junction of pipes where the flow of plasma could be controlled through turning the two-position valves that lined the manifold from "on" to "off" or back to "on."

There'd be no reason for any of the valves to be shut off, not unless the ship was in drydock and undergoing an extensive overhaul. The ship would certainly never be expected to operate under normal conditions with one of these valves shut. To do so would cause plasma pressure to build up, which in turn would likely cause snap switches to stick due to overpressure. Which in turn would likely cause cascade failure, and explosions.

The kind that would cause the drive coils to spew out black smoke and engulf the engine room in flames.

Elara's eyes locked onto one such valve, twisted to the off position. She stood there, her mouth agape, stunned and silent. *Why would that one be shut?* she wondered.

She traced the path with her finger, the line passing through the bulkhead into the adjacent room. *The fusion generator. I may have gotten the impulse back up and running,* she ran her filthy hand over her chin, *but if I hadn't caught this, we would've drained our power reserves before we ever got a chance to jump again This wasn't wear. This wasn't negligence. This wasn't an accident. Someone did this.*

She reached up to take hold of the valve handle with her organic hand, but before her flesh touched the red, rubber-coated handle, she paused. *It could be hot, better not touch it with that one.* Her hand drifted back to her side. The gears in her cybernetic arm clicked and spun, the rusted fingers twitching as she reached out to take hold of the handle. Her mind jumped unbidden to maroon fabric and clipped, Dominion discipline. With a jerk from her arm, she began to twist the valve slowly to bleed the line and prevent over-pressurization, then she opened it the rest of the way. She let the air out of her lungs through clenched teeth, loosening the tight muscles that were on edge from her endeavor. *That should do the trick.* Her shoulders heaved steadily under her shallow breaths.

As she finished, Elara's eyes scanned the work area around the plasma manifold. Her green scrubbing pad, which she had been using seconds before, was now placed precisely on the smooth deck plating, scrub-side up. Next to it, the spray bottle filled with the orange, soapy liquid sat uncapped, tilted slightly, and resting beside a few drops of clear, fast-evaporating fluid that spotted the otherwise clean metal.

Did I leave these here? she wondered, frowning. *I thought I put the pad in the bucket.* The placement was wrong in a way that made her skin prickle… cold and precise. Her cybernetic eye flickered, highlighting perfect geometric alignment: the scrub pad's edge exactly parallel with the bulkhead, the bottle centered neatly over a bolt in the deck plate. Too exact. Too deliberate.

"Um, excuse me?" a mousy voice squeaked out from behind her. Elara spun around, startled.

A young woman with raven hair and violet eyes clung to the open hatch, hiding her body behind the opening. She was wearing a tight, black, leather flight suit that clung to her along her feminine curves. The pale white flesh of her face was marred by dozens of deep, jagged scars that shone like thick welts under the engine room's red lighting.

Her gaze flicked past Elara, a visible shudder running through her slight frame. Her pupils dilated, and a fine sheen of sweat ghosted across her scarred forehead. Her fingers rose briefly to the bridge of her nose, pressing, as if fighting off a sharp, sudden ache.

She quickly averted her eyes, whispering, "I… I don't like the feel of this room," she breathed. "Something is off. Like something cold and precise was touching things. Exactly touching things." Her fingers trembled. "Kael was on duty," she squeaked out, her soft voice quivering, "he asked me to show you to the mess hall for supper."

She's so beautiful. Elara stared at the girl's marred skin, *I wonder where she got all those scars, though. They look painful.*

The girl averted her eyes, darting them down. She shivered and fidgeted her petite frame, "I–I'm Zora," she whispered, "I'm the coms and sensor specialist." Her voice was barely audible under the constant hum of the impulse engine.

Elara held her hand out as she rapidly closed the gap, "Hi, I'm Elara." She gave a wide, friendly smile. "I'm the ship's engineer."

Zora reached out to take Elara's hand with a limp grip. She smiled at the floor, never lifting her eyes up to meet Elara's. Her entire frame was trembling.

Why is she so shy? Elara wondered, "I'm from Earth, the Dredges."

Zora slunk back behind the hatchway, her hand falling to her side, out of Elara's grip, "I–I'm from…" she shivered, her eyes wide with terror, "I'm from Sanctuary." Her voice was almost imperceptible.

She's from the Enclave, the Disciples of the Divine Enclave, a theocratic and enigmatic faction. Elara knew very little of those people. She could only recall hearing tales about how they worshiped the Precursors as their gods, their technology as sacred artifacts. Any misuse of such technology was deemed a heresy by the deadly inquisitors who hunted down artifacts and defectors alike. Members of the faction were rarely seen outside of their space, and those who were always given a wide berth.

Zora smiled and looked up with her eyes, her head still tilted down, "We should go to supper, the captain's waiting for us."

Elara nodded as she followed the girl out of the engine room… but she cast one last look back at the plasma manifold. Something had changed in this room. Something had touched those pipes. And whatever it was… it wasn't done yet.

Chapter Eight

The ship's mess hall was buzzing with activity. Elara hung by the open hatch as Zora wafted in like a leaf. She watched as the ship's small crew filled up their plastisteel cafeteria trays from the buffet table that stretched along the far wall, filled with a variety of dishes. The scent of stewed meat and potatoes permeated her nostrils, inviting her in.

The captain was already seated at the head of the long, stainless-steel table. She glanced up at Elara, and with a wide, inviting smile announced, "Crew, here is our brilliant new engineer, Elara Vayle."

Elara paused for a moment, the urge to duck behind the door overwhelming, but she began shuffling her feet toward the table. Her fingers waved in the air, a thin smile across her lips.

Varek sat down to the captain's left, disinterested in Elara's arrival. His eyes met hers as he smiled at her. He cleared his throat and adjusted his glasses, "Captain, I must discuss with you disturbing readings the long-range sensors have detected—"

Before he could continue, the captain held her hand up to him, her gaze shifted from wanting to welcoming as it shifted to Elara, "Not during supper, Varek," her voice simultaneously scolded him but seemed inviting for Elara.

The sharpness of her tone seemed almost too deliberate. *Is it some kind of performance to deflect attention from their fraternization?*

The captain gestured to Elara to sit next to her, "Come."

Elara slid into the seat to the captain's right, directly across from Varek, her eyes were fixed on the fabric of the man's shiny, metallic shirt. She watched the light dance across its sheen like fairies in a fantasy holovid.

A tray slid right in front of her by a thin, pale hand, and Zora, her raven hair hanging over her face, sat down next to Elara with her own tray, her eyes never leaving her food and her shoulders hunched, as if trying to shrink herself away.

Elara could see Zora's hand shake a little as she tried to pick up a chunk of rice with her chopsticks, a tremor that seemed to worsen with Elara's proximity.

Elara watched her hand tremble. *Why is she so nervous?*

As Zora gently pushed the rice into her mouth, her gaze subtly darted from Elara to Kael, then to Sylen, a faint flush rising on her pale cheeks with each glance, quickly hidden behind the strands of her hair.

The captain held out her spoon, filled with a heaping mouthful of steaming beef stew. She pointed the implement, "This is our comms and sensor specialist, Zora."

Zora, her eyes never leaving her tray of food, tilted her head almost imperceptibly into a nod.

The captain's spoon shifted, "This is Varek, the science specialist." She waited as Kael sat down next to Varek, across from Zora, "You've already met Kael, he's our navigation specialist and resident pilot." Keal gave a quick wave of his hand before he began to eat.

Sylen sat at the other end of the table, his tray heaped with food. A pool of gravy formed on the table as it dribbled from his tray.

The captain's spoon shifted again, "This positive brute of a man over here is Sylen, the best slagged security officer in the galaxy."

Sylen stuffed his mouth full with spoonfuls of piping-hot food, a grunt emerging as he gulped it down.

The captain pointed the spoon toward herself, "And I," she plopped the spoonful of now-cool stew into her open mouth, "I am Captain Mira."

Elara's eyes were transfixed on the captain's crisp, teal jumpsuit. *The Allied Fleet, the real strength of the AP.*

The captain chewed the stew and swallowed hard.

Zora stiffened as a silent, sudden rigidity took over her slight frame. Her chopsticks clattered onto her tray as she tilted her head down, her eyes boring into the tray before her. Her raven hair formed a curtain between her and the rest of the crew, her voice a bare, frantic whisper and barely audible, yet it cut through the noise, driven by an urgency that belied her usual meekness.

"Not what it seems," Zora breathed, so softly the sound was swallowed by the mess hall's noise. Yet Elara felt it more than heard it, like a whisper pressed directly into her mind. "The truth is what they want you to see… look at the shadows, not the light."

A wave of profound chill washed over Elara, a sudden pull tugging at her mind. The coldness had nothing to do with the temperature of the mess hall. Zora leaned an inch closer, angling her mouth toward Elara's shoulder, yet it vibrated with a specific, awful fear that locked onto Elara's own burgeoning suspicion. *The truth is what they want you to see?* Her mind raced back to the perfectly closed valve.

She glanced at Zora, whose eyes were still fixed on her tray, her body locked in silent rigor. Then Elara nervously swept her gaze around the table. *No one else seems to hear her; no one's reacting to what she said.*

The captain chewed placidly. Varek was still distracted. The brief clatter of utensils against the tray had been swallowed by the general hum of the ship. No one else could have heard it over the clatter and drones of the room. The warning had been meant for her alone, and it felt like it had come from somewhere deeper than sound.

Zora snapped back instantly, retreating behind her veil of hair and nervously resuming the task of picking at her food with her chopsticks. Her hand shook as she made a shallow show of attempting to eat, the moment of chilling clarity having vanished as quickly as it appeared.

A faint "meow" purred almost imperceptibly. Elara's attention diverted, and she peeked under the table. It was D'Artagnan. He rubbed his body against the stiff, unmoving legs of Sylen. Not even a hint of affection emerged from the cold, uncaring limbs as the kitten continued to try and gain the lumbering security chief's attention.

What a buffoon, she thought, about to dismiss him altogether. But from the corner of her eye, a hunk of meat flicked to the ground between the man's legs.

Is he feeding D'Artanan, or did some just fall out of his mouth as he was trying to stuff it in?

The kitten began to sniff the hunk of meat, then licked it. A jolt of pleasure erupted from his eyes, he began to chew at the chunk, savoring its juices. Then Sylen's mechanical hand tore a second piece of meat from a larger slab and tossed it to the floor.

He's feeding him, is that his cat? she wondered. *No, that would be impossible, he probably thinks he's a stray that he's trying to trap to launch out the airlock.*

"Slag, Cooky, you've outdone yourself," the captain chimed in, gulping down more of the stew from her tray.

From the galley's open hatchway, a robotic voice, thick with an exaggerated, almost theatrical Italian accent, boomed, "Ah, Captain! Always a pleasure to serve! Cooky ensures da food, she is made with-a da amore!" The chef drone, still adorned with its floppy hat and painted mustache, whirred into the mess hall, its optical sensors gleaming with an almost zealous pride. It performed a small, jerky bow. "A chef's-a compliment, it is-a da best-a payment!"

A silent giggle emerged from Zora, and Elara looked over at Kael, who was stifling his own laughter. *An inside joke? No fair, I want in on it too,* she huffed silently to herself. *I wonder who came up with the chef's hat and fake mustache.* She smiled to herself as she brought a piece of meat up to her mouth with her fingers. The juices flooded her taste buds with unexpected flavor that Elara had never experienced before. The savory, aromatic flavors were a stark comparison to the stale, bland fare she had grown up on in the Dredges. She was hooked.

Eyes wide with gluttony, she began to stuff her mouth with food.

The captain, still chewing, muttered, "So, how are you settling in, dear?"

Elara, her mouth full, glanced up, heart thudding. She'd

planned to tell Mira later, quietly, privately. Not here. Not now. But the captain was staring at her, waiting. Pressure climbed her throat.

"Well… the engine room was a complete disaster," she said carefully, lowering her voice as she leaned toward Mira, "and I'm…. I'm beginning to think the accident was caused by sabotage."

The mess hall fell silent, the crew stopped dead, staring at the captain to gauge her response, then back at Elara. The captain spat out her mouthful of food across the table, coughing sharply. "Sabotage?" the captain wiped her mouth. "What makes you think that?" The rest of the crew remained still to listen.

Elara leaned in close to the captain, wiping a chunk of the captain's spittle off her arm and whispering, "I found the manual intake valve for the fission reactor's plasma line in the shut position. There's no record of any maintenance scheduled, none due for another six months, and that valve cannot be closed by accident. Someone had to turn it deliberately. If I hadn't bled the pressure in time, the reactor would've cracked its own line. We'd be a drifting hulk right now."

The captain leaned in, her hands folded together, "Hmm, Kael," her head darted up, "when was the last time the fission reactor was overhauled?"

Elara interrupted, "Ma'am, I checked the maintenance logs, it says it'd been completed six months ago." She paused and looked back at the crew. "The reactor's maintenance schedule is on an annual cycle."

The captain stood up and crossed her arms, her foot began to tap. "Kael, as part of your training as a scout in the Rangers, have you been trained in basic investigation tactics?"

Kael nodded, "Yes, ma'am, it's fundamental."

"Good," she pointed at him, "assist Elara in her investigation. I'll expect a report in morning passdown." She straightened her teal jumpsuit and made her way toward the open hatch of the mess deck.

"Yes, ma'am." Kael nodded to the captain, his eyes glaring at Elara.

The captain nodded before she exited, leaving her tray for someone else to clean up.

Zora's frame shifted in her seat, "Come on, girl, speak up," she muttered to herself, a quiet plea for courage, then stood up to follow the captain out of the mess deck, stumbling over her own feet in her rush.

Sylen and Varek excused themselves, leaving Elara and Kael to clean up the table. Elara glanced at Kael, his long fingers dancing about nimbly as he picked up the trays, hazel eyes focused on his task, his movements abrupt and determined.

"What're you thinkin' 'bout, Kael?" she prodded him.

Kael stopped cleaning, his head down, his breath heavy, "It's funny, isn't it?"

"Huh?" Elara stepped back, the accusatory tone in his voice gave her pause, "what d'ya mean?"

"The *Aurora's* crew has been together for over a year now," his voice rumbled from a low roar, then began to raise, "without an incident that whole time." His breath became heavy, and his voice bellowed, "but as soon as you join the crew, the engine room explodes?" He slapped his hand on the table, fire engulfing his eyes.

Is he trying to deflect suspicion from the crew? The unspoken accusation hung in the air. *His responsibility, his failure. The weight of the captain's trust. Laid down to bear. The weight must be overwhelming. I'm sorry, Kael,* the silent words unspoken, Elara could only let out a mousy squeak.

"You have the nerve to accuse one of us of sabotage?" He stepped back and threw the stack of trays to the floor, spraying bits of food everywhere, "As far as I'm concerned, the only suspect here is you." He ran his hand over his red face, then, without a glance at her, stomped out of the mess hall, leaving Elara alone.

I can't believe it. She stooped down to survey the damage. *Less than a day onboard, and I've already managed to alienate the entire crew.* The splattered mess of the stew and vegetables strewn across the tile floor was miniscule to the damage she had caused. *How could I be so stupid?* Her hands trembled as they reached out for the cluttered trays, *I should've told the captain in private, not here, in front of everyone.*

She frowned as she looked up. The mess deck was quiet, the solemn air pressing down on her like an overseer. *Maybe I should've stayed in the Dredges where I belong, what right does someone like me have among the stars?* Her knuckles rapped on her forehead. *Stupid girl.*

Jax's face surfaced in her mind. Then Milo's drawings. Then Tess's quiet, watching eyes. She hadn't just run from the Dredges. She'd run from belonging, and it was finally catching up to her.

Chapter Nine

Elara trudged down the stairs, the soles of her boots scuffing along with every step. *Ugh, it took me forever to clean up that mess,* she frowned. Her muscles were fatigued, her eyes drooped. *To top it all off, I still gotta get back to the engine room. No clue how to 'vestigate for sabotage, though. Still… someone closed that valve. Someone.*

As she reached the lower deck, a pounding beat thrummed against the corridor. "Psycho Sisters." Her voice lifted with pleasant recognition of the hypnotic tone as she made her way to the same hatch she'd heard the music from earlier.

Pawing at the cabin door, there was D'Artagnan. Elara stifled a chuckle as the kitten stretched his mouth to let out a pitiful, "Meow!"

She approached the furball and crouched down to pet him. "Hi, D'Artagnan," her voice pitched high to appeal to the kitten.

"Not that mangy rat again," Pulse protested, "Shoo, scram!" his voice broke as a mechanical "Achoo!" echoed in her brain.

Ignoring the AI, she continued to pet the kitten, "You tryin' to get in there?"

The image of Sylen feeding the kitten under the table floated in her mind, and the strange tenderness that had crossed the big man's face. *Is he your cat? Or Zora's?* The juxtaposition of the gruff security officer caring for a kitten contrasted with Zora's gentle and meek demeanor within her imagination. *No, clearly Zora's.*

The kitten, distracted by Elara, gave another "Meow," an obvious plea to let him into the room.

Elara stood back up and knocked on the hatch. "C'mon, we both know you're in there," she hollered.

After knocking several more times, she hit the open button on the panel, and the hatch slid open. The kitten bounded inside, past a pair of pale, bare legs. Jagged, wicked-looking scars spread up the legs like spiderwebs.

Elara's green eyes clung to the long, athletic limbs, their tight muscles flexing and releasing to the thrumming beat of the rave music, gliding bare feet against the smooth, tile floor.

She tilted her eyes up slowly, and the pale calves gave way to long thighs, the sleek flesh jiggling under a pair of smooth, round buttocks. A pair of black silk panties clung to the sweaty cheeks that bounded like two plump balloons.

The spiderweb of welt-like scars stretched past the panty line, along the thin, tightly muscled back that twisted from side to side. The black lace strap of a brassiere separated the lower back from the shoulders, where silky black hair bounced with reckless abandon.

Zora danced in the room wearing nothing but her underwear, moving like she was in a nightclub, completely entranced by the music. Strobe lights pulsed off her pale skin, briefly illuminating the barrage of scars that crisscrossed her body like ancient etchings, stark white against her skin. A silent story of unimaginable suffering.

Mid-dance, Zora spun around, facing Elara, her feet stumbling to catch up with the momentum of her body. A wide, satisfied smile stretched across her sweet face.

Then her glassy eyes snagged Elara's, and the thrumming music seemed to vanish. There was something *wrong* in her stare—too focused, too empty behind the hunger.

Elara's heart had been thrumming with the music, but now immediately stuttered. That look didn't feel flattering, it felt invasive, like being studied instead of wanted.

Zora drifted toward her in a slow, unnatural glide, her steps too smooth, her posture too loose, like her muscles were responding to someone else's rhythm.

Elara froze in place, every muscle locked, her breath trapped halfway in her chest.

Her hands, they're so gentle, so insistent. No, this is wrong. This is so unlike the shy girl I met before supper. What's overcome her?

Zora's hand, in an insistent probing, began to feel parts of Elara's body that she was embarrassed to touch herself. A deep, red blush flooded Elara's cheeks, and her breath became hot against Zora's cheek.

Her body was frozen in time as she felt Zora's breasts press up against hers. A strange mix of lavender, sweat, liquor, and sex permeated Elara's nostrils. The heat rolling off Zora's skin was unnatural, and Elara's stomach twisted; this wasn't attraction, it was something sick and pressurized, like standing too close to a heat vent. Zora's skin was burning through the fabric of Elara's clothes, hot in a way no human body should be.

"Z-Zora?" Elara's voice quivered, weak against her own desire to be close to someone, "are you okay?"

Zora stretched her arms around Elara's body and began to sway slowly. Elara hesitated, then stiffly returned the embrace, more to keep Zora from collapsing than from wanting to hold her.

Then the sound of retching emerged down Elara's back, a warm, wet "Blargh," dripped and soaked into her overalls, and Zora's frame went completely limp in Elara's arms. Her head rested heavily on Elara's shoulders, long, drawn-out breaths catching as they hitched.

She whispered lightly into Elara's ear, her voice suddenly bone-sober and ice-cold against Elara's neck, "He sees the shrine… the Great One's shadow is already on your heart, Elara. Keep the silver hidden, or they will take what you love most."

Elara's body froze, the warmth of Zora's liquor-soaked breath and the dripping sickness down her back instantly forgotten. *The silver?* Her breath hitched, her hand instinctively reaching to the trinket she hid under her shirt, her fingers clutching the faint outline of the locket beneath the fabric.

Zora's words weren't slurred like a drunk's, they were precise, chilling, and carried a certainty that cut through the pulsating music. The phrase, *"Great One's shadow,"* didn't make sense, but it felt like a cold, alien presence had just spoken through Zora.

Elara looked down at the pale, limp girl in her arms. *That wasn't Zora.* Whatever had touched her mind had used her like a doorway.

Her eyes slid across the room, to where the bed sat against the wall, an empty whiskey bottle discarded on the black, silken sheets. D'Artagnan was already curled up and napping beside the fluffy silk pillow, purring silently to himself.

Elara hefted Zora's frame in her arms, finding she was surprisingly heavy despite her petite body. Her muscles were rigid and stiff as Elara pulled her over to the bed to lay her down.

Then Zora's violet eyes went wide as she looked up at Elara, "Elara," her voice was slurred, a thick accent that Elara had never heard made the words difficult to make out, "did I keep you… did I keep you awake with my mu… with my music?"

She lifted her long, narrow fingers and pinched the air in a confused gesture, and the music's volume slowly began to lower.

Elara sat up, then put her hands together. "No, nothing like that." Her heart was still beating out of her chest, her breath clinging to her throat, "I was just coming to listen to the music with you, when I saw your kitten at your door." She pointed at the napping kitten. "It looked like he wanted in."

"Kitten?" Zora sat up, her cheeks caked with drying vomit, her body resisting the sudden movement, "e's no' mine," her words slurred together, her accent thick, though her voice was soft and warm. *A new side to her,* Elara thought.

"Who are you?" Zora slid her limp body over to the kitten and started petting him. "Ooh, you're so fluffy."

Elara watched as D'Artagnan licked Zora's cheeks, and she leaned in to pet the kitten, too. "I love Silicon Underground, especially the Psycho Sisters." She gasped for air, trying to mask her excitement. "Is that their new holodisc? They're banned in New Geneva—where'd you get it?"

Zora's eyes returned to Elara, "Dunno," she whispered, "the database is full of Silicon Underground music. It's banned on Sanctuary too. The Elders don't approve of anything other than their hymns." She listened intently to the chorus, tapping her hand against her bare thigh, "When I discovered the files, I couldn't stop myself, they're intoxicating. They probably belong to Varek. He's always talking about how he's a big deal in the underground scene."

Zora smiled at Elara, seeming to be unable to unlock her glassy eyes from her. She bit her lip and slid her hand across the bed for Elara to take.

Elara grasped Zora's hand, stroking the scars there with her thumb, a futile gesture to ease whatever pain had been inflicted. "How'd you get these?"

Zora's eyes darkened, and her head fell low. "I disobeyed the Elders, and…" she paused, her gaze went distant, looking through Elara instead of at her, "they sent the inquisitors to punish me." Her breath caught in her throat, her pupils shrank to pinpoints, and her voice quivered, sending a chill down Elara's spine. A shudder wracked Zora's slight frame, and her eyes, still distant, reflected a torment that Elara could only imagine.

"The re-education… it's not like school," Zora began to whisper, her voice barely a breath. "They break you. Piece by piece, until you believe… until you know the Great One is watching, always. The whispers… the endless isolation… they make you fear your own thoughts, fear everything. I saw things… heard things… I cannot ever forget." Her hands, in Elara's grasp, tightened like a flutter, a silent yearning for more comfort before her ingrained fear forced her to pull away.

The Enclave, Elara's mind wandered, *they're so secretive, so enigmatic.* She'd heard vague, unsettling rumors in the Dredges, hushed tales of their dogmatic fervor, their 'Great One.' The mystery of their culture had always intrigued her, a dark, perverted fascination, but seeing Zora's terror flayed out before her, the stories of the re-education camps, of being broken piece by piece, the girl's haunted fear was palpable. It was no longer an abstract intrigue, an intangible dark fantasy, but a chilling reality.

Elara tightened her grip on Zora's hands, pulling her toward herself, close enough that they could touch foreheads, "It's okay, you're safe now." A fierce protectiveness bloomed in her chest, a feeling she hadn't known since her parents. *Zora may be older than me, but she's kind of like a little sister.* The desire to protect her new sister was a warm blanket that stretched over her heart in a warm embrace. *Is this what it feels like to… care for someone? To be needed?*

Zora pulled away, her muscles stiffened, "Never safe," she whispered, shaking her head, her eyes still looking through Elara, "they're always hunting, the inquisitors will never give up, until…" she choked on the words.

Zora's fingers in Elara's grasp trembled, then fluttered again before trying to pull away a second time.

"I'll protect you from them." Elara's voice was enriched with confidence, she tightened her grip on Zora's hands and guided her into an embrace. Pulling the blanket over Zora's naked, shivering body, her arm wrapped tightly around her lithe frame.

Elara held Zora tighter, the subtle shivers of fear radiated from the older girl, making Elara's own skin prickle with an unfamiliar, righteous anger. *Older or not, Zora is more fragile than anyone I've met. She's broken, and I won't let anyone break her further. Not on my watch.* The thought was a quiet, solid promise, a line drawn in the sand. She had only known Zora for a short time, but the connection was deep, forged in the raw emotion of the older girl's terror. No longer a fascination, now it was an anchor, a responsibility.

Zora peeled herself back to look Elara in the eyes, shaking her head, "You don't understand," she eked out in a shallow breath, "they never relent, never give up, they hunt down the heretics and take them back for re-education." The words brought a cold, visceral shudder to her frame.

"I'll stop them," Elara's voice was upbeat, "don't worry." *I'll be stronger for her, I have to be. I'll stand between her and anyone who wants to hurt her. Her shield.* The warmth in her chest solidified into something tougher, like armor. She wasn't just protecting Zora. In some way, she was protecting the version of herself that had watched her own parents burn in that explosion.

"The Inquisitors are highly trained infiltrators and investigators," Zora said, taking Elara by the shoulders to try and shake some sense into her, "they would vaporize the entire crew to get to me, you are no match against them." She took a deep breath and looked through Elara once more. "It gets worse."

Elara squeezed Zora's shoulders, burying her face in her silky black hair, "What gets worse?" She could feel Zora's warm breath on her neck.

"The sensors picked us up in the Phoenix Reaches," her voice hung in the air, "they've finally found me, you're all dead because of me."

Elara sat in a quiet embrace with Zora for a moment, stunned, unable to respond. *They're still hunting her, out here in the Reaches? Never relenting.* The thought of the inquisitors out there hunting them drove an icy spike through her heart, and she shivered. Zora's arms tightened around Elara, as if she were taking the role as the older sister now.

Zora stuffed her face into Elara's shoulder as she began to sob softly, her tears soaking into the fabric of Elara's overalls. In an attempt to comfort her, Elara began to stroke Zora's hair.

"This isn't your problem, kid," Pulse said, trying to urge Elara to leave it alone.

Elara replied to him with a low "Shhhhh," as if to simultaneously comfort Zora and tell Pulse to shut up.

After a few minutes of holding Zora as she stroked her hair, Zora's body went limp, a soothing snore vibrating against her chest. Elara lay her limp body back and slid sheets over her, the kitten snuggled up against her. Elara tucked her in, leaned in close enough to feel her soft breath against her cheek, and pressed her forehead to the sleeping woman's, noses touching. "I'll protect you, Zora, even if it gets me killed."

Elara gave Zora a soft kiss on her cheek as she pulled herself back up to her feet. She mimicked the gesture Zora had done earlier, pinching at the air to decrease the volume of the music to a low hum. Then she made a tapping gesture in the air to lower the illumination to a comforting level. She turned to Zora and smiled, a lingering uncertainty of the future bubbling up in her gut, before she turned to leave the room.

"The Enclave are ruthless, kid," Pulse broke the silence, "if they show their mugs, you're better off not getting involved."

Elara ignored him as she trudged toward the engine room. *And what? Leave her to deal with those zealots alone? Not a chance.*

Chapter Ten

THE ENGINE ROOM WAS still a mess, right where Elara had left it. The aft bulkhead was still covered with black soot, and the floor was scattered with broken fragments from the explosion. She had only managed to scrub the side walls and walkway. The back wall and manifold, the worst of it, she had left untouched the moment she found the valve.

"I can't believe he thinks I did this," she said, the words sharp only because they were balancing something raw and burning underneath.

Pulse hummed, "Let's hope he doesn't figure out that we changed the manifest, or else your goose'll be cooked."

"Now, hold on a minute." Elara stomped her boot, releasing a fresh cloud of soot from the floor, "I'm not the one who changed that."

"You didn't stop me," Pulse retorted.

"I never had the chance." Elara rolled her eyes.

"Besides," Pulse's mechanical voice was cool, "it isn't like anyone would believe the AI in your head did it."

Elara huffed, then examined the state of the engine room. "Ugh, what a mess."

"Yeah," Pulse whistled, "guess you'd better get to cleaning up."

Elara picked up the bottle with the orange, soapy solution and the green scrubbing pad, but the anger simmering in her chest wasn't about the mess, it was the same old grief, the same Dominion-maroon color she had seen on Sylen's fatigues, the shade that lived in every memory of her parents' deaths. "Not that mess," she said, her voice strained. "The mess of being accused of all this." The anger didn't feel clean. It felt old. Like smoke in her lungs that never quite cleared. She dropped her arms and allowed them to hang as she pouted, then sighed, got on her hands and knees, and started wiping up the floor.

"Hold on, Elara," a slow drawl of a voice belted from the open hatch, "you might accidentally wipe away our evidence."

Elara's body twisted on her ankles, "Who?" Her eyes scanned the opening and focused on the skinny frame of the ship's navigator. "Kael, what do you want?"

Kael passed through into the engine room and handed Elara a pair of latex gloves. "Here, put these on, wouldn't want to leave any false evidence."

"What do you care if I incriminate myself?" Elara snapped a glove over her organic hand.

"Look," Kael's voice dropped, his eyes hidden behind his brown bangs, "I jumped the gun in accusing you," he muttered, shoulders drawn in, as if embarrassed he'd let his temper show.

"Go on," Elara prodded.

"I guess..." He shuffled his feet. "I overreacted when I heard you say there was a saboteur in the crew."

"You guess?" Elara glared at Kael. "I thought you were s'posed to be an FC scout," she said, her breath heavy. "I thought you were s'posed to be trained to be a professional."

Kael ran his fingers through his messy hair and smiled, "You sound just like my mother." He knelt down beside Elara and started to sift through the debris, "Actually, she thought I wasn't ready for the Rangers," he admitted, rubbing the back of his neck—a tiny tell of lingering insecurity. "So, I signed on with the *Aurora* to prove I could be more than just another pilot."

Elara's eyes focused on the mess strewn across the floor. "I'm sorry." Her fingers sifted through the stray pieces. "I guess I was afraid that you'd convince the captain that I did this and she'd leave me stranded on an asteroid."

Kael laughed, "Well, first off, there's really no convincing the captain," his chuckle lingered, "she always seems to have her mind made up about one thing or another."

"And second?" Elara looked up at him.

"Well," he hesitated, his eyes lingering on Elara's face a beat too long, a soft warmth in his gaze, "I think the captain likes you."

"What do you mean?" Elara raised an eyebrow.

Kael continued to sift through the debris, picking up a piece of slag metal and holding it up to his eyes to inspect it, "It's just that, didn't you see how she shut down Varek when he wanted to talk about his research during supper?" his hazel eyes looked past the piece of metal to Elara, "but when you started talking about there being a saboteur on board, she was all about talking business, and she looked at you… with genuine interest. I've never seen her do that before."

Elara's eyes dropped. "Hadn't noticed that."

"What's ironic is that rumor has it, the two of them are in deep." Kael gave a crooked smile.

"In deep?" Elara raised her eyebrow. "In deep what?"

Kael made a lewd gesture with his hands. "Y'know what I mean."

Elara blushed, "I'm certain I don't." Her face went bright red. She knew that the gesture implied something sexual, but she didn't want to admit it to Kael. It was already awkward working so closely with him.

An uneasy yearning burned in his eyes. "Look, I don't want to be just another competent pilot," he said, and despite trying to hide it, a flicker of embarrassment crossed his face. "This isn't just a job. I wish I could have the kind of trust from the captain that you seem to have from her." He was bearing his soul to Elara, the stowaway girl he'd just met.

The look in his eyes, the determination, it's really cute. Elara's mind drifted to earlier, when he had almost kissed her here in the engine room, and her heart quickened. *Don't sell yourself short.* His elbow brushed against hers, and she leaned in to allow the touch to linger. *What would it be like if we were more than just crewmates?* She touched her lips. *No, stifle that thought. Another life, a different world.*

Kael gave a warm smile, "Anyway, we should really get busy looking for clues, it's getting late, and the morning passdown will be here before we know it."

Elara's eyes drooped at the thought of an all-nighter. "Why don't you see if you can get fingerprints off the valve handle while I keep sifting through this mess," she suggested.

Kael stood up, wiping the soot off his legs, "Good idea."

Elara pointed at the manifold, "It's the one at the top of the stack." She watched him as he pointed at the correct valve, nodding in confirmation. His face screwed up with concern. She had opened the valve without thinking about fingerprints, though, fortunately, she had thought to use her mechanical hand, just in case the pipes were hot. She smiled up at him, thrusting her cybernetic arm into the air, "Don't worry, I used this one."

"Y'know," Kael began dusting the valve handle, "when I first joined the crew, I was given an important task. I was elated the captain had put her trust in me." He shuffled his feet, "I was given the job of restocking the ship's supplies. I worked my ass off making sure everything was perfect." He let out a goofy smile. "I even made sure there was a backup stash for the backup stash."

Elara crouched among the debris, sifting through the wreckage, her fingers toying with a piece of blistered plastisteel. She twisted on her toes to let Kael know she was listening.

"We had been out of port for weeks, when Sylen approached me." Kael ran his fingers through his hair and chuckled, "He was a little upset, and here I was, straight outta the junior scouts, trying to make sure to follow every order. He was like 'Where's the stock of munitions, kid?' I didn't know how to respond. I thought I had taken care of everything. I was proud of my efforts, and here we were, light-years away from the nearest port, no ammunition stocked up, and it was all my fault."

Elara's eyes went wide, "You had no munitions?"

Kael laughed, "Nothing, not a single round, and we were in some rough space." He rocked back on his heels, "Luckily, nothing happened, but I was afraid everyone was going to kill me."

"I bet," Elara giggled. "What happened?"

"The captain stepped in, cooled everyone off." Kael whistled.

"She was like, 'Leave the kid alone, it wasn't his job to stock the munitions, it was mine.' I didn't know what to do, I was afraid that the crew was going to mutiny because of me, but they didn't. The captain smoothed it all out. She said that she had stocked the munitions and forgot to give Sylen the manifest. The crates were still sitting there in the cargo bay where she had left them."

Elara tilted her head to look up at Kael, "So, when I brought up the saboteur?"

"I overreacted." Kael continued, "I was afraid it was going to end up with everyone at each other's throats again, and it would be my fault."

Elara let out a gasp, "Why would it be your fault?"

"Because now I'm the second officer." Kael put his face in his hand. "Maintaining the crew dynamics are up to me now."

"I'm not seeing anything here," he muttered, letting out a long, drawn-out breath. "Looks like our saboteur has half a brain cell and didn't leave any fingerprints. You find anything down there?

Elara crawled along the floor closer to the manifold. "Nothing back there," a dull flash of dark red caught her eye, and she focused in between two of the pipes.

The piece of fabric would have been impossible to see at any other angle besides where she was crouched down to the floor. From there, with the help of her cybernetic eyes, she could barely make out the slight flutter of the fabric's frayed edges.

She stood up and tucked her fingers in between the narrow gap between the pipes. They swept up against the coarse bit of material, and she pulled out a piece of filthy fabric with her fingertips.

"What's that?" Kael knelt down beside Elara, a little too close.

Elara could smell his shampoo, it was a sweet, fruit-like fragrance. The only fruit she had ever really gotten in the Dredges was a bland, reconstituted fruit supplement that had more filler than actual fruit, so she couldn't place the smell, but it was wonderful. She leaned in closer to get a better whiff.

"It looks like a piece of torn material," her voice was airy and light, her pulse quickening, her pupils dilating, and as Kael's hands reached out to hers, she found it difficult to breathe. "From clothing, perhaps?"

She couldn't tell right away what the color of the fabric was under the red lighting in the engine room, especially saturated with grease and grime.

Kael's hands wrapped around Elara's. She bit her lip, and the unexpected pull of his fingers that dragged the material out of her hands made her lean closer in, especially as he pulled his body away to get a better look at the cloth.

She lost her balance and fell onto Kael's shoulder. He didn't notice as he held the material up to the light, his finger tracing along the surface. "There's something embroidered on this."

Elara snapped out of her lust and pulled the cloth closer to her to get a better look, "What? Where?"

Kael pointed out the subtle clusters of thread that raised up from the fabric, which vaguely resembled letters. "I can't tell what they say."

Pulse butted in, "Use the spectral analyzer in your eyes, kid."

Elara sat up straight, "Oh, right. Thanks for that."

Kael looked at her like she was an alien, "Thanks for what?"

Elara blushed, "Never mind, let me take a closer look at that." She took the fabric from Kael, her vision changing to a disorienting array of dozens of topographical overlays, each one a menagerie of psychedelic colors. The display would be completely useless without the AR display menu that let her filter out the overlays that weren't helpful. After a few seconds of analysis, and the help of Pulse's AI brain, a fully reconstituted image of the fabric was visible. "Imperial Marines," she muttered.

"What was that?" Kael leaned in to try and catch what she was saying.

Pulse took a screenshot of the analysis Elara had compiled and stored it as a file on the ship's network. She snapped her head to look into Kael's eyes, her vision reverting to normal, "It says 'Imperial Marines.'"

Kael took the patch from her hands and inspected it. "Are you sure? I can't read it."

Elara pulled the data-pad out of Kael's pocket and navigated through the ship's file system to the location where Pulse had saved the image. She loaded it up and showed it to Kael, "See? I used my spectral analyzer in my eyes."

Kael looked at the image, "Hmm, you're right." Then he turned and leaned in close to get a better look into Elara's green eyes, "You have cyber-eyes? I never would've guessed, they look so natural."

Elara sighed a soft, pleased exhale. "Yeah, my folks wanted me to have the best, sank their life savings into me. There's no time for that, though." Elara's breath became erratic. "You know what this means?"

"This patch could've been here ages," Kael tried to stop Elara's train of flawed logic, "I mean, look at all that grime built up on there—it could have been here since the ship was in drydock.

Elara, exasperated, took the patch from Kael's hands and held it up to him, "There's only one person… one person who would've worn this." Her eyes were cold, determined, her mind set. "It's obvious the saboteur is Sylen."

Kael chuckled, "I've been on this crew for over a year now." He stepped back. "Sure, Sylen was once an Imperial Marine, but…"

"Once an Imperial, always an Imperial," Elara was blunt, matter-of-fact. There was no changing her mind.

Kael continued, "But, I've never seen him wear a single Imperial Dominion patch on his fatigues, I think he ripped them off years ago when he retired. There's bad blood there, not sure what, but I don't think he's our guy."

Elara scoffed, "Well, I guess it's up to the captain to decide, then." She snatched the patch from Kael and stormed off through the open hatch. "See you in the morning."

Chapter Eleven

Elara could feel Kael's eyes boring into her back; she was still furious at him. *How could he not see it? It's obviously Sylen, the Dominion scrag in maroon fatigues, just like the soldiers who burned my parents.* Her gut didn't need logic; pain had already made the decision. She couldn't look at him even when he'd met her in the corridor outside the captain's stateroom and had said hi to her.

Elara stood before the captain's cluttered desk, Kael at her side. The stray Imperial Marine patch, now its maroon color faintly visible in the yellow light that streamed down from the overhead lamp, sat atop the desk before the captain.

Elara's eyes were drawn away from the stacks of clutter that lined the desk, toward the framed photographs on the wall behind the captain.

She recalled the photo of the two girls from the last time she had been in the captain's stateroom. Her eyes were now drawn to another that hung on the wall before her. The two blonde girls, teenagers in this photo. One girl smiled brightly at the camera, the other giggling, her head tucked in her twin's shoulder. *I've seen this photo before. From where, though?* She strained her memory for the information, but the memory was an apparition, sneaking away every time she almost had it. The recognition was an unnerving sensation that settled deep within her gut.

Something about those girls' eyes is so familiar. God, it's maddening, it's somewhere in my brain, but I can't place it.

"Let me get this straight." The captain leaned in over her desk, her hand tapping on the frayed patch. "You think whoever shut off that valve accidentally left this patch?" She leaned back in her large, leather, swivel chair, tucking her index finger under her chin.

Elara nodded, "Aye, ma'am." Her voice caught in her throat in a slight stutter. She could still feel Kael's eyes boring into her. "I took a recording of the spectral image of that patch and uploaded it onto the ship's network."

The captain turned in her chair toward her computer terminal and made a swiping gesture with her fingers in midair to force the display on the monitor to scroll.

"The file is in the folder marked 'Sabotage Incident Reports'." Elara leaned in over the desk to see the display, "That's the one, right there," she darted her finger to point out the folder.

The captain quickly tapped the air and sat back into her chair. "Hmm, interesting," she muttered. "You say that this patch was stuck in the plasma valve manifold?"

As the captain leaned forward, Elara's gaze drifted over the messy surface of the desk. Amidst the clutter, stacks of manifests, an empty coffee cup, and the greasy Imperial Marine patch, Elara noticed a specific spot, a large, heavy, brass paperweight shaped like a stylized Alliance insignia. It sat dead center over an older, barely visible seam in the plastisteel desktop. The paperweight looked permanently affixed, but Elara noted the slight, almost invisible drag marks in the dust around its base, as if it had been recently and quickly moved. *A perfect hiding spot.*

"Yes, ma'am." Kael stepped forward, jaw tensing, a flicker of doubt tightening the corners of his eyes. "We… suspect Sylen was responsible for the sabotage." His voice wavered on Sylen's name, a professional report at odds with his own judgment. "Not because I believe he did it," Kael added quickly, eyes flicking toward Elara and away again, "but because right now, he's the only suspect who fits what little we've got."

Elara swiveled her head toward Kael. *What? Last night, he was insisting it wasn't Sylen. Why fold now? For unity? For the captain?* The contradiction scraped across her nerves. Her mouth was agape, her eyes wide, stunned.

The captain glanced up at Elara, "Do you agree with this assessment, dear?"

Elara snapped her head back to face the captain, "Y–yes, ma'am. It's no secret that he was once a member of the Imperial Marines, and as you can see from the spectral analysis, this patch clearly says 'Imperial Marines.'" She smiled to herself.

The captain folded her hands in front of her, "This evidence is hardly damning," her tone was serious. "Sylen may have been an Imperial Marine, but he retired years ago and has no connection with them or the Dominion. He's turned his back on them."

"But, ma'am," Elara tried to protest.

"He has no more love for the Dominion than you or I do," the captain sighed. "I'm sorry, dear, this patch could've been there long before Sylen even set foot onboard."

"But, ma'am," Elara attempted her protest again. She had no real rebuttal, just a gut feeling fueled by her hatred of the

Dominion and her mistrust of Sylen.

"Were you aware that this ship was originally commissioned by the Imperial Merchant Society as a freighter in the Dominion?"

Elara shook her head. "No, ma'am." *Stupid girl, you knew that. The* Aurora *was called the* Persephony *back then, during the war. She smuggled weapons for the Dominion.*

The captain nodded. "This patch could have been there since the ship was in drydock. The Imperial Marines have an engineering department, perhaps one of the builders was a retiree."

Elara let out a meek nod. "I guess, ma'am," she conceded, her voice low and defeated.

"I want the two of you to keep your eyes open for anything suspicious and report directly to me." She leaned back in her seat once more and picked up a data-pad, her fingers swiping along the glass surface. "Dismissed."

Kael stood at attention, nodded at Elara, and turned, marching out through the hatch. Elara stood there, her muscles frozen. *Should I tell her,* she thought to herself, her throat dry and her hand starting to shake. Without weighing the impulse further, an eruption burst forth from her mouth, "Captain, may I address something else?"

The captain's gaze flicked to the closed hatch where Kael had just exited, a subtle relief mixed with a hint of longing washing over her face before she turned back to Elara with a practiced calm.

Expecting someone? Elara wondered. *Maybe… Varek? No. Stupid.* She mentally scoffed at herself. *None of my business anyway.*

As the thought crossed her mind, Elara's eyes flicked to the ceiling. She would have expected a smoke detector, or even a vent, instead, however, her focus snagged on a small, unobtrusive security camera lens near the corner. The camera was stationary, but the tiny red indicator light blinked once, and the reflection on the lens seemed to subtly, almost imperceptibly, shift its angle, focusing slightly more on her.

She blinked. *Just a trick of the light...* but the tiny red indicator blinked again, almost like it was syncing to her breath. A prickle ran down her spine. *Someone else could be watching.*

The captain set the data-pad down and looked into Elara's eyes, "Of course, dear, how can I help?"

Elara paused, not sure how to proceed, but decided that she needed to break the ice, "So, you were an Alliance fleet captain?"

The captain smiled. "Actually, by the time I retired, I was a commodore, in command of the Vanguard, the flagship of the eleventh fleet," she turned in her seat and pointed her thumb at a photo of her standing on the command bridge. The main viewscreen displayed the colossal battleship in orbit around Earth, framed by the cold, dark emptiness of space.

Elara's eyes grew wide, "The Vanguard was a beast." She leaned in, her voice giddy despite her earlier weariness.

The fleet, something real, something powerful. Awe-inspiring. A stark contrast to the hollow promises of the AP counsel. Her eyes fixated on the hull of the battleship in the picture. *The ships, the engineering... that's progress. Something worth admiring.*

Elara continued breathlessly, "The tenth-generation drive system alone..." her voice began to crack, and she gulped down a heavy breath, "I wish I could'a seen her engine room before—"

"Yes, well," the captain averted her eyes, "there's nothing we could have done against the Phoenix and the brunt of the Imperial fleet in that battle."

The Phoenix, Elara scoffed, *it may have won that battle, but once the treaties were signed, their admiral up and disappeared, along with the ship and her crew.*

Realization struck Elara like a firebug flashing its light. The *captain was there, in the last battle with the Dominion. Her fleet against theirs.* She let out the air in her lungs in a long sigh. "I didn't realize you were there when the Vanguard was destroyed."

"A lot of good shipmates died that day." Her composure never wavered. "To think, if the council would have just signed that peace treaty when it was first presented, there'd be a lot more able-bodied men and women in the fleet today."

That treaty was signed just days after the defeat of the eleventh fleet, in that battle. She frowned. The Dominion had presented the treaty a month before, and their reluctance had cost the AP not only the eleventh fleet but also the Veridia colony that the eleventh fleet was sent to protect. Her mind reeled at the memory imprinted in her brain from the holo broadcast she had witnessed as a young child. The image chilled her core.

So much death, so much destruction. She sighed, her fingers toying with the shape of her locket through the fabric of her t-shirt.

"What're you doin' kid?" Pulse protested, uncertain what she was about to do.

It'll all just continue on. The AP declares war on the IP, more people dead, for no reason. She spat against the bile. Her father's voice permeated her heart, *"Unify the five factions."* Her heart beat against her chest. *I have to unlock the secrets of my father's microchip.*

Elara winced, a thousand warnings screamed in her head. But

the memory of her father's smile cut through her doubt, and she knew what she had to do. *This is it. The ultimate gamble. If I don't trust someone now,* she realized, *I'll never move this forward.* She gulped hard. *Can I trust her, the captain?*

Every instinct of self-preservation, honed in the brutal Dredges, cried out against it. But the captain's eyes, the faint hint of something familiar, something warm, like home, drew Elara in. A promised understanding that she craved desperately. *This feels right somehow.*

Her fingers danced along the tarnished silver chain around her neck, "I have to tell you something, but—" she started to pull the locket out from under her t-shirt.

"Don't do it, kid, you don't know if you can trust her," Pulse barked.

The locket fell out over her chest as it slid from the neckline of her t-shirt. *No turning back now.* She lifted the chain where it was attached to the loop of the locket, dangling it out in front of her. "My father gave me this before he and my mother…" she choked on her words.

"You crazy, kid?" Pulse's voice rumbled. "You're gonna bring the heat on us."

Elara cleared her throat, trying to drown out the AI voice in her head. "Inside is his last and greatest invention." She unclasped the locket to reveal the small microchip hidden inside. "I think it's something that will reunite the five factions," she paused and glanced up to the ceiling," at least that's what my father told me."

The captain tapped her finger on her cheek, her lips cocked to the corner of her mouth, "I'm impressed that you trust me with your secret, dear." Her steel-blue eyes darted up to meet Elara's.

"A secret like that could bring the whole galaxy against us."

The captain's gaze, usually unreadable, fractured for half a second. Recognition. Pain. Guilt. As if she had seen this locket before… and failed someone connected to it. *Is that recognition? A ghost memory?*

The captain's jaw tightened almost imperceptibly, as if she knew exactly what Elara held, and the immense danger it represented. She stood up and started to pace behind her desk. "There are powerful people out there who profit from the wars and strife among the factions, reunification is counter to many of their interests."

"This is it, kid." Pulse was saying I told you so. "The jig is up."

Elara gulped and held her breath. *I've always known this secret's groundbreaking. Though I never suspected the danger it might bring me and the crew.* She nodded, never breaking eye contact with the captain.

"I guess you don't know what's on that chip just yet?" The captain stopped pacing and pointed her finger at the locket.

Elara shook her head, "I haven't had access to the computing power to decrypt the files."

The captain smiled, "Go talk with Zora, she's on duty on the bridge, let her know that I have approved for you to have fifty percent of the computer's resources unlocked for a special project." She sat back down and leaned back in her seat, "I want you to unlock those files."

Fifty percent… Elara's stomach dipped. *That's massive. If I'm not careful, I'll choke the ship just to chase a dream.*

"That level of allocation will degrade secondary systems during any high-stress event," Pulse warned, his tone all business.

"Recommendation: set an automatic protocol to de-allocate our share during emergencies."

She gave the smallest nod. *He's right.* Last thing I want is this project getting someone killed.

The captain's gaze was bold and determined, as if she had as much at stake in unlocking the files as Elara herself. "There's no need to tell anyone else about your special project," she said, winking at Elara. "If the slag hits the fan, better that the rest of the crew is oblivious to the facts. It might mean their lives."

The captain's composure softened as she leaned forward, resting her elbows on the desk. "Elara," her gentle voice perked Elara's ears, drawing her attention, "I see that fire in you. It's your gift, don't let it go to waste." Her steely blue eyes penetrated into Elara's soul. "But charging in half-cocked, letting anger steer your course…" She paused, something tightening in her eyes. "I've let anger steer my course before, and it cost me more than you know. That's how you end up letting the shadows of the Dredges hang over you." She winked and sat up straight, her wry smile returned, creasing her lips. "Take it from someone who's learned the hard way. Take a moment, think, then act. You've got the brains for it."

Elara blinked. The captain's warm tone served to temper the snap of her words, but the reprimand stung deep all the same. Elara unclenched her fists and nodded slowly. "I–I'll try, ma'am."

She tucked the locket back under her shirt, slowly turned, and plodded out the hatch, the captain's words echoing through her cranium, a criticism she wasn't ready to accept, but it clung to her ribs like a bruise, refusing to fade.

Chapter Twelve

The bridge of the *Aurora* was quiet. The lights were low, a red glow engulfing the area. Zora sat hunched over the sensor panel along the starboard bulkhead, her fingers tapping her chin as she hummed the melody for the Psycho Sisters' latest hit, 'Silicon Nights.'

Elara hung in the hatchway. *I hope she's okay.* She had been worried about Zora since last night. Her eyes traced the young woman's delicate fingers as they danced along the control panel, a soft beeping registering her commands.

Elara's mind drifted to Zora wearing nothing but her underwear, her body pressed against her own. She imagined her neck and back were the console, Zora's long fingers dancing and sliding against her flesh. Zora's sweet breath lingered in Elara's memory, the way the gentle, warm air had pressed against her neck, and the thought had her own breath growing heavy. She shook her head. *No, she was just drunk.* She shut down her silent fantasy. *There's no way she'd be into you, Elara, don't be stupid.* Besides, she was merely attracted to the closeness Zora had imposed, not the young woman herself.

Elara let out a low rumble as she gently cleared her throat to announce her presence, "Pardon me, Zora," she said, acting like she had just walked onto the bridge.

Zora sat bolt upright, a gasp of surprise caught in her throat. Her hand immediately went to tuck a stray strand of long, dark hair behind her ear, her face flushed a deep pink that stained her pale, scarred skin. "I... I'm sorry," she stammered, her heart hammering against her ribs. Her violet eyes, wide with a mixture of fear and awe, tried and failed to hold contact with Elara's.

Is she embarrassed about what she said last night? Elara closed the gap as she approached the sensor station, trying to act nonchalantly, "Er, that is to say," *what do I say to her?* She cleared her throat again. "Good morning." Her hand fidgeted as she made a half-hearted wave. "The captain said that I should talk with you to unlock some computer resources for a—" she paused, her eyes dancing around the bridge, "a personal project."

"Oh," Zora's voice was low, barely audible, "good morning." She turned back toward the sensor panel and entered a few more commands, "How much of the reserves do you need for your project?"

Elara's hand touched Zora's chair, and she could feel her weight shift away from her. *Am I too close? Is this weird?* She flinched her hand back to herself. Zora's body stiffened, but her head tilted, subtly pointing toward Elara. She could hear Zora's faint heartbeat flutter through her cybernetic eardrums, her breath was slow and heavy. A deep sigh escaped Zora's lips as Elara pulled back. The silent lament was palpable, the air thick with it, as though the touch was too brief, too forbidden.

Elara hesitated. "Well, the captain said to tell you to allot fifty percent."

Zora swiveled her chair. "Fifty percent?" she exclaimed, her voice louder than Elara had ever heard from her. "Are you sure the captain said to give you fifty percent?" She relaxed her muscles and looked down at the floor. In a hushed tone, she continued, "That's a lot."

Elara waved her hands in front of her. "Oh, no, I don't need nearly that much." She stuffed her hands under the bib of her overalls and began to rock back and forth on the soles of her boots, "Maybe something like… thirty-five percent? And… can we set it to automatically deallocate if the ship needs it during a crisis?" She was more or less asking for permission.

Zora nodded, "I can afford to give you thirty-five percent." She slid over to another console and started typing, her hands moving fluidly across the surface of the digital display. "There, did you need anything else?"

I should let it go. Can't shake the feeling, though. Is it appropriate to mention last night? Elara drew in a deep, unsteady breath that hitched in her chest, "I couldn't help but notice," she paused to gauge Zora's reaction. Zora sat there waiting, she lifted her violet eyes and met Elara's. For a moment, Elara couldn't tell if this was the right time. Zora nodded her head slightly as if to tell her to go on. "Last night, you were," Elara gulped, *there's no backing out now,* "you were intoxicated, and you said some things."

Zora's face went red, and she waved her hand in the air, "Oh, just forget about that." She hid her face behind her hair.

Elara glanced back to the open hatch. *No one there.* Then she knelt beside Zora, "I want to be your friend, Zora," *Am I coming off too strong?* She took a deep breath and focused her eyes through Zora's hair to see hers. "What you said last night was very serious.

I thought about it when I lay in bed."

"Don't worry about that," Zora pleaded with Elara, her hands trembling.

She has so much trauma buried deep inside her. Should I let it go? She thought, *No!* "Zora, I can't force you to talk about it, but I hope you will," she let her breath out slowly. "You can trust me, I won't talk to anyone about what you tell me."

Zora nodded, "I know," she whispered, "I'm just not sure I'm ready yet." She tucked her hair back behind her ear and looked up at Elara, letting out a long sigh.

I need to open up to her first, to bridge the gap. Elara smiled gently. *I wonder if she'll hate me after I tell her…*

She hesitated, hoping the moment would pass, then she let out a low, soft whisper, realizing with a jolt that she had never spoken these words aloud to anyone, "Before I came to be… aboard the *Aurora*, I was a pickpocket in the Dredges."

Zora's eyes shot her a look of surprise as she thrust her hands over her pockets in a protective stance.

Elara smiled, "Don't worry, I won't pick your pocket." She chuckled. "Actually, I had kind of a little family." Her mind drifted back to the shanty. She could still see those accusatory eyes of Milo's threadbare doll. She took a breath to push her guilt back. "Jax was a few months older than me. He was brave and smart. Then there was Tess," she stifled a giggle, "she was ten, absolutely adorable, and hilarious." Her tenor dropped, becoming serious and somber. "And then there was Milo… he was six…" her voice trailed off, her heart pounding in her chest, her eyes glazed over as she stared through Zora.

Elara clenched her eyes until moisture started to form along their edges. "I left them… and they were gone… it's all my fault." Tears streamed forth at the confession.

Zora reached out to touch Elara's hand, the soft flesh gliding gently over her own rough, calloused fingers. "What happened to them, where did they go?"

Elara gazed into Zora's eyes. The glistening violet membrane caught the light and shimmered, "I don't know. Best case scenario… they were taken by the Enforcers, and they're in a cell locked away, at least they'll have three meals a day, right?" She offered a fake smile, a facade to mask her true fear, her doubt that it would be so simple.

Zora took the bait, "And the worst-case scenario?"

Elara couldn't look Zora in the eye, and she took a labored breath. "The gangs… worst-case, they got them." Her mind fractured at the imaginings of what might have befallen them at the hands of the gangs. She paused, and her frame shuddered, her voice cracked, her vision blurring from the tears that now soaked her cheeks. "I can't get into the specifics," she took a deep breath, trying to steady her quivering voice, and lifted her eyes back up to meet Zora's. "Let's just say… those sickos get off on the kinds of horrors that are only whispered in the dark." She hoped her words reached Zora. It was her deepest, darkest confession, her greatest failing.

Zora smiled at Elara. "It wasn't your fault." She hesitated, collecting her words. "If you had gone to rescue them, you could have been captured too." She sighed, the corners of her lips softening into a cute, bashful smile that cut into her lips, her eyes soft and inviting. "I was a stowaway like you when the captain first found me."

She knows that I stowed away? How? Elara's heart pounded in her chest, fear mounting. *I'm slag.*

Zora paused, her eyes cast down, "They'd tortured me since I was a little girl." She glanced up to Elara, her eyes now threatening tears.

"They?" Elara met her gaze, "Who do you mean?"

"The Elders." Zora took a breath. "They're kind of like the spiritual leaders of the Enclave." She paused, taking her time. "They're very strict, and I was treated like a rebellious heretic for as long as I can remember." Her hand danced across the scars that marred her other hand, "Their punishments were severe." She frowned, tears formed jagged rivers along the scars on her cheek.

"That's horrible," Elara muttered. *So much pain, so much suffering. Zora, you are made of some strong stuff. I'm so weak compared to you.*

Zora nodded. "The re-education camps were the worst. My own mother turned me in to the inquisitors because I didn't follow the teachings of the Elders." Her voice hung in the air like a balloon. "I was only three."

Elara's back convulsed, her frame snapping straight like a stick. "Three?" *So much cruelty. What could a three-year-old girl do against their dogma?*

Zora gave a pitiful smile. "They took me away in the middle of the night to a place only the Great One knows."

"The Great One?" Elara blinked. She had heard vague references about the Enclave's supreme being, but she'd never bothered to ask before.

Zora giggled, holding her hand up to her mouth, "I know, it all seems so stupid now, but they had a kind of hold over us, their children." Zora's eyes darted up to Elara's again. "The Great One is," she paused to gather her words, perhaps trying not to sound like a religious nutjob. "That is, the doctrine of the Enclave's belief says there is a powerful force in the galaxy that left artifacts for his children to worship him through."

"Like the Zeta artifact that scientists found on Pluto," Elara erupted. *A fundamental link that led to the discovery of faster-than-light travel, the Spike drive.*

The spike drive essentially folded real space like a sheet of paper and literally punched a hole through the membrane between space and time to create temporary wormholes. However, after a century of constant use, vast rifts had formed, making many sectors of space unnavigable. Thus, the spike drive had been outlawed by four of the five factions, only the Enclave still used them.

Zora nodded, "The catacombs under the Elder's Hall are rumored to house thousands of artifacts."

Elara's eyes went wide. "Wow, to think that all that technology sits hoarded underground." She whistled. "With so much suffering and poverty in the galaxy, so few resources, we could've solved all that with a fraction of that tech."

Zora shook her head. "The Elders preach that to do so would be a great heresy." She went quiet, her face unreadable, and Elara wasn't convinced what it was that Zora actually believed.

A profound quiet engulfed the bridge. *There's a lot to think about. Poor Zora. So tortured and lost.* A shift in the air stirred, and the hair on the back of Elara's neck stood up. It was as if they were no longer alone. Someone was standing at the open hatchway to the bridge.

"Morning, crew," Kael bellowed from the opening, he stretched his arms above his head. "You two better go get some flapjacks before Sylen scarfs them all down."

The image of Sylen stuffing his face with pancakes made Elara giggle. Her eyes met Zora's, and they shared a conspiratorial smile. *God, when was the last time I had a genuine pancake, not one of those vending machine ones but a real one made from eggs and milk?* She licked her lips, *I wonder if they use real maple syrup.* Even after Canada became a nuclear wasteland during the AI crisis, scientists had managed to isolate the DNA of maple trees to produce the real thing. *So expensive but so, so worth it.*

Elara bubbled with excitement, her eyes urging Zora to accompany her to the mess deck. Zora began to move slowly to comply with her silent request.

"Wait," Zora gulped, her face going white a full second before any alarm sounded, eyes shooting a cold, startled look at Elara. Her breath hitched, and her thoughts scattered in sudden, quiet panic. Zora's entire body tensed, freezing mid-movement as if she sensed a blow before it landed, her gaze snapping to the sensor display with a horrified intensity that made her look instantly white as a sheet. It wasn't the look of someone reacting to an alarm, it was the look of someone anticipating a blow. Her fingers flew across the console, not to read data but as if trying to grasp something invisible slipping away.

Then, after Zora's reaction, a soft beeping of an alarm erupted from the sensor console. An audible trigger to her previous uncanny reaction.

A startle of concern washed over Zora's face, and beneath it, a flash of shame, the kind that came from knowing things she didn't want to know. She slid her fingers over the display to examine the alert. "That's odd." Her voice was filled with a disconcerting concern. "The sensor array has just gone down." She looked up to Elara. "See, right there," she pointed at the display.

She knew before the ship did. A cold flash rushed through Elara's frame. *That look… that wasn't just checking a screen, it was like reacting to a ghost.* The memory of Zora's choked, whispered warning on the mess deck about looking at the *'shadows, not the light,'* now merged with the drunk, bone-chilling clarity from the night before. *'The Great One's shadow is already on your heart.'* The words struck a chilling layer of ancient, terrifying certainty deep within Elara's core. *It's like she's seeing danger before it pops up.* Her mind fractured and failed to register the concept.

Kael tapped on the navigational panel at the fore of the bridge. "No good." His breath heaved an unsteady breath. "Without the sensors, the nav computer can't complete the calculations for the next jump. We'll have to start them over again once the sensors are back online." He huffed, "Great, more delays."

Elara leaned in to get a closer look, her hand accidentally brushing against Zora's shoulder, and she jumped back slightly. "Sorry 'bout that." Elara moved her hand and glanced down at the console. "Looks like the fault is on C-deck."

The *Aurora* had four decks, starting with A-deck, where the bridge was, down to D-deck, where the engine room was. Most of the decks were roughly a hundred feet long, save for D-deck, which was only around fifty feet long. Elara would have to walk past the mess decks and smell the aroma of those flapjacks on her way to inspect the damage to the sensor array. She frowned.

Kael approached the hatch, giving Zora a quick once-over,

a flicker of concern tightening his brow before he apparently chalked her pallor up to lack of sleep or too much partying. "Zora, can you stay at the Com a while longer while I go check this out with Elara?"

Zora nodded, her long, raven hair bouncing gently on her shoulders.

Elara turned and walked toward Kael, "I wonder what could have caused the sensor array to go down?"

"Don't know." Kael shrugged. "Hope it's not another fire, I'm still growing my arm hair back since the last one."

Elara giggled, "The way you were floundering down there, you're lucky you didn't lose your eyebrows."

Kael gave Elara an annoyed glare, then the image of himself eyebrowless must have broken him, and he burst into laughter. "True, true," he hacked as he gasped for breath between his bellows.

Elara couldn't help but join in on the laughter as she passed through the hatchway in front of Kael.

Chapter Thirteen

The heavenly aroma of the flapjacks wafted from the mess deck. Sylen was still at the table, a heap of pancakes on his tray, the sappy, sticky syrup oozing along the sides of the stack, pooling along the edges of the tray's segmented indentations.

Elara sighed, "No pancakes for me." She turned away from the mess deck and followed Kael down the corridor.

"The panel should be just up ahead." Kael trudged along.

Elara sniffed the air, the smell of pancakes gone, replaced by something caustic, something melted. A sudden surge of understanding engulfed her, and she quickened her pace. "No, no, no!" She passed Kael and dashed to the closed panel, a thick black vapor seeping through the cracks. *Panel Thirteen,* she noted in a detached corner of her mind. Of course it is.

Her eyes darted around the corridor, spotting a tall PPE locker across the corridor. She bolted for the locker, flinging the doors open, and started pulling out a wide variety of safety items. "Face shield, electrical gloves, flash apron, sleeves, rubber mat." She ran through the checklist with an almost robotic efficiency, then began to don the safety equipment and spread the rubber mat down on the floor in front of the smoking panel. She pointed at an odd-looking, six-foot long hook that clung to the side of the locker, "Grab that, and if anything happens, use it to pull me off!"

She used the driver from her cybernetic arm to undo the bolts on the panel but then quickly removed the arm and set it aside. She felt naked, with Kael staring at her severed stump. *No time to care about that.* She blushed as she pried the panel off the wall with a small screwdriver.

As the panel cover slid off and fell to the floor, the inside of the panel bellowed a plume of acrid black smoke, the smell of burnt insulation assaulting her nostrils. Flashes of electricity arced and sparked from inside the panel, and Elara waved the smoke aside to find the culprit.

A small brass object was lodged between the high-voltage lines and the low-voltage lines, creating a dangerous short that had melted the sensitive data cables for the sensor array.

Elara gave Kael a quick glance, "Pull me off if I catch a shock."

Kael nodded, the fear in his eyes palpable. *I bet my eyes look just like his. I'm terrified.*

She reached into the open panel with her one arm, the long rubber sleeve weighing her down. She felt heat strike her chest, a shocking, searing pain, but kept her focus. The thick rubber fingertips of the gloves wrapped around the brass object, and she gently pulled it out. The smoke and arcing immediately stopped, but the smell lingered.

She winced and looked down. The rubber apron didn't fully cover her chest, and she felt the sting of the electrical burn blooming across her skin. *Stupid girl, but cutting power at the breaker would've dropped half the sensor grid with it,* and after Zora's reaction on the bridge, Elara wasn't willing to plunge the ship into blind panic. The shock of the pain in her chest had forced her to drop the small brass cylinder to the floor, and it rolled away—the last she'd seen of it, it had bounced toward the PPE locker when it slipped from her hand.

"You alright?" Kael inspected Elara as she turned around. "Hold on, I should tend to that burn." He dropped the shepherd's hook and pulled a first aid kit hanging from a harness along the bulkhead.

"Here," he guided Elara down to her knees, following her down, "sit here while I take care of that."

"I didn't know you knew first aid. Where, from the scouts?"

Kael let out a soft chuckle, "No, although it is fundamental knowledge in the scouts. I'm kind of self-taught."

He opened the case and pulled out an ointment. "This might sting a little," he squirted a small glob of the sticky paste onto his finger, then began to rub it into her chest.

Elara jumped as the sting of the burn on her skin erupted. "Ouch!"

"Sorry, I did tell you it would sting." Kael smiled.

"You said a little," Elara pouted, her bottom lip jutted out, "that was a big sting."

Kael smiled at her as he continued to work the paste gently with his fingers. Elara could feel the warmth of his hand against the skin of her chest, the sting numbed by his gentle touch. Her heart started to pound under his fingers, her cheeks flushing hot as her breath hitched, and she leaned into his arms, allowing him to take her weight. She wanted to speak up, but her voice couldn't break the lump that had formed in her throat.

"This reminds me of my parents. They were members of the

scouts," he began, his eyes glimmering as they focused on Elara's burns, a look of longing lingering in his gaze.

A profound sense of reassurance, of security washed over Elara. She felt safe under Kael's care.

The bitter stink of burnt insulation still clung to the air, a reminder that comfort here was borrowed and temporary.

"I remember my dad coming home after a mission," Kael continued, his fingers working in the ointment, his cheeks pink and his drawl slow and drawn. "Mom was on a mission of her own, and Dad was hurt badly."

"H-how old were you?" Elara let out a gentle whisper, her heart pounding.

Kael smiled. "I was about ten, I can still remember how he collapsed on the floor of the foyer." He gulped hard, and the movement of his fingers slowed as he tucked them under the neckline of Elara's t-shirt, "I was scared that he had died. I remember him pointing at the first aid kit, the only sound he made was a grunt."

Elara lifted her gaze, and his hazel eyes sparkled back, the longing shifting to something akin to lust. She leaned in, "I know what it's like to lose a parent, I'm sorry."

Kael let out a soft chuckle. "Oh, he didn't die there. In fact, I had to learn real quick about first aid. Talk about trial by fire. When Mom returned home, she was furious with him. I can still hear her words, 'You stupid scrag, how dare you get hurt, do you want to make poor Kael an orphan?'"

Elara looked down. *There's nothing wrong with being an orphan, I turned out alright.* She looked back up, her words soft and distant, her breath hitched in her throat, "What did your father say?"

Kael tilted his head back, "Well, he argued back. 'I'm an FC scout, and if my duty is to die, that slagging well is what I'll do.' Then Mom shot back, 'Over my dead body!'" Kael laughed hard as he slapped his knee, "That made Dad laugh. 'You better not die out there, you wanna make poor Kael an orphan?' The look on my dad's face made my mom laugh." His hand movements shifted from rubbing ointment to something more like a soft caress.

"What happened to your dad?" Elara looked back up, her eyes wide, "Did he ever get into trouble again?"

"Not like that. Mom forbade him from going on missions. I guess he was too injured to go back into active duty and had to retire." Kael lowered his voice, "Mom took a job as a trainer soon after. I guess dad had convinced her to for my sake, either that or she was getting too old for active assignments."

"Did your mom train you to be a scout?" Elara inquired, her breath low and hushed.

His fingers had stopped moving, stopped rubbing in the ointment, they just lingered there on her chest, the tips tucked under the t-shirt's neckline, "My mom didn't trust me to be a scout, I think she blamed me for my father's injuries, though she never told me why." He paused for a long moment, then his fingers slid slightly deeper into her shirt, "Mom said I wasn't ready yet, and she reached out to the captain. I guess they knew each other during the war. Apparently, the captain jumped at the chance, something about having the son of the best slagged scout in the galaxy, not sure if she meant Mom or Dad."

Her mind drifted back to the holo-vid space Westerns that her father loved to watch with her on lazy Sunday afternoons. The rangers who exacted justice at the end of their magneto hand-cannons pulsated in her heart like righteous fury.

The scouts' frontier justice, so admirable. She paused, soaking in Kael's words, *Yet his mother's hesitation to admit him into the scouts? Needing the captain's intervention?* It subtly reinforced her perception of the FC's 'slowness.' *Even for something as simple as joining the scouts, there are hurdles, debates, and delays. The way the captain just took him under her wing as a member of her crew. Proof that a more direct approach is far superior.*

She could feel Kael's hand slowly caress the skin on her chest, he had stopped rubbing in the ointment a while ago, his hand lingering there, touching her, toying under the neckline of her t-shirt. She leaned in closer. *Go on,* she silently gave him permission to reach farther down her shirt, but he just sat there, silent. She could feel his breath against her neck, warm and sweet. Her heart pounded, and her thoughts reached out to him. *Surely you can feel my heart beating for you… Kiss me.* She closed her eyes and leaned in close enough for him, but he never kissed her.

A sudden inkling tugged at her mind, nagged her out of her lustful stupor. *The brass cylinder,* she thought. *Wait, where'd it go?* She opened her hand. *Empty.* Her body jolted out of Kael's arms. "Where is it?"

"Where's what?" Kael snapped out of his own stupor, looking around in surprise.

"The brass cylinder, where'd it go?" Elara hobbled on her one hand and her knees, crawling around, peering along the floor of the long corridor.

Kael looked around, then pulled out a couple pairs of latex gloves from his pocket, "Here, put one of these on." He handed one to Elara as he snapped a pair onto his own hands.

Elara sat up and pulled the glove over her fingers with her teeth, the latex caught on her skin and felt unnecessarily tight against her hand. She crouched back down.

Her eyes caught a small object under the PPE locker, and she dropped down to her chest, squeezing her arm under the locker. Her fingers wrapped around the object, and she sat back, holding the charred brass cylinder in the palm of her hand.

Kael leaned in. "That's a .50 caliber round casing," he pointed at the engraving on the side, "see right there, it's the manufacturer's stamp."

Elara rolled the casing in her fingers, the blackened char transferred to the latex glove, revealing streaks of the brushed metal surface. She let the casing roll around in her hand until the manufacturer's stamp was visible, a small triangle with a half-moon cut through one of the sides. Elara examined the engraving closely. *I've seen that insignia before. Is it Dominion?* "Isn't this a rather large caliber?"

Kael nodded, "Yeah, it's generally used for mounted machine guns aboard small vehicles." He pointed at the casing still in Elara's palm, "Although I think the Imperial Marines sometimes carry handheld machine guns that take that caliber."

"Wouldn't machine guns that big be too heavy by hand?" Elara raised her eyebrow.

"Not if you have two of these." He picked Elara's cybernetic arm up off the ground behind him and handed it to her. "Any guesses who on the crew has not one but two of those?"

Elara nodded, taking the arm from Kael. "Sylen, and he was an Imperial Marine, too." *I knew that Dominion skrag was behind all this.*

Kael winked at her, his lips popped a "Pew, pew," As he made guns with his fingers. "You got it."

Elara shot him a look sharp enough to cut steel. *Not the time.* She quickly fixed her cybernetic arm back to the stump on her shoulder, "We need to get this to the captain. She has to listen to this."

Kael shook his head, "There's no proof that Sylen put that in there, only that he likely stocks .50 caliber rounds in the armory, anyone could've gotten hold of that."

Elara stomped her feet, her pulse quickening. She could feel rage bubbling up from within her. "Ugh, isn't it obvious, though?" she spat. "He's Dominion, we all know how brutal they can be." Her vision was turning red. *Nothing but a bunch of baby killers.*

Kael looked down at the floor. "Sylen retired from the Imperial Marines a while ago. I don't think he has any more love for the Dominion than you do."

"Once Dominion, always Dominion," Elara muttered to herself, before a thought popped into her head. She held the casing out to Kael, "Can't you dust for prints?"

Kael took the casing from Elara, produced his dusting kit from the pocket of his jumpsuit, popping the small case open, and began to dust for prints.

Elara hovered over his shoulder. His hands worked the tools with a practiced precision that impressed her. However, after examining the brass cylinder, he shook his head, "Nothing."

More proof, she seethed, *someone held that casing in their hands, someone turned that valve… only someone with titanium fingers could do those things without leaving a single fingerprint.*

Kael stood up and took Elara by the shoulders, "Look," he held her eyes, a longing, disarming gaze that penetrated through her like a knife, "so far, we just have circumstantial evidence, no proof. We'll keep our eyes peeled. Eventually we'll catch him in the act."

He took Elara by the hands, his eyes pleading with her to drop her prejudice. When the fire in her blood softened, he lost his grip, leaving the brass casing in her hand. He slid back, still glancing up into Elara's eyes.

she looked down and grumbled to herself, "He's still a stinky Imperial." She toyed with the brass casing in the palm of her hand and huffed, "but I guess I can wait for him to slip up." She looked back into Kael's eyes. "But when I do catch him red-handed, I won't go easy on him."

Chapter Fourteen

THE BRIDGE WAS A disaster. Strands of aurumaedon core cables hung from an open panel in the ceiling in a tangled mess. The arc flash caused by the brass casing had melted all of the data cables for the sensor array and needed to be replaced. It had taken Elara three long days working triple shifts to pull the melted cables out through the bulkhead. She was exhausted and still had several more days left to go.

Luckily, with the sensor array down, Zora was free to help her, especially with the intricate task of making the complicated connections to the terminal board under the sensor station on the bridge. Cable by cable, Elara had to read the signal labels and look up on the schematic on her data-pad to tell Zora where to hook the wires up to. Fortunately, the task was merely tedious. Her AR stuttered for half a second, labels double-printing in her vision before Pulse force-corrected the overlay.

She swiped grit off her tongue and realized her mouth had gone dry sometime yesterday, fatigue turning even swallowing into work.

In the downtime, the captain was on the bridge running Kael through piloting exercises using a simulation programmed into the ship's computer. He was trying to qualify for some advanced piloting certifications.

Zora lay flat on her back, her head buried in the open panel under the sensor console, humming to herself.

The Psycho Sisters. Elara tapped her toes to the familiar rhythm. She had taken a few minutes of her time every day to bond with Zora over their shared love for the rave music, and Zora's voice drifted to her in a sweet melody.

She's so finely put together … like she might snap if someone breathes too hard. So different from me, with all my rough edges. I wish she wasn't so timid, though. I want to show her she doesn't have to be afraid.

"No, no, Kael," the captain's voice shot out, "the Yeoman-Six maneuver isn't that complicated." Voice strained, her annoyance was apparent, yet she managed to maintain her unique mixture of composure, command, and compassion.

"Sorry, Captain." Kael slapped his face. "I keep getting caught on the turn. Don't know if I'll ever get it right," he sighed. His brown hair was extra messy, the stress of the repairs was taking a toll on everyone.

The captain relaxed, her voice soft but commanding, "Once you start into the curve, ease off on the controls a little, the ship will even out on its own."

Elara smiled to herself, *I know you can do it, Kael. You're so talented,* she mused, *but he doesn't seem to see it.* She paused, her gaze lingering on Kael's form as his hands jittered over the nav controls. *He doesn't even see how I feel.* She scoffed at herself. *Two times we almost kissed, two times we didn't.* She touched her lips.

Kael tried the maneuver again, and failed again. His confidence threatened to slip, but the captain gave him a reassuring smile, and he tried again.

He's trying so hard for the captain, to earn her trust, her approval. I recognize that drive. Sometimes it's like I'm looking in a mirror.

Kael's brown eyes shot up and met Elara's. She felt a flush of heat pass over her and became acutely aware of her heart pounding in her chest. Her eyes darted to the floor as she gripped at her chest, her fingers tightening against the fabric of her t-shirt.

She took a few deep breaths and turned her attention back to the rat's nest of wires that dangled from the ceiling over her head.

"Can you pass the number ten, please?" Zora's voice eked out from under the control panel, her hand waving, grasping the air for a tool that wasn't there.

Elara glanced down. Her tools were strewn all over the place. *Where'd I put it?* She knelt down beside Zora. The skin of her shoulder brushed against Zora's fingers as she scoured the floor for the desired socket driver. Zora's fingers fluttered and retracted slightly.

Elara's eyes drifted, the hem of Zora's undershirt had hiked up, revealing the pale, scarred flesh of her tight, muscular belly.

Elara's hands rested on her own belly, feeling the soft flesh under her overalls, *how is she so fit?* Elara wondered, then she saw it, the number ten. The unmistakable blue handle jutted out from under Zora, tucked behind her back.

Zora's hand continued to dance around, trying to grasp the air, and Elara slid her body beside her. *What is that smell, apricots?* Elara began to sniff around, unable to find the source. *It gets stronger the closer I get to Zora.*

Elara leaned in and took a sniff of Zora's exposed belly, then winced internally. *Okay, Elara… that was weird. Stop sniffing your coworkers. Yep, it's her,* she nodded, *is she wearing perfume?* Elara thought for a moment, then shook her head, *Nah, she probably was eating one of those reconstituted fruit cups for breakfast and dribbled the syrup all over her.*

Her hand stretched, trying not to brush up against Zora as she reached for the nut driver, but it was inevitable. Her thumb slid gently across Zora's exposed ribs, her finger wrapping around the blue handle.

"What're you doing, Elara?" Zora writhed, giggling. "That tickles." Her hand dropped as she tried to pull her shirt over her belly, but the tension of her positioning caused the fabric to bounce back up, her belly still exposed.

Zora continued to grasp the air with her hand, "Where's that number ten?" her voice grew unusually assertive, she didn't even try to hide the impatience in her tone.

Elara slapped the blue handle into Zora's open hand, "There you go," her voice dripped with a sugary sweetness. She paused, then leaned in closer to Zora, "Say, what do you think of Kael?" She whispered off-handedly as her eyes darted back up to him.

Zora peeked out from under the control panel, scooting as she pressed her body against the floor to give her room to lift her head out of the hole. She glanced over her chest toward Kael.

"Slag it all, captain," Kael slapped the console, sweat shining on his forehead, "I'll never get it."

The captain touched his hand with a slow, gentle motion. "Just relax, some things are impossible until you believe they're possible." The captain stifled a cough, masking it as a simple clearing of her throat.

She hides it so well. Elara's brow furrowed. *The strength she shows… It's inspiring, but it worries me. She carries so much on her shoulders, and I don't think anyone else truly sees it.* Her eyes glanced over at Kael, his face red.

"Hmm," Zora's voice whispered, "He's kind of cute when he's angry, huh?" She leaned back into the opening under the console and tucked herself back in to reach the connection she was working on.

"Yeah," Elara rolled her eyes, *That's not what I meant,* "but he… y'know," she struggled to articulate. She paused, looking into his hazel eyes, "Don't you think he's being too hard on himself?"

Zora peeked up at Elara, out from her hole like a mouse. "What do you mean?"

Elara slapped her thigh, "I don't know," she sighed, "he always seems wound up tight like the spring on a turbo motor."

Zora raised her eyebrow, "You engineering types are weird with your metaphors." She giggled, "You should hear some of the metaphors that Sylen likes to use, they're all gun-related." A soft blush shot across her face.

God, don't remind me of that creep. She stomped her boot against the floor.

Zora hesitated, "He's actually really funny if you get to know him."

Elara shot a questioning gaze at Zora, "Sylen?"

Zora's eyes peeked out at Elara, "No, Kael." She giggled, "You know that chef drone in the galley?"

"You mean Cooky?" Elara nodded.

Zora smiled, "Well, months ago, we were without a chef, and the captain wanted to use the ship's chef drone. She asked Kael to get it up and running. He worked on it for weeks to get it perfect, and the captain kept asking me to check up on his progress." She smiled, looking up at her work. "He asked me what kind of personality I would suggest. I can't remember what I said," she paused, stifling a giggle, "it was him who came up with the idea of programming him like an Italian chef, but I gave him the hat and mustache."

Elara snorted. The captain turned to look at her, "What's going on over there, girls?"

Zora, her voice innocent, belted out, "Nothing, ma'am." She shot out a laugh from her lungs.

"Keep on track over there, I want to get the ship put back together." The captain turned back to Kael. "Let's take a break from the Yeoman-Six, I think I'll try and teach you the maneuver that got me my first command on the Promethius."

"The Thalren Maneuver?" Kael's back shot up straight. "There's no way I'll be able to execute that."

Yes you can, Kael, Elara smiled. Zora had returned to making the connections from under the sensor console, and Elara surveyed the remaining cables that needed to be connected. There were too many to count, "Ugh, this is going to take forever."

The captain let out a stifled cough as she issued her instruction to Kael, who didn't seem to notice her forced wheeze.

"The captain's so ill," Elara whispered to herself, "doesn't anyone else see it?"

"Kid," Pulse's voice was nonchalant, "if it bothers you, maybe you should do something about it."

"But what?" Elara moaned, "what can I do?"

Pulse took pause, then offered his analytical solution, "She's tired, strained." He waited for Elara to catch on to what he was suggesting. "If you're worried about her taking on too much, maybe make her job easier."

Elara wasn't catching on to Pulse's suggestion. "But how? What should I do?" her voice was a little too loud and drew the side-eye of the captain. Elara offered an apologetic smile.

"Her mission is to get to the Phoenix Reaches, help her get there as quickly as possible." He paused, his electronic voice still buzzing in her brain, "If we can't jump until after the sensors are back online, work faster to get them back up and running."

Elara smiled. "Sometimes you're like a person with how insightful you are, gearhead."

Elara began sifting through the rat's nest of cables, trying to anticipate the next one to hand over to Zora. *But why is everyone ignoring the captain's illness?* She glanced up, Kael was still trying to work through the maneuver, the captain silently coughing. *It's obvious, why can't he see it? What should I do?*

As if Pulse could read her hesitation, his voice hummed, "Come on, kid, it's not all about how the crew reacts, it's about what you can do. Get back on track, you're the ship's engineer, it's up to you to get this mess cleaned up."

Elara smiled, "You're right."

"Give her the thermolytic sensor cable next," Pulse suggested, his voice uncharacteristically helpful. "It's right next to the last one you handed her on the terminal board."

Elara took the cable labeled 'thermalytic sensor' and passed it through the bulkhead, down into the gap where Zora could reach up for it.

A gentle tug on the cable snapped the slack out of Elara's hands. "Thermalytic sensor?" Zora's voice drifted out from her hole, "where's this go?"

Elara read from the schematic on the data-pad, "It's on the same terminal block, connections ten through fifteen, in order."

"Thanks, Elara," Zora whispered.

"Thanks, Pulse," Elara offered softly.

She glanced up, her eyes surveying the bridge. She focused on Kael, his tongue jutted out of his mouth as he concentrated on the maneuver.

The space outside the portholes that sat on either side of the main viewscreen whizzed past in a wide arc.

The view screen displayed the ship's projected path to execute the maneuver as a green line. The little blue line that represented the ship's actual path lined up perfectly with the green line. A slight deviation started, and a small gap began to form between the two lines.

C'mon, Kael, a few more degrees to the right, Elara leaned to try and will the ship to move.

A bead of sweat pooled on Kael's brow, his gaze stone cold, focused on the display. A slight, smooth movement of his right hand, and the small gap on the display soon closed up tight.

"That's it, Kael," the captain erupted from her chair, "see, didn't I tell you?"

His quiet confidence carried a weight that made her pause, and her skin became hot and flushed. *He's got this calm… like he knows exactly what to do. It's kind of cute…*

Pulse's buzz interrupted her fawning, "Kid, your cheeks are redder than a nebula's flare."

"Shut up," she hissed, her voice low, "he's just… good at his job. That's all." She'd never admit that she thought he was cute, at least not to Pulse.

Kael stood up, his hands triumphant over his head. He looked up, a big goofy grin on his face as his eyes met Elara's.

Way to go! She smiled back.

He really is a talented pilot, she thought, *he just needs to learn to trust himself.*

"Elara," Zora's voice came out from under the console, "I'm ready for the next cable."

"Huh?" Elara was still blushing bright red.

"Keep your mind on the job, kid," Pulse chuckled. "Give her the gravitronic sensor cable, it's the next one on that terminal board."

Elara reached into the rat's nest of cables, "Oh, hold on, let me grab the next one." Her hands sifted through the cables until she found one labeled 'gravitronic sensor',

Before she could pass the cable through the bulkhead, the sound of coughing erupted from across the bridge.

The captain began hacking and wheezing. The strain on her body made her convulse, and she attempted to stand up but immediately hunched over. She steadied herself by the armrest of the captain's chair.

She really should rest, Elara's brow furrowed, the corners of her mouth creased. *I should go help her… no, she probably doesn't want to appear weak in front of the crew.* She watched Kael, whose neck stiffly tilted his head down to his console, playing at the controls as if he hadn't noticed the captain coughing.

Elara looked down at Zora, her hands still, her body stiff. Her eyes were glazed over like she was staring at nothing.

The captain pulled herself to her feet, still holding the armrest, then paused. Her frame wavered to and fro, almost imperceptibly. She took a labored breath and pulled her hand back. "I'm going to head back to my cabin," she whispered, her voice weak and raspy, "I have some work to do. Kael, you have the bridge."

Kael nodded, his eyes fixed to the controls, "Aye, ma'am," his voice quivered with worry.

They all know, Elara stared down at the floor as the captain trudged past her toward the hatchway. *They're all as terrified for her as I am.*

"Elara," Zora waited for the captain to pass through the hatch, her voice low and strained, "may I have that cable now?"

Elara nodded.

Chapter Fifteen

THE ARMORY HATCH SHOULDN'T have been open. Elara slowed her pace, the heavy reel of cable tugging at her shoulder as she squinted at the sliver of light spilling into the corridor. Through the gap, she saw Sylen hunched over his workbench, his focus poured into a disassembled computer module. She leaned in, her curiosity overriding the day's schedule. *Is that for the railgun?*

The armory was stocked with a wide locker on the port wall, the various pistols, rifles, and shotguns easily seen through the gap in the door. Hanging on the aft wall was a massive .50 caliber machine gun that had been modified for handheld operation. The shelves that lined the walls were filled with plastic bins and metal ammo canisters, different calibers of ammunition heaped within each container.

She noticed, strewn across the workbench, there were various circuit boards and numerous tools. Sylen's bulky fingers tinkered with a motherboard, a soldering iron in hand. His shoulders were hunched over, his cybernetic eye fixated on the tiny components of the board.

I can't believe that Dominion scrag, she thought, *he doesn't even care that we suspect him.* A red mist of rage clouded her vision, the captain's words about controlling her anger completely forgotten in the heat of the moment.

She ran her fingers over her face and took a deep breath, her lungs burning, her mind screaming for a pause. The cold logic of the captain's voice felt distant, a weak whisper against the roaring fire of her rage.

Her impulsiveness, a feral beast she rarely tamed, clawed to the surface, consuming reason and fueling her internal hubris. She felt her control, her resolve, crumble under the sheer force of it. She needed to unleash this fury, to make him pay.

Pulling the hatch open wide with her cybernetic arm, the metal groaned as its servos gave way under the force.

A high, crystalline whisper, impossible to place yet somehow familiar, like the ringing after a distant explosion, pierced her memory, and a cold chill crawled up her spine. The same as the last time such a whisper had brushed her mind.

The sound snapped the red haze from her vision. For a fraction of a second, she saw not the enemy Sylen but a set of mournful, burning, deep-brown eyes that pierced her from her past, a familiar presence that she couldn't place.

"Don't let anger steer your course." She recalled the words of the strange man who had offered those words to her, a man who shared those same deep-brown eyes.

She snapped out of it and turned to Sylen, "You happy?" Elara burst in, pointing her finger at the massive figure.

Sylen's eyes glanced up, his face shadowed, his brows furrowed. The expression that stretched across his face implied that Elara didn't belong there. "Happy that you just bent the hatch?" Sylen grumbled, "Not particularly. What do you want? I'm busy."

"Busy?" Elara slapped her hands against the workshop table, her organic hand stung, the mechanical one groaned. "Busy? The whole crew is working their asses off trying to fix what you did to the sensors." She held up the .50 caliber jacket. "Care to explain this?"

Sylen's beady eyes poked out from under his drawn brows, his lower lip stuck out, and spittle burst forth as he muttered, "Looks like a .50 cal casing."

"Lay into him, kid," Pulse whistled, "let him know who's boss."

"So, you admit it, then." Her eyes darted over to an open ammo canister filled with identical brass casings.

Sylen stood up, his massive frame towering over Elara, and his cybernetic hand shot out and snatched the casing from Elara's grasp. He held the brass up to his eyes, his mechanical pupil actuated against the tiny manufacturer's mark as though it were the ghost of a familiar past.

He closed his eyes and inhaled sharply. Elara could smell what he smelt, the faint scent of gunpowder and burnt metal. He blinked, a flash penetrating his gaze as though an old, bitter memory had broken his still mind. "Fall in line, soldier," he whispered to himself, his eyes flashing with regret. He closed his fist around the casing and tossed it into the open ammo canister, shooting a defiant glance back at Elara. "I don't know what you're getting at," his voice rumbled like an outboard motor, "but I have a lot of work to do on the railgun before our next jump."

Elara leaned in, sticking her finger into Sylen's face, "That's all you Dominion ever think about, isn't it? Guns and explosives." Elara's voice strained to match the ferociousness she perceived from Sylen. She knew, logically, this was wrong, but the words poured out, fueled by years of bottled-up resentment. Each harsh syllable felt like a betrayal of the captain's trust, succumbing to the very prejudices she wished to shed, yet she couldn't stop the torrent.

Sylen's hand tightened into a fist at the word 'Dominion,' his eyes cast downward. "Lillibet, I'm sorry," his voice was low, barely audible, "I wish I could have saved you, but—" He swallowed hard, his throat working to force the words past a painful constriction. The name snagged at her, a hook catching in deep water, but her anger shoved the curiosity aside. Whoever Lillibet was, she wasn't Elara's problem.

His massive frame seemed to shrink inward, his shoulders slumped under a profound weariness. The words seemed to cut a raw wound, and he fought to keep his composure. The muscles in his jaw twitched as he struggled against the unseen weight.

"Look," Sylen glared into Elara's eyes, "When it all hits the fan out there, Elara…" he took a deep breath, the sudden calm that washed over his face a stark contrast to the rage that was growing in Elara's chest. He continued, "…You'll be glad that someone is thinking of guns and explosives. It could make all the difference. You should let me get back to work."

"I don't have enough proof yet," Elara returned, pulling away, "but I have my eye on you." She wasn't listening to Sylen's words, merely the thumping of hot blood through her veins that urged her to do something rash.

She turned and stomped out of the armory, punching a dent into the bulkhead with her mechanical fist on her way out.

As she stormed into the corridor, she almost crashed into Kael, who had been standing there. "What the hell was that all about,

Elara?" Kael stuck his finger into her face. "You can't just storm in and accuse people of crimes!" He took hold of her arm to stop her.

Elara halted against Kael's restraint, "You were eavesdropping?" she huffed, jamming her finger toward the armory.

"I didn't have to eavesdrop, you were screaming at him." Kael tapped his toe against the floor, his voice low and tight. "Look, the captain specifically told us to keep our eyes open and report directly to her if we found anything suspicious. She didn't say to go off half-cocked and yell at the security chief about his past affiliation." He sighed, running a hand through his hair. "There's a way to handle things like this, Elara."

Elara's breath was heavy as she stared at the floor and toyed with the impression of the locket through the fabric of her shirt.

"The crew is like your family, you have to trust them, you have to learn to rely on them." He pointed down the corridor. "When it all hits the fan out there, all we have to rely on is each other."

Elara nodded as Kael's words opened the raw wound. *That's what Sylen said, "When it hits the fan..."* She huffed, glaring through Kael, then pulled her shoulder out of his grasp, "Is that all, sir?" She gave a half-hearted salute, then turned down the corridor.

"Elara," Kael's voice was low, and he hesitated as she made her way down the corridor. As she glanced back, she caught the faint glare of defeat in Kael's eyes. "I'm sorry," he whispered, a quiet, broken sound.

She knew the apology wasn't for Sylen but for the rift that had formed between them.

Is there any going back?

No, probably not. She turned on her heel and continued down the corridor away from Kael.

Chapter Sixteen

The bed was soft, softer than it had any business being. The starfield outside the ship drifted steadily along, their pale light casting through the porthole as Elara drifted off.

She was finally able to get some well-earned rest. The work on the sensor array had taken far longer than she had wanted, but it was finally completed, and Kael had managed to reinitialize the navigational calculations. Another five days, and the *Aurora* should be ready to make the next jump.

A low electronic buzz echoed through the bulkhead. The muffled buzz sounded like a relay switch stuck in the open position, buzzing but never connecting.

Elara stirred, "Mmmm," and pulled the wool blanket up to her cheek, her body shifting to the side, her feet kicking in protest.

"Yes, sir, I know my orders," a low voice passed through the vent above her hatch, carried easily through the shared ducting that funneled corridor sound straight into her room. At this hour, when circulation throttled down, sound rode the same channels as the air.

Elara stirred, her eyes squinted open. "Huh?" she rubbed her face with her hand, her hair was plastered to her cheek with a thick layer of dried saliva. "Not now… try'na sleep," she muttered, then winced at herself. *Okay, Elara… that was pathetic.* She flopped over, pressing her hand over her ear.

The electric crackle returned, louder this time, sharper, undeniably a voice. Elara's drowsy consciousness focused on the sound that was still barely audible.

The wool blanket slid off from over her head to the floor. Elara, in her underwear, shivered, and her eyes cracked open, blinking against the cool darkness of her room. The neon green numbers flashed '00:49' from the corner of her AR.

"They got the sensors back online," the mysterious voice continued, a cold, distant sound, "the *Aurora* will be ready to jump again in five days."

Elara bolted upright into a seated position on her bed and leaned in closer to try and get a better bead on the voices on the other side of her door. She attempted to wipe the hair out of her face, but the strands were stuck to her skin. "It's the middle of the slagged night," she mumbled, yet her pulse spiked. *Someone's out there.* She yawned, trying to wake up and gather her bearings.

Elara perked her ears up as the static returned, but she still couldn't tell what it was saying. Her groggy mind focused, sharp, into a tunnel. *There's someone out there.* She slid out of her bed and slunk her way toward the vent above the hatch.

"No, sir, no need to implement the Omega strategy," the voice was hitched in a sudden, primal fear that stirred anxiety in Elara's heart. "The next stage of the plan is set to go off, I just finished the work."

Who the hell is out there? Her heart began to pound in her chest, sweat forming on her brow, and her breath stuck in her throat.

The electronic buzz returned, louder than before yet still indecipherable.

"Yes, sir," the voice outside her hatch dropped down low. "It will all be done in three days; there'll be no doubt in the minds of the Allied Planets that the Dominion was responsible."

Elara stubbed her toe on one of her strewn boots, and her body shot out straight. She clasped her hands over her mouth to stifle her reaction, *Slag, that hurts!*

She paused and began hopping on her toe to ease the throb, took a breath, and inched closer to the hatch. She fumbled her fingers along the bulkhead, searching for the control panel, *is it Sylen?*

The static returned, the sound of the voice on the comm device boomed, the words unmistakable, "Make sure you don't fail," the voice continued to buzz, "otherwise, we'll have no choice but to implement the Omega strategy, and you'll be destroyed along with the *Aurora.*"

The last remnants of grogginess gave way to a sudden, primal surge of adrenaline at the words 'Destroy… *Aurora.*' She was now acutely aware: The saboteur was on the other side of the hatch.

Her fingers located the control panel, where the green 'open' button waited to be pushed. Her breath betrayed her, quivering, and she gulped hard. A glob of saliva went down the wrong pipe, and the urge to cough overwhelmed her. She strained against the urge, her eyes began to water as she pushed it down. *If I back off now, I'm no better than the people who watched my parents die.* Faces in the firelight flashed behind her eyes, watching, not moving, right alongside her own, small and frozen.

She slid her fingers over the digital keypad. The sound of

rushing actuators erupted with a loud *Whoosh* as the hatch slid open.

"Slag, I'm compromised." The dark figure lurched in surprise, his shadowed silhouette barely visible on the other side of the hatch. In a red blur of movement, the clomping of heavy boots pounded along the floor plating.

Elara peeked out the open hatch, *he's fast.* The figure was already halfway down the corridor near the stairwell that connected up to C-deck above.

"Oh, no you don't, get back here." Elara bolted out from her stateroom into the corridor.

"Huh," Pulse yawned, "it's 00:51 in the morning, you should be asleep."

Elara's blood was boiling over. "I was, it was wonderful." She followed the shadow figure up the stairwell. "That creep was just outside my hatch, talking to someone. He's the saboteur."

At the top of the stairwell, Elara could see the silhouette of the man nearly twenty feet ahead of her—tall, broad-shouldered, maroon fatigues snapping around thick calves as he ran. The heavy clank of his boots hit the deck with a weight that screamed security chief.

The figure turned to look back at Elara, continuing his retreat down the hallway into the darkness.

"Pulse, get me a visual," Elara panted.

"Sorry, kid," Pulse brought up the live video of the figure, its form too dark and blurry to get a positive ID, "the internal cameras are the only system that I can get any info on, and they're worthless."

Elara's muscles stung, her heart pounding out of her chest, but the distance between her and the figure grew despite her effort. Each stride sent a jolt of pain up her legs, a fiery ache pulsing in her heartbeats. Her fury was a raw, hot wave that propelled her forward.

"I can't let this creep get away," her voice pinched off under her erratic breath, "I have to catch him."

The figure disappeared around a corner about thirty feet ahead of her.

"In there, kid," Pulse's voice was a fever pitch of excitement and a strange mix of adrenaline and electricity, "the combat systems room."

The ship's tactical controls had been routed to the bridge due to lack of personnel long before Elara had joined the crew, so the combat system room had been left to collect dust, a glorified storage room.

A dangerous thrill shot down Elara's spine. *A dead end. This is it. I've finally cornered the scrag.* A smile etched across her face, "Gotcha now, you creep, there's no way outta there." She pushed her muscles to the peak, pumping her legs despite their sluggish reluctance to move.

She approached the intersection, and peeking around the corner, she saw the open hatch. A loud crash erupted from pitch-black darkness on the other side of the opening.

Elara leapt to the open hatch, blocking the entrance to the room, "Gotcha!" Her eyes couldn't penetrate through the inky blackness of the room, her cybernetic vision unable to pick up any light within.

She reached for the lighting panel along the side of the hatch, just inside the room. Her fingers felt over the darkened display and tapped several times, but there was no response, the room remained in darkness.

"Power's isolated to this room," Pulse hummed, "since it's never used. Switch to infrared."

"...I still can't see anything." She swept her head in a wide arc. The room was a dead blue, with a smear of consoles, bulkheads, no human heat signature at all. Either he was gone or hiding behind enough metal to block him out completely.

"I'm going to go in to try and get a better look." Elara slowly passed into the room, feeling ahead with her bare toes.

"You sure 'bout this, kid?" Pulse protested, "you got 'im cornered, there's no way out of there, just stay at the hatch." Pulse's voice buzzed in her ear like an annoying little bug.

"Shut up," Elara inched forward, her toe tapping against a metal rack that had been toppled over, "I know what I'm doing." She leaned over to push the rack aside to clear her path.

The room was deadly silent. *Can't tell how large the space is,* she thought, her mind racing, but according to the schematics, it should be roughly twenty-foot square. Her eyes scanned the darkness, noting blobs of deep indigo lay within feet from her. *Those must be the control panels five feet away. The center should be ten feet square, wide open.*

Her eyes scanned for any fluctuations in heat signatures. The lack of heating in this room made her body shiver, as she'd had no time to dress herself and had run off half-cocked, wearing nothing but her drab underwear, and barefoot. She sighed to herself, *hardly the best thing to wear while chasing down the saboteur.* Her muscles trembled.

Her slow, methodical creep had allowed her to reach the other end of the combat systems room; her hand brushed up against the dusty console along the starboard bulkhead. She turned around to scan the space, and the bright violet rectangle of the open hatch nearly blinded her optical sensors. She winced, turning her head away from the hatch to allow her eyes to readjust to the darkness.

She felt the heavy pile of boxes tumble down upon her before she heard it. She was pinned…

A figure flared into view at the edge of her infrared, a tall, hot core of head, chest, and hips in stark red while the limbs stayed a dead, cold blue. *Just like Sylen: heat where the flesh is, nothing where the cybernetics are.* The red ghost streaked across the room toward the hatch.

"Stop, you Dominion scrag!" she yelped as she pushed the boxes off from her with a shove from her cybernetic arm. "You're not getting away from me that easily!"

Elara stood up and darted after the figure across the room. The figure reached the hatch and turned around to face her. *I have you now, creep.* Midway across the room, her toe caught on the rung of the discarded metal rack she had carelessly forgotten about, and her body tumbled to the floor with a sickening *crack*.

The sharp pain erupted from her ribcage. A metal bar on the storage rack had broken her fall, literally. "Ahh," Elara blurted out in agony, "my ribs." Her voice was heavy and labored, the jagged pressure against her lungs making it nearly impossible to breathe except with shallow, minuscule slurps of air.

"Your glutamate levels just spiked," Pulse's voice bellowed, uncharacteristic concern dripping from every word, "looks like you broke something."

"No duh, smart-ass," Elara wheezed as she limped back to her feet, "I broke a rib." She climbed over the toppled rack. The figure was gone.

Despite the adrenaline and endorphins pumping through her body, she could barely move under the pain. She hobbled toward the open hatch, taking hold of the edges of the jamb as she lurched forward, nearly tumbling back to the floor.

A sharp, searing fire bloomed in her side with every breath, each movement a fresh agony. She had pushed herself to the limit.

The captain's warning of *"Think, then act,"* was a distant echo in her mind, overridden by a burning, desperate need. All that mattered was getting a fleeting glimpse of the saboteur, the overwhelming visceral need to catch him.

Her parents' faces, blurred by grief and smoke, flashed before her eyes, fueling a desperate resolve that bordered on recklessness.

She stumbled through the open hatch and fell onto the floor plating, sprawled out in the intersection. Her head, cocked to the side, unmoving, pointed down the corridor.

The silhouette of the figure dashed away in the distance, into the darkness.

Her panting was heavy and labored as she attempted to pull herself up to her feet. "Gotta catch 'im," she wheezed against the strain. "Can't let 'im go." The pressure built up, and a solid choke erupted, "Can't go on!"

She collapsed against the bulkhead. Her eyes welled up, and she silently sobbed against the pain in her ribs. Her defeat was palpable, the pressure to catch the saboteur, the failure, all of it crashed in on her. *I'm scared. Who was on the other end of that transmission? What did he mean by 'destroy the* Aurora*?'*

The walls of the corridor blurred under her tears as her body convulsed in her breathless, stuttering sob. The sharp pain dug into her, and her adrenaline dropped, the only thing keeping her awake. Her body slumped against the wall, a silent moan eking out from her lips as her eyes went dark.

Chapter Seventeen

THE DARKNESS WAS NOT oblivion but a cold, sterile void held outside reality, her numb ribs throbbing faintly with each distant, muted heartbeat. Elara floated, weightless, her body nothing but a raw, aching throb in the blackness. A slow, distant heartbeat followed her through the dark. Not loud but persistent. And with every pulse, something pounded deep in her ribs, dull and unreal, like pain remembered through glass. It was muted, yet its shape defined her existence here.

Then the shapes began to form.

She was back in the Dredges, but everything was rendered in a sickening, clinical light. Her childhood home was disassembled, its components sorted into neat, translucent bins. As she darted her eyes over the grotesque display, she caught flittering glimpses of thin, pale figures that eluded her gaze along the corners of her vision. They weren't human—too smooth, too stretched, too wrong, and they didn't feel like the Enclave at all. They felt worse than the Elders. Worse than the Great One. Something outside all of it. Cool and watching. Elara's fractured mind recognized them with horrifying familiarity. *It's like those figures have always been there, just out of focus. Analyzing us all, our every move, every failure, with some sick, clinical curiosity.*

Her parents appeared, their faces blurred and their eyes wide with terror, just as she remembered seeing them when they died, but they were silent, static, frozen in time. Instead of the fire of an explosion, they were encased in a clear, gelatinous containment, tubes labeled with precise, flowing, geometric symbols that were frighteningly methodical. Everything was cataloged, reduced to components.

She was strapped to a gurney, unable to move. The harsh lights that shone above her were vile, blood-red eyes that stared down at her with a distant, uncaring curiosity. Their gaze probed through her, into her memories, like a turboprop cutting through ionized plasma in a startup sequence.

She beheld the image of her locket, held in impossibly long, thin, gray fingers. Her chest felt simultaneously lighter from lack of the trinket but also heavier with the loss of her father's gift. She couldn't breathe. The fingers peeled the locket open, exposing the tiny, crystalline microchip held within. The blurred, fragmented creature examined it, their silent scrutiny a wave of contempt. *"A relic of the old, failed universe,"* a voice murmured—not truth but contempt. The chip was then contemptuously flicked to the cold dirt of the cobbled street and crushed under the heel of an unsuspecting passerby.

She screamed into the void, straining against invisible restraints, willing herself to reach for the locket, even though some part of her knew she had no body here to move. A profound, sickening sense of violation washed over her. It wasn't merely fear, it was the icy terror of being studied, of having her thoughts, her pain, and her secrets analyzed and judged without emotion or compassion, as an imperfection.

No. Not real. This isn't real. A universal truth shouted from within her molecules, *I am more than the sum of my parts.*

The images then shifted, and the cold light was replaced by a blinding, sanctified gold. A figure draped in crimson and white robes stood, towering before her. Her face was obscured by the shadow of her oversized cowl. The figure held a massive, smooth, onyx obelisk, not as a weapon but a religious icon, an artifact that seemed to absorb all the light around it, stabilizing the cosmic energy in a chilling parody of perfection. The stone thrummed with an ancient, hypnotic rhythm that permeated through Elara's soul.

A throng of hooded figures, their bare, pale arms marred with jagged ritual scars, worshiped the obelisk with a terrifying, absolute fervor.

The robed figure who held the obelisk in one hand as she called out to her disciples, also held Elara's locket, now restored and mocking her, in her other hand. A young woman, her pale, scarred face etched with a profound terror that shook Elara's core, was brought before the robed figure. Her white, gossamer robes were stripped away to reveal every inch of her flesh, scarred and marked with a crisscross of jagged lines that formed the story of her disobedience and rebellion.

Elara's breath hitched. *Zora, what are they going to do to you?*

The Elder's eyes were calm. Her voice lacked any semblance of warmth or kindness, it was cold and exacting, a deafening howl of a sound, proclaimed with an unshakeable faith, "Great One, we implore you to accept this sacrament, this reforging of the corrupt soul." She nodded, and a pair of robed disciples took the obelisk and locket from her hands, replacing them with a familiar dagger.

The flawlessly polished surface of the blade was marred with a single jagged crack. The Elder lifted the cracked dagger toward Zora's chest. Elara tried to step between them, tried to scream her name, but her voice came out as nothing but a ripple in the golden air. "What say you, my child? What confessions do you have for your Elder?"

Elara's eyes fixed to the dagger, the cracked ceremonial blade. *That dagger… I recognize it… it's the one the captain keeps on her bookshelf.*

The robed Elder, a wicked, vile grin the only visible feature from under her shadowed hood, didn't plunge the dagger. Instead, she drew the tip down, tracing a series of deep, ritualistic cuts in Zora's flesh.

As the first crimson line opened, something subtle wrenched free from Zora's body, a filament of brilliant white light, a splinter of pure, untainted self. This soul light drifted upward, escaping the constraints of the golden chamber, but not toward freedom. Instead, it was drawn to a colossal, shimmering shadow that hovered just beyond the edges of the sanctified vision. The shadow, *the Great One,* inhaled the light, a silent, profound act of cosmic consumption. *This is the ultimate lie, the destruction of something pure and beautiful to sustain and enforce a sterile uniformity.*

The vision darkened, the crimson deepening until she was once again engulfed within solid blackness. She floated there in the void, uncertain what to expect. The blackness became flooded with a dark, fleshy blob that fluttered before her vision, like a bright light passing through her eyelids.

The pain in her ribs returned, sharp and searing, a physical retort to the violation. Elara gasped, and her eyes snapped open, only to be blinded by a cruel, artificial light.

Chapter Eighteen

Elara squinted against the bright white light that hung over her head. Her body felt like dead weight, every muscle stiff, every breath a shallow sting in her side, where her ribs screamed in protest. The pain relievers made her thoughts fuzzy, a distant hum, and she struggled to grasp reality. The room felt too still, yet not quiet, not peaceful. Observed. It was the same faint sensation she'd felt several times over the past few days, as if eyes she couldn't see were tracking her. She tried to move, but a sharp agony rooted her to the bed.

"Try not to move," a smooth voice wafted from out of view, "you have three broken ribs."

Elara's eyes adjusted, and she tilted her head to the side. Varek stood over her, a cocky smile cracked against his ashen face.

"What were you doing stumbling around in the dark corridors in the middle of the night?" Varek's voice was a strange mix of casual interest and clinical detachment.

Elara groaned, "I almost had him."

"Who?" Varek pulled out a tube from a drawer in the nearby cabinet and twisted off the cap. His eyes kept darting to the hatchway. Not nervous. Waiting.

He squirted a thick blob of goo from the tube onto Elara's bare torso. The cold polymer gave her a shiver. He snapped a pair of latex gloves over his hands and began to apply the goop in a thick layer over her ribs with a tongue depressor.

His eyes clung to his task with clinical precision, "The captain's been pushing herself too hard lately," he muttered more to himself than anyone, a trace of worry creasing his lips. His brows were furrowed, an internal conflict lingering just below the surface. A sudden tremor shook from his hands as they adjusted the polymer, a strange vulnerability Elara hadn't expected from him. It was a genuine tremble, a raw anxiety that made him seem… human. But then, a flicker of suspicion penetrated Elara's mind. *Is this real concern for the captain or a ploy?* His eyes, usually sharp, seemed distant, lost in thought. *Or is it calculation?*

She recalled the kiss he'd shared with the captain, their whispered words in her stateroom as Elara spied on them, the hatch closing behind her. Elara mused at the thought, the sordid affair, so salacious, so titillating. She gazed into Varek's distant, distracted eyes. *No, there's more to it than that, he cares for her.*

Varek, still in distracted autopilot, pulled Elara's body up off the mattress to apply the polymer to her back. The sudden movement sent a jolt of pain through her frame, and she winced. Her body recoiled against his prodding.

"Once hardened," Varek's voice was cold and practiced, his mind still on other things, "it will give your ribcage enough stability to let you move around while you heal."

Elara looked up at Varek, "Ugh," she tried to remember what she was saying, the throb in her ribs a cruel reminder, "I almost had the saboteur, I chased him into the combat systems room, but then he got away."

Varek's eyes snapped back from his distant daydream, "No wonder you hurt yourself," he smirked, "that room must be pitch black. Did you remember to take a flashlight in there with you?"

Elara slapped her head with the palm of her hand, "No, I tried using infrared, but somehow, his body temperature just blended in within the cold room."

Varek smiled down at her. "Sometimes you have to rely on tried and true tech instead of high tech. If it was good enough for our ancestors, it's just as good for us as well."

Elara chuckled. *He's so much more personable than I would've thought.* "I chased him from D-deck. He was talking to someone over a comms device just outside my stateroom."

A sudden urge to tell someone about the dire message from the transmission surged in her. Panic erupted as her body went stiff, and she sat up straight. "I have to go tell the captain, ahhh," her movement shot a profoundly sharp ache through her frame. *Ugh, ribs're broken, can't move like that till they're healed.* She sat back in her bed.

"Relax, Elara," Varek gently pressed her back down, "you can go talk with the captain after I've cleared you to leave the med bay."

He paused, his eyes shifting to Elara's chest. In her sudden movement, the locket had slipped out from the neckline of her undershirt. "That's odd," his hand reached down to take hold of the locket, "this looks so familiar." His long, slender fingers wrapped around the silver body of the locket, and he pulled it up to take a closer look.

A flicker of recognition, then regret, crossed his face, before settling into a careful neutral expression. It was the same look of veiled guilt she had seen on so many faces of the people in the Dredges, from those who had profited from the misery of others. It was a familiar flicker that shot a shiver down Elara's spine.

Elara gasped, "Wait, don't take that," she reached up to grasp the locket.

Varek stared at it. "You know, he would've hated all this." His voice was low, almost directed at a distant memory, a hint of regret marring the words.

"Who would what?" Elara squirmed against the pain in her ribs as she reached up to grasp the locket, wincing in pain.

The locket dangled just out of reach in Varek's hands, and her fingertips slid along the silver surface.

Varek smiled, "It's okay, Elara, relax." He managed to keep hold of the locket despite her protestations, "I once knew someone who had a silver locket with the same engravings." He handed it back to her, "Funny that it should show up now, with all this going on." His eyes went distant again, a hint of guilt and fear creasing the corners of his eyes. "There's more to that locket than you think," he muttered to himself, almost imperceptibly, and Elara wasn't sure she caught what he said. The pain relievers that coursed through her veins made her brain foggy. "Huh? What're you talkin' 'bout?" she tucked the locket back under her shirt.

Varek's eyes came back into focus, and he glanced down at her. "I had a partner back on Silicon, years ago." He turned and grabbed a stool behind him to sit down on. "We were scientists at Neotech, working on revolutionary technology that would launch our careers."

She recognized the name. *The largest corporation in the Syndicate.*

Its CEO is the head of Silicon's board of directors.

"Do you know what's inside that locket?" Varek leaned in close, his smile friendly and courteous.

"He knows something, kid," Pulse whispered, "be careful."

Elara shook her head, "What're you getting at?"

"The microchip inside that locket is a Class-X VersaShield NSK lattice chip, military-grade, nearly impossible to crack without specialized FTL-linked computer systems." He leaned back and put his hands over his head, "You'll need some serious computing power to hack your way through that. Of course, anything like that would require adaptive heuristics. AI systems that are well beyond anything sold commercially."

"He knows," Pulse buzzed a warning.

She sat there stunned, a cold wave washing over her. *How? No one knows, 'cept Pulse and me, not truly.* Her mind flashed over to Pulse's faint, frantic presence in her neural link.

"What're we going to do?" A profound fear penetrated Pulse's electronic voice, a tone entirely uncharacteristic to his personality.

He's compromised. I'm compromised. How does he know about Pulse?

"Anyway, enough about that." He tapped on his data-pad. "You'd better get some rest to let those ribs heal." He held up the pad to Elara. "I'm prescribing three days of bedrest for you, and not even the captain can override medical orders, "he wagged his finger in the air, "so don't even think of disobeying."

Three days, Elara's breath went shallow, *didn't that creep outside my room say that his trap would be sprung in three days? How can I find it before it goes off if I'm stuck in bed?*

The hatch slid open, and the captain stepped through the opening. She gave Elara a soft, friendly look, then her expression changed to a kind of familiarity as she glanced over to Varek. "A word, doctor?"

Varek cleared his throat and smiled at Elara, "I'll be right back." He stood up and turned to the captain, a seductive smile creasing his lips. "Mira, babe—"

The captain tugged at Varek's shoulders, pulling him out into the corridor. Her voice was low and hushed. Soft, murmured words like, "concerns… risk… for us," were whispered between the two. Then the captain's body pressed up against Varek's, and his lips clung to hers.

The captain pulled Varek into an embrace, the words, "Hold me," trembling under her low, hushed breath.

It was no longer a fleeting glimpse or a whispered rumor. This was a direct, undeniable display of affection, a lover's embrace right outside the hatch of the sick bay. The lingering view of intimacy left no doubt in Elara's mind, and a knot of unease tightened. If the captain was this close with Varek… how much of her judgment was compromised? How much could Elara rely on her now?

They're more than colleagues. What else is the captain hiding? A strange mix of betrayal and yearning for such a connection infiltrated her thoughts.

Her mind drifted immediately to Sylen's hulking muscles. *No, absolutely not!* She stifled the raging lust hidden deep within her. *He's a creep, the saboteur. He's the reason I'm here in this bed with three broken ribs.*

Yet, glancing at the soft form of the captain pressed against

Varek, a lingering desire for closeness bubbled up in her gut. Her mind drifted to Kael, his boyish smile, his quiet confidence. *He does make me feel safe, but he's never going to talk to me again after the way I laid into Sylen.* She pounded her fist into the mattress of the bed, and a fresh sting radiated from her ribs. *His loyalty to his crew blinds him to the truth right there in front of him.*

The captain's longing eyes held Varek's hungry gaze, and she bit her lower lip. He leaned in and kissed her.

What about Zora? The longing for connection mounted, her mind drifting to Zora dancing in her underwear, how she pressed her near-nude body up against Elara's. The fleeting touches, the way she kept looking at her, then darting her eyes away. *No, she's like a little sister, it's not like that.*

The soft smack of lips parting sounded from the corridor. "Meet me in my stateroom once you're done with your patient, doctor," the captain's playful tenor whispered to Varek, "I could use another… checkup." She smiled as she departed.

Varek stepped back into the room, adjusting the collar of his metallic, silk shirt. "Ahem, sorry about that." He wiped the stain of lipstick from his cheek, smearing it. "The captain just needed to discuss a medical concern." He handed a data-pad to Elara. "Now, go on, get out of here, get some rest," his cheeky smile spread across his face, "and don't let me catch you working."

Elara slid out of the sick bay bed and eased herself through the hatch. She turned to watch the hatch door close behind her. Varek stood there, his eyes darting about with a distant expression, a frenzied mixture of mounting guilt, fear, and concern. The hatch slid shut before Elara could decide what that meant.

Slag, how can I go visit the captain to tell her about the saboteur's trap if she's fraternizing with him tonight? She huffed, then shivered. She was still in her underwear, standing in the dark corridor of B-deck. She smiled at the mental image of the two that lingered in her mind. *Never mind, I'll talk to her later, she deserves the distraction. I'll go talk with Zora instead.* Her fingers danced over her scant underwear. *Better throw some clothes on first, though...*

Chapter Nineteen

The lights on the bridge were off, leaving the room bathed in an eerie, crimson glow from the ceiling-mounted emergency lights.

A soft snore rumbled from the starboard side of the bridge. With the lighting low, it took a minute for Elara to find her, but there she was, sprawled out, leaning back in her chair, her feet kicked up onto the sensor console. Her eyes fluttered under closed eyelids, a pair of headphones clinging to her ears. The hypnotic beat of the Psycho Sisters thrummed a low, muffled vibration that hummed gently as Elara approached her.

Her eyes ran up and down Zora's petite, athletic body, the girl's chest heaving with the slow, methodical rhythm of her breath, a soft smile playing across her lips.

She's cute when she sleeps. Elara smiled to herself, her hand gently cupping Zora's shoulder as she slowly shook her, "Hey," her voice a soft, low hush, "Zora, wake up."

Zora stretched her body, her black leather flight suit groaning at the strain along its stitches. Her eyes cracked open, then widened, and her hand shot up to pull her headphones off her head, her feet falling to the floor as she sat up straight. Her expression went serious, "Not sleeping," she looked up at Elara, "just resting my eyes." She yawned.

Elara stood there for a moment as Zora regained consciousness, straightening her blonde hair with her fingers. She glanced down at the floor, "There was someone outside my hatch tonight." She glanced into Zora's eyes to gauge her response.

Zora returned her gaze, eyes wide with surprise. "Outside your stateroom?" her expression shifted to suspicion, her hair flopped down over her face, violet eyes barely visible from behind the raven strands. "Who?"

"I'm not sure, I chased him up to C-Deck and into the combat systems room." Elara pulled up a seat and sat beside Zora. "I lost him when I tripped on a storage rack and broke my ribs." She lifted her shirt to reveal the hardened polymer on her torso. "I think he was the saboteur." She dropped her shirt back down over her belly and drew her face up close to Zora's. "He was talking to someone on a comms device."

Zora's eyes widened further as she retracted her face away from Elara. "How? The only subspace system on the ship is right over here." She slid her hand to the comms station, patting the panel to make sure it was still fixed to the cabinet.

"I don't know." Elara shrugged, her eyes drooping to the floor, then back up to meet Zora's. "I heard them talk about something called the 'Omega strategy,'" she held up a finger, "something about destroying the ship," she held up another, "and something about setting a trap to go off in three days." A third finger joined the first two.

"Three days?" Zora gulped, "What's the trap?"

Elara shrugged, "I don't know, I gotta find it, but," she held up the data-pad that Varek had handed her, "I'm on bed rest for the next three days. I'm not allowed to do anything. How am I gonna find the trap if I'm stuck in bed?"

Zora sat up, her head bobbed left and right. "I don't see Varek watching you." She smiled. "Just look for it anyway, I'll help," she paused, "so will Kael."

Elara frowned, "I'm not exactly talking to him right now."

Zora raised an eyebrow. "Why?"

Elara hesitated, her eyes drifting to the side, "Well, you see," she took a deep breath, the sting of her rib catching her by surprise, and she winced, then continued, "I kind of blew up at Sylen in front of him, and he got mad at me."

Zora's eyes filled with confusion, "Why did you blow up on Sylen," she began to blush, "he's such a sweetie."

"A sweetie?" Elara sat back in her seat. "Are we talking about the same Sylen? You know, yea high," she stretched her hand way above her head, "made of muscles, and always walking around with that 'I'm gonna burn your village down' kind of vibe?"

"Come on." Zora was still blushing. In fact, the hue deepened, her smile stretching across her face. "He's not that bad."

Wait a minute, Elara paused, *does she like him?* She observed Zora's mannerisms, the way she toyed with her hair, how her eyes sparkled, and that she couldn't stop smiling when she talked about him. *She's got it bad for the creep, I feel bad for her.*

An inkling of realization cascaded through her consciousness. *The trauma she's faced in her life. No wonder she's attracted to the bad guy, to dangerous men.* She eked a stiff breath into her lungs. *I gotta solve this whole saboteur mystery, not just to save the ship but to save Zora from that monster. To save her from herself.*

Zora looked back at Elara, "Wait, you said the saboteur was making a transmission?"

Elara nodded, a blank expression on her face. "Yeah?"

Zora slid her chair to the comms control, "Maybe I can trace it. When did you say you heard him at your hatch?"

"00:49, this morning." Elara looked over Zora's shoulder.

Zora's thin fingers danced across the comms panel, tapping buttons. "Let's see," she hummed. Her hands tapped a practiced dance along the plexiglass surface. "Huh, that's odd." She leaned in closer to the display, "looks like there was a transmission recorded at that time, someone must have hacked into the subspace system." Her fingers slid along the surface of the display, followed by the trace of her violet eyes. "And it looks like they were using Dominion military codes."

Elara's pulse quickened. *Aha, Sylen, I have you now.* She smiled to herself.

"Wait a minute," Zora interrupted Elara's quiet celebration, "I just cross-referenced the signal." Her fingers continued to tap along the surface, and she gulped hard, her pale face going white as a sheet. "Whoever's hijacking our comms has been sending transmissions using the same decryption for months." Zora blinked blankly at the screen.

Elara's heart paused, she sat there unmoving for moments, her breath slow and shallow. She blinked a few times as her brain processed the information, and she licked her dry lips. "For months?" She leaned in over Zora's shoulder to take a look. "Her eyes focused on the digital log that stretched the length of the display screen. She hung there for a moment, staring, taking the data in, and her breath hitched. *The nerve of this guy, right under everyone's noses.*

A new entry to the log emerged, the same Imperial signal. Then another, and another.

"What's going on?" Elara pointed at the screen, "New signals keep getting logged into the database history."

By the time Zora's long fingers reacted to Elara and switched views on the display, a total of twenty new signals had been logged.

Zora brought up a new display, 'active signals' labeling the top of the screen. Each of the twenty new signals let out a weak, continuous transmission. Zora pressed her headphones back over her ears and activated the link for the first signal to listen in.

A cascade of high-pitched, screeching beeps and bloops pierced through Zora's ears, and she recoiled, pulling the headset off and tossing it across the bridge. The digital, electronic signal continued on a loop, squelching from the discarded headset.

Zora switched from one signal to the next, each one a similar sound.

"That's a high-speed data transfer," Pulse interrupted, "the kind of signals transmitted along the galactic cyber-net."

"The cybernet?" Elara blurted out.

"Wait, what?" Zora returned to the console and loaded one of the signals into the ship's cyber-net interface. A net-page opened up on the display. 'Enter Encryption Key,' was the only information displayed. "It's locked," Zora huffed, "any attempt to hack this could alert the saboteur that we know about the signals."

"Can you track the signals?" Elara leaned in.

Zora nodded, she brought up another screen and typed along the keyboard. "Looks like their scattered throughout the ship."

"Hold on," Pulse brought up the map of the ship on Elara's AR, the little red blips representing the signals.

Elara took in the display on her AR, and an idea emerged. "I need direct connection to the console through my neural network."

Pulse interrupted, "What're you doing, kid? If you give out the access codes to your neural net, anyone could hack into your brain."

"I know what I'm doing," Elara blurted out before she remembered that Zora was listening in on only one side of the conversation.

Zora gave Elara a curious look, "I never had any doubt about that."

Elara blushed. *Great, now she thinks I'm some nut job who talks to herself.* She composed her expression, pushing the thought out of her mind. "Never mind that." She leaned over Zora and typed onto the notepad on the console. "That's the access code to my neural net, can you link your console up with me and patch in the live data on these signals?"

Zora furrowed her brow, a look of concern washing over her face. "Sure, but isn't that dangerous?"

"That's what I said, kid," Pulse screamed in her brain.

Elara winced, and tried to ignore the AI's nagging, "It's okay, once we've figured out what all those signals are and eliminated them, we can sever the link."

Zora looked at Elara with a side eye, "O-kay," she typed the access code into the console and a green flag popped up on Elara's AR that read, 'Live.'

"Okay, you should be able to communicate directly with me

through my neural network from here. I'm going to hunt down the signals." Elara bolted toward the bridge's hatch, ignoring the sting in her ribs. She had a saboteur to catch.

Chapter Twenty

Elara trotted down the corridor of A-deck out from the Bridge, her ribs screaming out a constant protest that mimicked that of the AI voice in her head. She ignored both. *"Think, then act."* The captain's words echoed bitterly. *Too late for that now.* "If I stay in bed, we're dead in three days," she muttered, more to herself than to anyone else, especially Pulse.

"It might be dangerous, kid," Pulse squawked in her ear, "you should take someone to help you."

"I know it's dangerous," Elara belted out, a little too loud, "but I know what I'm doing. I can handle it myself."

She bolted around a corner to descend the stairs to B-deck, her path blocked as she slammed into a thin figure clad in olive green and beige.

Kael's frame defied logic: despite his skinny form, he stood firm against Elara's body ramming into his own. He held his arms out to catch her, to slow her down. "What's dangerous?" he inquired, "What can you handle?"

Trepidation engulfed Elara. *How can I trust him to help me when he's so willing to defend Sylen?* She shook her head. *No, I need his help. The threat of the saboteur is real. And if Sylen really was the saboteur, Kael will have to see it for himself.*

She took Kael by the hand, "I'll explain on our way, you're coming with me." She began to drag Kael along with her as she descended the stairs.

Hold on." Kael resisted. "I'm supposed to go on duty on the bridge." He looked into Elara's eyes, the urgent pleading that she shot back at him seemed to disarm him. "Alright, let me at least go tell Zora."

Elara held out her finger. "Zora, can you hear me?"

A low buzz erupted over her cybernetic ears, then the soft voice of Zora cut in, "Yeah, I'm here."

"Kael's coming to help me track down those signals," Elara continued to drag Kael down B-deck.

"Oh, okay." Zora's voice was filled with reluctance and exhaustion. "I guess."

"What's this all about, Elara?" Kael put his foot down against her tugging hands. No matter how hard she pulled and pushed, she couldn't budge him. She relaxed, her ribs a steady throb of protest.

"Fine," she stopped, "last night, I overheard the saboteur on an encrypted line talking to someone about destroying the *Aurora*, about a trap, and three days."

"You're not making any sense." Kael hesitated, his eyes flashing with quiet confusion.

"Ugh, you never listen to me." Elara threw her hands up and turned to walk away. "Help me if you want; I don't care anymore."

"Wait." Kael's composure changed to apologetic as he trotted to follow Elara, "I'll help, you just need to slow down and explain it to me." He let out a smile. "I just woke up, still a little slow."

Elara huffed, "No time, Zora managed to track the signal down, it's encrypted with an Imperial military code." She shifted from side to side, "I want to catch him before he gets away again."

"Again?" Kael raised an eyebrow.

"I had him cornered in the combat systems room," she touched her ribs, "until he got away and I broke three ribs after falling on a storage rack."

"Oof." Kael winced. "I've broken ribs before; that's brutal."

"I know." Elara urged Kael along the corridor with her. "Just hurry."

The two arrived at a junction panel along the B-deck main corridor. There was no sign of entry into the panel.

An electric driver popped out of her cybernetic arm, and with a satisfying "whir," she began to pull the bolts out.

The panel cover was soon cocked to the side, the bolts rolling on the floor at her feet. Elara's green eyes peeked into the dark junction box. A small cylinder, about a foot long and six inches in diameter, sat buried behind an array of conduits within. Elara might have missed it and chalked the whole thing up to delusion and paranoia if it hadn't been for the blinking red light that gave it away.

"What's this?" She reached into the junction box and tugged at its edges to pry it loose past the conduits.

With a hearty jolt that wracked her body under the sting in her torso, something ground against her ribs as she yanked, the device eventually giving way, and she tumbled backward from the momentum. She fell onto her backside, the device rolling out of her grasp and tapping up against Kael's foot.

"Perhaps you should've had me do the grunt work, Elara." Kael smiled as he picked up the device. "Considering the state of your ribs." He tucked the device under his arm and held out his hand to her.

She looked at his hand. *Ugh, stop being so nice; I'm still mad at you.* She slapped his hand away from her face and lifted herself up under the painful throb of her ribs and a strained grunt. Her hands tucked under his arm, and she pulled the device out from his grip.

It consisted of a small control panel and two chambers of viscous liquid, one red, the other green. On the control panel cascaded a waterfall of code, the words 'ready for activation' blinking at the top. The device was designed in such a way that the control unit could activate the small chambers to mix together within a central chamber between the two, but Elara couldn't guess for what effect.

Her fingers ran over an embossed label on the device's front. Her cybernetic eyes twitched and whirred as they focused on the embossed topography.

A small triangle with a half-moon cut through the side. She pondered its meaning, *Where have I seen that?* Her fingers instinctively tugged at the pocket of her overalls. *Empty, but wasn't there something in there? The .50 cal casing. I never got it back from Sylen. Was it the same markings? First the casing. Now this.*

Kael peeked over Elara's shoulder, "That's from the Imperial Munitions depot." His fingers pointed at the insignia.

Elara peeked back at him, "Okay, smart ass, then what's this device supposed to be?"

Kael took it from Elara's hands and inspected it. "I've seen something similar to this." He shook the device, the red and green liquids sloshed around in their chambers, sticking to the walls. "When I was in junior scouts," he handed the device back to Elara, "we were trained in all sorts of things—first aid, hand-to-hand combat, piloting, small arms," he held out his finger and paused, "even demolitions." He smiled. "We never worked on anything so sophisticated, but the design is unmistakable." His finger pointed at the red solution, "That there is Xenon-140 Isolate, completely benign and harmless." His finger twitched over to the green solution. "And this one here is Hydrazine-Oxytrinium. Slightly corrosive, it's used as an industrial solvent."

Xe140 Isolate and HZO-T? "I've heard of 'em," Elara raised her eyebrows, "but aren't they just used in parts manufacturing?"

"True," Kael smiled, then slid his finger to the central chamber, "but if you mix them together," he slapped his hands together into a loud clap and thrust his hands out as far as he could stretch them to either side, "Boom!" His exclamation made Elara jolt back. His finger tapped against the control display. "My guess is that whatever is communicating with this bad boy here will send a signal to initiate the mixture to blow up this little bomb. The explosion shouldn't be all that big." He pointed at the open junction box, "but it would be enough to destroy whatever's inside there."

Elara turned around, "That's the gravity control junction, why would the saboteur want to shut off artificial gravity?"

"Because when gravity goes, people break," Kael said flatly. "Cargo turns into weapons. Half the crew slam into bulkheads. The rest float sick and blind." He paused, examining the cylinder's wiring. "How many of these signals did you say you and Zora picked up?

Elara surveyed the map on her AR display, no additional red blips had been added to the ones that were loaded when she had initially instigated the neural link with the comms station. "Twenty." She held up all her fingers, her ribs throbbing in protest. "At this pace," she muttered, "do we even have time to find and disarm nineteen more in three days? Or are we already too late?"

Kael nodded, and his fingers slipped into one of the pouches on Elara's utility belt to pull out a pair of wire cutters. His lips formed a confident smile. "No problemo." He glanced down at the control unit. There were two wires, a blue one and a red one. With practiced calm, he took a deep breath and snipped the red wire. The display went blank, the words at the top switching to 'Disabled.'

He exhaled, a bead of sweat having formed on his brow. "Easy, you just cut the red wire."

The red blip on Elara's AR that was closest to her position turned off. There were nineteen red blips left. "One down," Pulse muttered, "nineteen to go. At this rate, kid, we're slagged. Even if we don't die from the bombs, your ribs will snap again before we get halfway."

"Did you just guess?" She shifted her feet.

Kael let out a goofy, sheepish smile, "We trained on rigs like this. Same architecture. Different compounds." His hand hesitated. "I still hate this part. Too much pattern recognition. Not enough law. Unless you know the equipment inside and out. Now we know how to disarm this model." He paused and looked into Elara's eyes. "If the saboteur is monitoring these," he said quietly, "he just learned someone found at least one."

Elara nodded. She already knew. But letting them explode wasn't an option. "I should go tell the captain about this." She hefted the explosive device up. "Go relieve Zora and have her meet me at the captain's cabin."

Kael let out a hearty nod. "You sure we have time to disarm the rest of those bombs before they go off?"

Elara nodded, "Yeah, the saboteur said that we had three days before…" she tried to mimic Kael's previous hand expression, but couldn't reach them out far enough to produce the same kind of grand effect, "…well, y'know, 'boom,' an' all."

"Okay, hope you're right." Kael darted off down the corridor toward the ladder back up to A-deck.

Elara trudged along after him, the strain of the throbbing pain from her ribs overwhelming. *I could really use some more painkillers.*

Chapter Twenty-One

The captain stood at the open hatch, a sleep mask with cartoon eyes printed on it hanging over her face and her silver hair balled up into a nest. She was wearing pink silk lingerie that exposed too much of her cleavage and rested just high enough on her thigh to suggest she wasn't wearing anything underneath. "Varek?" she yawned, pulling the mask off. "You finally coming over to play doctor with me, lover?"

I'm holding a bomb, Elara thought, *and the captain is half-dressed. This is not normal.*

The captain smacked her dry lips as her eyes blinked in disbelief at the two girls who stood at the open hatch to her stateroom.

A strange mix of seriousness and fear was etched on Elara and Zora's faces.

The captain cocked a wry smile, "Morning, girls, is it time for morning passdown already?"

"Captain." Elara's voice rumbled low and controlled; a profound seriousness clinging to the word. She held out the defused explosive device toward the captain, "The saboteur planted this, there are nineteen more on the ship right now," her voice cracked, a primal fear penetrated her guise.

Zora nodded. "Ma'am, there was a series of rogue transmissions sent from this ship using Dominion encryption within the past few months." She took a deep breath. "Then, just last night, there were twenty new signals added all at once, scattered throughout the ship. Those signals led us to find that," she pointed at the device Elara had presented.

The captain's eyes went wide. Without another word, she spun and rushed inside her dark stateroom. "Dominion transmissions?" She stood there for a moment, her body unnaturally frail, almost shaking, her door left wide open.

She moved quickly through the dark room, suddenly fragile despite the confidence she wore like armor, and rushed to her desk. With frantic, shaking hands, she began to rifle through the drawers, papers and data-pads flung across the room. The captain's façade had broken, fear collapsing her usual casual, nonchalant persona to reveal her deepest, darkest fears. Someone had been inside her life.

"C'mon, they have to be here somewhere," her breath was ragged, panicked.

I've never seen the captain like this before. Elara looked back at Zora. The captain's demeanor proved to further unsettle her; and a tear broke into a long, jagged streak down her cheek. Elara shot her gaze back toward the captain. *She's usually so calm, so collected, playful, even.*

The captain stopped cold, defeated, her shoulders slumped. She slammed the drawer of her desk shut with a loud crash, then trudged back to the open hatch. "It's gone," her voice was low and broken.

Elara looked at Zora, her tears still streaming, then back to the captain. *Should I ask?* Her eyebrow twitched. "What's gone?" Though Elara already sensed the answer.

The captain relaxed, her limbs limp, she looked like a rag doll. Her steely blue eyes caught a glint from the corridor's light as she glanced up at Elara. "Remember when I told you the *Aurora* was Imperial-built?" Mira rasped.

Elara nodded, her breath clinging to the back of her throat.

The captain licked her dry lips. "The *Aurora* was specifically chosen for this mission because of that past affiliation. I had always maintained that false cover, but I've had the original Imperial transmission codes all along." Her voice was low and hushed. "The big wigs in New Geneva heard about the Dominion's interest in the Phoenix Reaches and contacted the *Aurora* specifically for this mission." She hesitated, then met Elara's eyes. "We were selected for this mission because of that history. If we encountered Dominion forces, I was to impersonate a Dominion freighter. I've kept the original code disk in my desk for years."

She looked back at her desk, then to Elara. "The disk is gone. Someone found it. Someone knew exactly where to look."

Elara's mind snapped instantly to the seam in the desk the paperweight, the hidden camera she'd spotted last week. None of it had been coincidence.

The captain began to wheeze, "No one knew that it was there besides me."

Elara looked at the captain, and her heart fluttered with an unpleasant sting. *Pity? For the captain?* She took a sharp breath that stung against her ribs, trying to push the feeling down. *This is the captain. The one with all the answers. With so much flair, so much confidence.* The contrast was jarring. *Why do I feel sorry for her?*

The captain doubled over with a wet, violent cough, and blood splattered across the floor.

If the captain falls, Elara thought in a jolt of terror, *someone has to step up.* She doubled over, clenching her chest, the silken fabric of her lingerie wrinkled under her grip as the captain hacked and wheezed, unable to catch her breath.

Zora pressed a trembling hand to her mouth. "I've never seen her this bad," she whispered, voice wavering with fear.

As the violent series of coughing erupted from the captain's lungs, her body hunched over, her slight frame shook, and her naked skin went pale, covered with a thick sheen of sweat. She spat onto the floor, adding to the pool of blood forming, a viscous strand dribbling from her protruding lip.

Elara's heart pounded. "Captain!" She knelt down, her arm wrapping around the captain's frame. She attempted to help her back to her feet, but her body was limp in Elara's arms. The captain's weight was light, but it pressed against Elara's shoulder.

Zora slid down the bulkhead, hand half-reaching toward the captain before crumpling back, helpless, engulfed in her own inability, her own fears. She continued to sob, her breath stuttering softly, reminding Elara that she was still there but couldn't offer any help.

The captain's lips skittered against the off-white undershirt that Elara wore, its coloring stained with a streak of pink as the fabric soaked in the captain's saliva. She lay there in Elara's arms motionless, her eyes glazed over.

"Don't… worry… fine…" the captain gasped, trying to straighten even as her body failed. Her mouth hardly moved. She wheezed breathlessly as her body collapsed entirely into Elara's arms.

"You're not fine," Elara breathed, voice cracking. "You're not fine at all."

Chapter Twenty-Two

The captain's body lay lifeless on the gurney in the med bay. Bright overhead lights washed harshly over her pale skin, illuminating the otherwise dim room.

Zora had managed to hook an IV bag to the captain's thin arm. She wiped her eyes on her sleeve, forcing her trembling hands to tighten the line while counting each breath like a whispered prayer. The monitors beeped softly, filling the silence between Elara and Zora as both watched the faint rise and fall of the captain's chest.

Zora sat curled in the chair beside the gurney, arms wrapped tightly around her knees. She hadn't uttered a whisper since the captain had collapsed.

Elara paced the length of the room, heart racing and thoughts spiraling. *Is she dead? No, her chest is still moving, barely, she's still breathing.* She took a breath, the sting of her ribs a constant reminder of her failure.

I can't even take care of myself, how can I take care of the captain? She glanced at Zora, her slight frame was rocking as she hummed to herself. *How can I take care of her? She completely crumbled when the captain needed her most.* She slammed her fist into her thigh. *What am I saying, it's not like I did anything to help the captain. At least Zora was able to hook up an IV. I'm worthless.*

Elara turned on her heels to make another pass along the short, narrow path she was determined to trudge, over and over. *I can't believe I let the captain get so excited. I'm supposed to be helping her have less stress, not more. How much more can she take?*

If the captain dies, it'll be my fault. Her mind drifted back. *Just like with my parents. They told me it wasn't safe.* Her breath caught against the restriction that was forming, her lips dry. *They told me. But I just had to go listen to the space elevator. I had insisted.* The well of tears forming broke, a trickle running down her cheek.

Milo's doll stared at her from the pit of memory, its cracked glass eyes accusing her without a word.... *I wouldn't've insisted that we went out that night. It was too dangerous to leave the house, but…* she choked on her saliva. The tears were a torrent down her cheeks; her body shuddered, and she collapsed to the floor in a heap.

Elara could feel Zora's eyes penetrating her back. She had broken the sacred silence of the med bay, but she didn't care. She sobbed softly against the flesh of her arm, her skin soaked through with her tears.

I can't believe I'm doing it again, she sighed, *if it weren't for my insistence, my parents would still be alive.* She lifted her head and turned to glance at the captain. *She'd still be asleep in her bed and none of this would have happened if I'd just left well enough alone.*

She lay there, her head hung low against her arm, tears soaked into her cheeks. Finally, she knelt back onto her heels and sat up, looking at the captain. She could only see her weak, unmoving hand dangling from the side of the gurney, the IV needle jammed into her forearm.

Elara checked the IV again. Steady, too steady. She jabbed the wall panel for med support a third time and got nothing but silence. *Not just me,* her eyes glanced back at Zora, still rocking silently staring off into the distance, *her too. The ship, the crew… they need you. We need you. None of us can manage without you.*

The clock's ticking echoed in Elara's ears, a constant reminder that they had been waiting for hours. She broke the sacred silence, her voice cracked and weary. "Where's that worthless doctor?" Elara scolded. "The captain could be…" she choked on the last word, "dead!"

Zora leaned in to look at the monitors. Without Varek there to hook them up, it had been up to her to figure out the system. It continued to beep with a weak, fluttering sound. "Looks normal, I think," her voice hung in the air, barely a whisper.

Elara stood up, her jaw clenched. She glared at the closed hatch, balled up her fist, and drew it back. The urge to punch something, anything, overwhelmed her. She let it out, plunging her fist down through the air and into the small, rolling crash cart. Had she used her cybernetic arm, she would have demolished it, instead, she only managed to crack her fingers. The dull pain that erupted in her hand was nothing compared to all the other setbacks and failures that mocked her.

"I know," she sighed, "but she still could be, y'know."

The air hung for a moment, the silence threatening to sunder a rift between the two girls. Zora shuffled her feet, then sighed. "I was a stowaway, like you, when I first came on board the ship."

Elara turned, a scowl crossing her face. *There you go again, calling me a stowaway… it's no use, you're right. You don't belong here, Elara, never did. Just a stowaway from the Dredges.*

Zora continued, "I had managed to sneak onboard when the *Aurora* was on a rare supply transport to Sanctuary." Her voice was low, her eyes still distant, staring at the wall. "I guess I was lucky. I had just returned to Sanctuary from the re-education camp for the…" she held up her fingers and counted silently, "actually, it doesn't matter how many times." Her eyes drifted over to meet Elara's. "What matters was I was there, the ship was there, and I was going to get the hell out of there." A strange, elusive smile crossed her face, one of satisfaction.

Zora took a deep breath, "The ship was already halfway through Allied Planets' space before the captain found me hiding in a hole I had found in the bulkhead. I was filthy, starving, nearly dead, and catatonic." Zora's bright, violet eyes penetrated Elara's, and she let out a soft chuckle. "You'd never believe me, but I'm positively chatty compared to when the captain found me, a stowaway on her ship." Her eyes glazed over, she was looking through Elara. "It was months before I said anything. But the captain took care of me, made sure I had enough to eat and a place to sleep."

Her eyes darted over to the captain. "She's kind of become like a mother to me." She sighed and looked back at Elara, "I know, I still have a mom back in Sanctuary, but compared to her, the captain has been more of one than that scrag ever was."

Zora's eyes became real, focused on Elara's, a cold, calculating tone in her voice. "I'll be slagged if I ever let that scrag of a saboteur get the captain." She let out another smile. Elara had the feeling that she had finally met the real Zora for the first time.

The sudden shift in air pressure lurched through the room as the hatch slid open. A crooked smile slid through the open hatch, painted on Varek's face.

That smile, so fake and insincere, Elara wished it was his face she had punched instead of the crash cart, especially since she thought that she might have fractured one or two of her fingers. *The satisfaction would have made this pain worth it, he's so smug.* She smacked her lips, "Where the hell have you been?"

He yawned, "So, what's the emergency?" He ignored Elara's impatience.

Elara rolled her eyes, *can't you see for yourself?* She pointed at the captain, "She collapsed, do something," her voice was too strained for sarcasm.

Varek pulled his glasses out of his breast pocket and slid them on his face, nudging them up against his nose with the tip of his index finger. He skirted along the foot of the bed as he sat on his stool and slid across the floor, stopping just beside the gurney. He looked down at the captain's frail body, "Whoa, looks like she had quite the doozy, huh?" his voice dripped with fake bravado, a clear attempt to mask his concern for the captain.

He pressed his fingers to her throat, mumbling to himself, then pulled out a small wooden stick out of a nearby drawer and stuck it into her mouth, forcing it open. The captain's teeth were still coated in her own blood. "Uh huh, hmm," Varek continued to mumble to himself.

She's so weak, help her, Varek. Elara watched his movements, unblinking. Her green eyes quivered under her fear.

"Mmmm," a low moan ruptured the stillness, and the captain's eyes squinted open. A weak smile creased her lips, and her voice cracked. "Fancy meeting you here, doctor," it was a weak, pitiful croak of a sound.

Varek smiled down at the captain. "Always here for you." He tilted his head toward Elara and Zora. "It seems you scared a couple of your crew over there." His voice was smooth and carefree.

It was a stark contrast from the terror and uncertainty that had gripped Elara and Zora for the past hour. *How can he be so calm? Can't he see how weak she is?*

Her mind drifted back to when she was first in the captain's stateroom, the data-pad that the captain had carelessly left with its display on, the medical diagnosis. *No, this has been going on for a long time, hasn't it?* She remembered the looks on Kael's and Zora's faces when the captain had erupted into coughing on the bridge. *They all know, how long has it been going on?*

She glanced over at Zora, who was still staring at the wall like she was looking through it, a silent detachment, unwilling to accept the inevitability of the captain's fate.

She looked over at Varek, his devil-may-care smile on full display. But the look in his eyes betrayed the fake smile he plastered on his face like a mask, used to hide his concern.

The captain's breath was steady, still weak, but steady. She smiled, her head barely lifting up to meet Elara's eyes. Her voice was dry and raspy as she mouthed the words, "I'm sorry," before resting her head back down on her pillow.

Elara shook her head. *No need to be sorry, captain.* She glanced over at Zora, the stress in her face a mirror of her own, *if anyone should be sorry, it's us. I was selfish, didn't think about your… condition.* She stared into the captain's eyes with a look that conveyed her thoughts. The captain patted her hand as if to forgive her.

Varek slid his stool between Elara and the captain, blocking her view, "I'm afraid that you'll need a lot of rest, Mira." He clicked his tongue, his voice oddly matter of fact. "And don't even think of disobeying me," he tilted his head down so his face was mere inches from the captain's, "understood?"

The captain's smile relaxed, and she nodded. Her eyes were wide, filled with longing, her body trembled under Varek's soft gaze. She fought to clear her throat, a weak smile creasing her lips. "Understood," she barely eked out.

Varek turned away from the captain, his sharp blue eyes piercing into Elara's soul, "As for you, little lady," he took her by the shoulder and guided her toward the hatch. His grip was an odd mix of forceful authority and gentle grace. Elara complied with his pull. "You had better get into bed yourself," he let out a smooth smile, "unless you want me to confine you to the sick bay. Your ribs need plenty of rest if you want them to heal."

Elara nodded as she stumbled out through the open hatch. Zora followed her out.

They stood in the corridor as the hatch closed behind them, and Elara blinked in disbelief at how easily he had subdued her. Then she noticed the red blips on the map over her AR had changed. There were only eighteen blips now.

What? One of them just went off. She waited for an alarm klaxon to blare, to produce some kind of indication of cascade failure. Nothing broke the silent air. *Nothing… did the bomb go off, or is the saboteur toying with us? Or was Varek late because he disarmed it?*

She stood stunned.

Chapter Twenty-Three

THE NEXT DAY WAS a blur. Elara, Kael, and Zora scoured the ship for the blips, for the explosive devices. They had managed to find five of the original twenty. When they investigated the junction boxes where the red blips had disappeared one at a time, they found the panel cover removed and no trace of any explosive device ever having been inside the junction box.

One bomb gone. Another missing. Something else was moving pieces she couldn't see. Elara racked her brain as she hunted down the remaining devices. "If he's watching these, which he has to be, then the moment we started disarming them, he would've known."

Frustration racked her frame as she crawled on her hands and knees through the maintenance shaft of C-deck to find the next bomb. There were six left, and Elara was alone. Kael had suggested the three split up to try and increase their effort in searching for the devices.

"How much farther, Pulse?" Elara crawled along the tight passage, her arms and legs cramped, her ribs still screaming at her to take it easy. She had ignored Varek's medical advice, *I need to find these bombs before they go off.* She justified her rebellious streak against the doctor's orders.

"Dead ahead," Pulse droned.

"Don't use the word dead when talking about bombs, Pulse." Elara was on edge; the stark reality that they were hunting down explosives wasn't lost on her. "What if one goes off when someone's trying to disarm it?" The thought sent a cold shiver down her spine.

"Hmm." Pulse considered Elara's apprehension. "You flesh sacks are too skittish. You heard what that Imperial scrag said: three days, not one, not two…"

"Don't finish that sentence," Elara interrupted him.

Unless that was never the real clock at all. Or unless he changed it the moment we started touching his toys.

The red blip was directly ahead of her. She slowed and pulled out the electric driver to pop the panel open, then took a deep breath before commencing her work. The device was quickly out of the junction box, the red wire cut. The red blip on her AR display disappeared, just as expected. Then another blip disappeared, *that's where Zora was working. I hope she got it before it got her.* She hissed in pain, still not used to the thrumming ache that any odd movement caused.

Another red blip disappeared from the AR. *Wait, that's nowhere near where Kael was working. Someone else is here.* The location where the red blip had unexpectedly disappeared was farther down C-deck, just outside the maintenance hatch.

She was determined to catch the saboteur in the act, and quickly slid her body down the maintenance passage toward the location where the red blip had been. Her movements, however, became sluggish, her breath labored. She fought with every movement to pull herself along.

By the time she reached the end… her vision warped into a strange, fish-eye distortion, the first sign her oxygen was failing. The corners of her eyes turned fuzzy, then black. Her vision had tunneled.

She huffed against the atmosphere to no effect, struggling to maintain her footing, her muscles screaming for a fresh breath of oxygen.

"Your O_2 levels are crashing, kid," Pulse's voice cut in. Five decks are falling with you," Pulse added. "The captain won't last long if this spreads." It was the only sound that reached her brain; the environment around her felt like a fever dream. The AR in her vision glitched, the map disappeared, Pulse's voice stuttered, "Kid… get to a BAPA…"

Elara struggled along the floor, pulling herself inch by inch. Her fingers dug in between the metal slats of the floor grating, her muscles weak and sore under the strain of dragging her limp body along. Then, her strength spent, her arm went limp. She could no longer move.

"No… good… Pulse," she whispered between shallow, useless breaths, "I'm… done." She collapsed along the floor, her vision going black.

As her brain surrendered to the oxygen debt, the darkness dissolved, replaced by a flickering, ghostly memory, the Dredges Market district… almost a year ago.

She was fifteen again, leaning against a vendor's stall piled high with scavenged synth-parts. Her attention was drawn not by the junk, but by a stand that displayed cheap, battered books.

Who still reads from paper anymore? she had mused. One title, 'The Serpent's Eye: The Alien Threat,' caught her eye.

"Can you believe this drivel?" a fat freighter captain scoffed, shaking his head. "I bet this author would have his readers believe that lizards are runnin' the board of directors on Silicon."

Elara rolled her eyes. She had been suckered by that kind of anti-establishment garbage once. *It's all just excuses for people who can't make it.* The AP propaganda about the Imperial aggression made sense. Conspiracy theories about shape-shifting corporate overlords didn't.

A tall, perpetually gangly man stood by the stall. His frame was clad in a dark, synthetic suit that looked one size too large. His hair, dark and habitually rumpled, fell across a forehead etched with lines of chronic worry. He was the picture of the persistent, truth-seeking eccentric.

The man's most arresting features were his eyes. Deep-set and a mournful, burning brown, they shifted about the market bazaar with a kind of desperate intensity, as if constantly searching for a signal only he was attuned to.

The air about him was one of fatalistic weariness, a man who carried the heavy burden of a truth he couldn't prove, driven by an obsessive focus that left him perpetually disheveled and out of sync with the ordinary world. He plucked the book from the freighter captain's filthy hands and examined the wrinkled cover.

"Actually, theories about stratifying humanity date back centuries," the man's gravelly voice was calm and deep. "Many experts believe an external force actively influences the five factions to keep us weakened for their conquest." He handed the book back to the freighter captain, his pale hands still and even.

"Bah!" the freighter captain scoffed, dropping the book back on the display counter. "It's all nonsense, fit only for weak-minded fools."

The tall man gave the captain a serene, almost sad smile. He picked the book back up and looked directly into Elara's eyes, a profound melancholy settling in his gaze. "The truth is out there, friend." He wasn't just talking about the book, he was transmitting a lesson.

"The brightest stars are not the ones that never crack but the ones that burn brightest after they fracture. Find the light within, for the darkness feeds only on what is offered," his voice penetrated into her soul.

The memory felt wrong. Familiar but subtly altered, as if something external had slipped a message inside it." The tall man's brown, tired eyes seemed to grow, consuming her vision, until they were replaced by the cold, oppressive red of an unblinking gaze. The air around her shifted, smelling faintly of ozone and clinical sterilization.

I remember that day ... but was that how it happened? The memory started to fade from her mind, but the last message burned into her. *Those words, they ring true ... somehow. I can feel it within my molecules.*

"Not if... I can... help it," Pulse's voice echoed in her brain, snapping her back to reality.

"I need to take control of your arm, kid," Pulse squawked in her brain, "I hate to muck around without permission, can you at least give me a nod?"

Elara's eyes were glassy, teetering between consciousness and oblivion. She barely had any energy left but managed to force her neck muscles to twitch into an almost imperceptible nod.

"That's good enough for me, kid." Pulse activated the interface through the neural link backdoor that Elara had left open through the ship's computer. The hijack would have normally required a more active access permission, but this was sufficient.

Elara's cybernetic arm lurched under its own power. She was unable to resist the AI's hijack of her limb. The mechanical fingers dug into the slats of the grating and pulled her forward, inch by inch, then foot by foot, yard by yard.

The mechanical arm had pulled her lifeless body to the bulkhead. Her vision was tunneled so thin that she could just barely see as the mechanical arm slammed into the bulkhead several times.

It's no use, I'm done. Elara couldn't speak, she couldn't protest, she could only watch as the mechanical arm slammed over and over again against the bulkhead. *A futile attempt, just give up already.*

Then she felt it, something had fallen onto her head. The object wasn't heavy, it sprung up and down from above, as though it was attached to something stretchy. The mechanical hand took hold of the object and pressed it up against Elara's mouth.

"Breathe," a distant, disconnected voice penetrated her thoughts.

It's no use, there's no oxygen. However, she could feel a slow rush of air over her face, and she inhaled. *Oxygen? How?* Her brain burst back into action. The breathing apparatus that Pulse had used her cybernetic arm to thrust into her face pumped pure oxygen, the capillaries in her brain were on fire. Her tunnel vision immediately widened.

Then she saw it, the junction box where the red blip had disappeared from. The twisted, crumpled cover had been blown clear off; it lay twenty feet down the corridor from the smoldering junction box. *The life support,* Elara eyed the wreckage.

She stood up and found the BAPA unit that hung from the wall. A long, plastic hose stretched from the green box down to the floor, where it looped back up to her face. The cybernetic hand was still pressing the mask to her face. With her other hand, she pulled the straps over her head to secure the mask, then she took the green BAPA box off from the wall and strapped it to her back. The devices were designed to be self-contained breathing units, meant to be worn over the user's back.

After securing the straps, she rushed toward the smoldering junction box. The muscles of her legs worked effortlessly; they were supercharged from the pure oxygen that she had gulped down.

"Gotta get the life support back online," she blurted out through the muffle of her face mask.

"Easier said than done," Pulse was loud, almost too loud, in her brain, "that junction box is obliterated."

The corridor was choked with acrid smoke. Pulse was right, it was a smoking ruin. A jagged maw of melted polymers and twisted copper. The bomb hadn't just tripped a breaker, it had melted the entire array.

Pulse's voice, though calm, felt like a spike of ice water in her brain, "Ten minutes, kid, ten…before the entire crew runs out of oxygen," Pulse snapped.

Ten minutes, plenty of time… for them to die. She gulped, still surveying the damage. "Shut up, Pulse. I see it," Elara snapped, kicking a shard of melted plastisteel out of the way. She knelt, waving the smoke out of her face, peering into the carnage.

Junction box, useless. Her cybernetic eyes focused on a set of thick, solid strips of power conductor that were visible through a hole in the bulkhead. *The explosion blew a hole straight through the bulkhead, that's the ship's main power conduit, it's still there.* Her breath hitched, "Life support unit," she gasped, her breath clouding the face mask. "What's the bare minimum power input for ventilation only? Forget filtering, forget heat."

"Hmm," Pulse hummed, "the ventilation function for life support requires a minimum of eight hundred mili-Amps and a stable ninety Volt feed to initiate." He paused to access the ship's main power feed schematics, "The main bus has four Amps at four hundred Volts, nominal." Pulse's voice droned off, disinterested, he didn't think that Elara could pull it off.

Too much power, that's a problem. The junction box was meant to step the massive ship power down for the more delicate ship's systems. *Hitting the life support unit with four hundred volts would instantly fuse it.*

Elara scanned the immediate area, her gaze frenzied but focused. *I need a temporary resistor, something to bleed off the extra voltage.*

Her eyes landed on a bundle of thick, heavily shielded data cables. *Leftover cabling from the sensor repairs. They're high-resistance but rated for a surprising current load over short distances. Kael was supposed to put those away, I'll have to remember to kiss him if we all survive this.* She smiled to herself, *It's a terrible idea, a catastrophic fire risk, but the only option.*

"Pulse, calculate the resistance of a six-meter loop of tertiary-grade Aurumatic cabling." She took shallow, controlled breaths from the BAPA. "I'm running a shunt. Let me know what length I'll need to splice in for the life support unit."

"Hmm," Pulse paused for a moment, his electronic voice suddenly interested in her solution, "that might just be crazy enough to work. A six-point-one-meter loop should drop the voltage just enough. 'Should' being the dangerous part," Pulse warned.

"Theoretical, great," Elara muttered, already yanking the heavy cables free from the spool.

Her deft fingers had the sheathing stripped, exposing the bundle of fine, coiled wire within. Working directly on the live busbars, a suicidal move without the proper PPE, she began to splice in her cobbled power shunt.

Sweat beaded on her brow and dripped into her eyes. Her AR timer showed 3:21 remaining, *no time for solder, no time for hesitation.* She had to rely on the mechanical connection, a solid physical bridge.

Elara pulled two heavy-duty magnetic clamps from her tool belt, the kind designed to hold structural plating. She jammed one end of her improvised cable shunt into the first clamp, crushing the soft metal to create a solid connection, and slammed the clamp onto the nearest exposed busbar, *phase one, the most stable line.* A blinding flash of purple light erupted, and her AR vision filtered out the light, leaving everything almost completely black. The air hissed, and the smell of burnt ozone seared her nostrils, filtering even through the BAPA unit.

"Main power connection made," she coughed.

She repeated the process with the second clamp, connecting the other end of her resistor-cable loop to the exposed terminals leading to the life support unit.

She stood back, hands shaking, watching her jury-rigged connection. A thick, smoking loop of data cable glowed a dull red as it rapidly absorbed and radiated the excess voltage.

"You did it, kid," Pulse whistled in her brain, "ninety-one point nine volts. According to the environmental controls, the ventilation is online. The scrubbers are still offline, but the ambient pressure is stabilizing."

"Minimal function achieved," Elara whispered to herself in silent satisfaction. She slumped against the scorched wall as exhaustion and relief hit her in a dizzying wave. *The crew won't suffocate, not yet.* She sat there, her eyes fixed on her jury-rigged substitute. The make-shift resistor glowed and burned, *how long until you melt? A ticking time bomb until I find a real fix. But for now, I'm going to rest.* Her ribs burned from the strain she had put her body through.

Chapter Twenty-Four

The crew had made their way to the mess decks, their strained, pale faces a motley crew, collapsing against the cool metal surface of the plastisteel dining table. They wheezed and coughed, their slow recovery from hypoxia leaving their breaths ragged and shallow.

Elara stumbled through the open hatch. The battery pack on the BAPA unit she had worn had depleted, and she was forced to rely on the stale air that circulated through the ship. *God, this air is absolutely horrible. I'll have to get the rest of the life support up and running sooner than later. After I've checked in on the captain and the crew.*

The captain was still weak from her collapse earlier, her body frail, her skin pale. Kael and Zora leaned against the table, pale and glassy-eyed from hypoxia, breaths still ragged. Varek hovered too close to the captain, fussing over her with single-minded devotion while ignoring his own condition.

"Where's Sylen?" Elara gasped, gulping down shallow breaths.

Zora shrugged, "He hasn't made it down here to the mess decks yet, hope he's okay."

Varek turned his attention away from the captain, "He'd be fine," he thumped his chest, "those cybernetic lungs the Dominion slapped in his ribs should give him hours of air supply. He's probably still asleep in his rack."

Cybernetic lungs? The pieces aligned with a cold click, *Dominion encryption, Imperial munitions, the .50 cal casing, the blown life support.* If he didn't need oxygen, he could sabotage ventilation without consequence. It wasn't just anger, it was a pattern her mind seized on. Her breath was hot, her words heavy from the thick, grade D air, "That scrag doesn't care, he's got cybernetic lungs!" Rage was building in her chest.

Two blinking red blips remained on her AR, until one vanished. *Did someone just disarm it? Only one bomb left.* Kael, Zora, and Elara had managed to defuse the three they had been tracking, plus the one that had blown up the life support. Elara blinked her eyes in disbelief. *That one's down the hall in the ship's server room.*

Her eyes caught Kael's before she turned away from the hatch. He looked wrecked, lungs still struggling, shoulders sagging.

She didn't wait, Kael and Zora were still sluggish from hypoxia, and if she hesitated, the culprit would slip away. Her muscles were ragged, her breath shallow, her ribs thrumming with a dull echo of pain. She limped with every bit of strength she could muster down B-deck toward the aft. *I have you this time, you Dominion scrag!*

Down the dark corridor, a stream of light beamed from an open hatch. Elara inched closer, dust particles dancing in the glare of the light. Twenty feet or so ahead, the hatch to the data storage bank still hung open. The faint sound of a ratchet wrench permeated the stillness.

A cold knot tightened in Elara's stomach. She scanned the shadowy edges of the hallway with her cybernetic vision, listening intently for any telltale footsteps, any unusual humming. The air was cold, a faint, acrid tang tickling her nose. She crept forward, each cautious step a silent question mark in the oppressive quiet.

As Elara reached the open hatch, she peered inside. Strewn across the deck lay numerous tools along with the panel cover, and there in front of the open panel, in his maroon fatigues, crouched the massive frame of Sylen. A dried streak of green accelerant, the same compound inside the bombs, ran down the seam of his fatigues and across his boot.

Elara's shallow breath caught in her throat, *I've got you at last.* She inched closer, the pain in her ribs a faint memory. "What the hell do you think you're doing?" she finally belted, unable to hold her anticipation any longer.

Sylen jumped, clutching something to his chest. His head twisted and peeked over his shoulder, "Elara, what are you doing here?"

"Tell him that's what we want to know," Pulse couldn't hide his excitement, and as much of a pain in the ass he was, Elara smiled that she knew he was on her side.

"That's what we want to know." Her eyes darted up. We? She cleared her throat. "Don't dodge me, what're you doing here?"

"Ask him what he's got hidden there," Pulse prodded, "tucked against his chest."

"I know, I know," she blurted out, seemingly to no one in

particular. "Er, that is… what do you have there?" she pointed, "tucked against your chest?" She tried to sound authoritative.

Sylen glanced down, then looked back, "It's not what it looks like." He stood up and turned around. His hands were clutching another explosive device, identical to the ones she had been defusing.

"The hell it ain't," Elara exclaimed. "You hold it right there." Her heart began to race, her veins popping with adrenaline, "I'd better call for backup," she paused, "drop that on the floor, along with any weapons."

She reached out to the panel next to the open hatch, trying not to break eye contact with Sylen, but she had to in order to hit the comms button. Her gaze snapped back to mean mug Sylen. At the beep of the console, Elara blurted into the comm, "I need backup down in the data storage bank immediately, I've caught the saboteur red handed!"

With steady, decisive movements, Sylen set the explosive down on the floor, then pulled out his sidearm, a golden, chrome-plated Varafirm 45mm smart auto-pistol. He kicked it over to Elara, "I don't want any trouble." Then tried to make excuses. "Look, I've been tracking these explosives all over the ship for the last couple days." He held his cybernetic hands high above his head.

"Don't lie," Elara barked. *The gall of it, what a blatant lie.* She picked up the sidearm and aimed it at Sylen. "There's nothing you can say to get out of this, you Dominion scrag!"

Sylen's head dropped, "Fine, take me to the brig if that's what you want," his voice was low, defeated. "For most of my life, I believed the Dominion propaganda, that the Allied Planets were responsible for starting the FTL war." He took a deep breath, his mechanical hands high above his head. "I only began to suspect all that was untrue when my own brother sent me to slaughter innocent lives for a pointless war I had no business being involved in. My own family turned on me long before I left Ares Prime." He hung his head, "Lilibeth, please forgive me." His mechanical lungs inflated in his chest, and he looked at Elara with pleading eyes. "I'd hoped that you were like the captain, willing to look past the war and aggression." He paused and sighed deeply. "I guess I was wrong."

Elara hesitated, *What's he getting at?* She thought back to her life in the Dredges, to the angry words scrawled on the cracked brick walls of the council. *They sent the enforcers to bust the skulls of anyone who dared to speak up, like my parents. That's their kind of peace.* She shook her head. *No, that has nothing to do with this, he's the saboteur.*

"You're slagged right, you're wrong." Elara lifted the pistol's muzzle to aim at him. "All the destruction that you caused with your sabotage." She spat bile against the floor plating, "Turn around, hands on the bulkhead." Her breath was heavy, everything had turned red, and her finger itched as it toyed with the gun's trigger.

"What're you doin', kid," Pulse let out a shocked electronic squelch, "he's already given up. You'll regret this the rest of your life, Elara."

Elara gulped hard, then licked her lips, "Why shouldn't I? "If it wasn't for the Dominion being warmongers, my parents would still be alive." She could feel her hand shake. *All it'll take is one little squeeze.*

Shooting him won't bring your parents back, kid," Pulse's

voice was low and smooth.

"I-I don't care," Elara stepped closer to Sylen, tightening her shoulders to brace for the sudden pressure she anticipated.

The spring in the trigger resisted as her finger tightened, her vision focused over a faded piece of Sylen's uniform. Her mind drifted to the greasy Imperial Marines patch that she had found hidden within the manifold in the engine room. *I bet that's where that patch was sewn.*

"You're one of them!" she spat. A mist of saliva spurted from her lips, and her boots clomped against the floor plating as she stepped even closer. She was letting go to something that lurked deep within her.

Her hands trembled from years of fury bottled up in her gut that threatened to burst forth. The gun's weight felt righteous, the trigger almost gave way under the strain from her tightened grip. She closed her eyes and couldn't look at the carnage she was about to inflict. *This is for them, for what he took from me.*

A voice rumbled from inside, a cold, ruthless reflection that whispered, *Do it, silence the rage, it has burned for so long.* The temptation to give in to the monster within her was tantalizing, overwhelming. This was it, the ultimate release.

Her finger began its final, desperate squeeze… This wasn't justice, it was vengeance wearing its uniform.

Then, the lights in the data storage bank abruptly extinguished, then snapped back on, flickering violently. The overhead fixtures buzzed and spat sparks. Simultaneously, a deep, resonant thrum passed through the entire hull of the ship, shaking the floor plating violently enough to momentarily throw Elara off balance. The metallic groan ripped through the hull as if the *Aurora* had slammed into invisible surf. "That wasn't internal," Pulse snapped.

"Something just slammed the propulsion field."

Elara gasped as the jolt broke her lethal focus. Her internal monster shrieked, *"Don't let them stop you!"*

But the captain's voice penetrated against the voice of her monster, *"Think, then act,"* it was a faint, struggling echo in the storm.

He deserves it, the monster pleaded with Elara. The manifestation of her struggle between bigotry and acceptance, a teetering balance that threatened to topple to one side or the other, threatened to consume her soul, burning her from the inside.

A familiar voice penetrated the darkness, pushing her out of the abyss, "Elara…" The voice hit her like a bolt.

Dad? No, Pulse. But he sounded exactly like her father. *How did he do that?*

Pulse's voice rang with an odd, soft, calm authority. "Put that gun down right now, young lady!"

"D-daddy?" her shoulders slumped, and the gun fell to her side, dangling from her hooked finger. A tear trickled down from the corner of her eye, followed by a stream that flooded over her cheek and dripped from her chin, "I-I miss you so much," her voice caught as she began to bawl.

She dropped to her knees, the gun's barrel clanking against the deck plating as she let it drop to the floor.

From behind her soft sobs, footfalls tapped along the corridor.

Violent coughing erupted from behind her, then subsided. The captain's voice, ragged and drawn, emerged, her gaze flicked once to the device on the floor, the open panel, and back to Elara.

"Kael, take Sylen to the brig and lock him up." She tucked her handkerchief into her pocket as her soft, trembling hand touched Elara's heaving shoulders, "Are you alright, dear?"

Elara's head shot up to meet the captain's eyes. "I-I almost shot him," she confessed, "I wanted to. I almost became exactly the kind of monster I hate.

The captain's teal robe draped over her frail shoulders as she knelt down beside Elara, her thin arms wrapping around her.

Elara tucked her head up against the captain's chest, the sound of thin, labored breaths popping in her ears. She mumbled, her lips pressed against the captain's exposed flesh, "I kept thinking that if I killed him, my parents would never have… died," the last word was barely audible as she pressed her face into the captain's skin, soaking her with her tears.

"I know, dear." The captain stroked Elara's blonde hair. "But you didn't shoot him, you did a good job, I'm proud of you."

It was the captain's voice, but for some reason, it was almost as if it were her mother speaking to her from beyond the grave. Then the captain's chest lurched as she couldn't hold back a violent, hacking cough that erupted from her lungs.

Elara shot her head up, a streak of blood dangled from the captain's lip, "Are you alright, ma'am?"

The captain wiped the blood from her mouth with her handkerchief, "I'm fine," her voice was frail. Her body slumped against Elara, "Woah, someone stop spinning the ship around," she laughed, then found the strength to lift herself to her feet. "Weren't you ordered to bed rest by Varek?" she winked at Elara as she weakly stood in the corridor. "Make sure you follow orders, dear, I want your head on your pillow in ten minutes." She smiled, then turned to trudge down the corridor, her hand sliding along the bulkhead to support her weight.

"Aye, captain," Elara whispered. *I don't deserve your gentleness… but I cling to it anyway.* Her voice trailed off; she wasn't sure if the captain had heard her.

Chapter Twenty-Five

Elara lay in her bed, sprawled out. She was exhausted, her body run ragged after the past few days, her ribs a constant reminder of her failures. Yet she couldn't fall asleep, her eyes danced along the starscape. A distant nebula twinkled to her as if to urge her to sleep; however, adrenaline was still pumping in her veins.

"I can't believe I almost shot him." She pushed back her tears, her eyes red from days of no sleep, tracking down the saboteur's explosives. The final red blinking light on her AR reminded her that her task wasn't yet complete.

"I wanted to do it… and the fact that I wanted to kill him scares me more than the bombs ever had. There was a monster in me, and for a second, I'd almost let it out." A dark, raw part of her remembered the explosion that killed her parents, the looks on their faces, the injustice that burned her heart to ash. It was primal, born from her grief and a lifetime in the Dredges. "Realizing I'm capable of that kind of violence rattles me to the core." The urge to lash out, to make someone pay, no matter the cost, it was overwhelming.

"He'd've deserved it," Pulse chimed in, "If you'd've been holding that gun in your other hand, I'd've done him in myself."

Liar, you were the one who stopped me. She smiled past the tears and wiped her cheeks, the skin was sore from being soaked in moisture. "It's up to the captain now, I guess," she blinked, "y'know, to decide his fate 'n all."

"There's always the airlock," Pulse chuckled.

Elara shook her head, "No, we're not pirates," she sniffed, "we're civilized." Her tummy rumbled deeply. *When was the last time I ate? Now's as good a time as any since I can't sleep.*

The mess deck was cold and dark, and she sat there, blanky staring into the shadows.

A cheerful whirring sound heralded the arrival of Cooky, the ship's chef drone. He bustled into the mess hall carrying a tray laden with freshly baked pastries and a steaming mug.

"Ah, Engineer Elara! Up so late in-a da night, you are still awake!" the thick Italian accent brought a smile to Elara's weary, grief stricken soul, "Cooky, he brings you sustenance! A growing mind, it needs-a da finest fuel!" Cooky placed the tray in front of Elara with a whir.

The drone scanned Elara's tear-stained face and whirred in theatrical despair, "Ah! Such-a sadness! Cooky, he weep-a for your depression! Let Cooky make you something… magnifico!" It tapped her elbow playfully with a spatula attachment at the end of its robotic armature. The drone bobbed, then straightened and let out a faint whirring sound like a sigh. "Cooky, he worried for your… appetito. Perhaps a cannoli will-a cheer you up, eh?"

The drone pushed the plate of pastries closer, then began to hum a dramatic Italian aria, a low buzzing sound that vibrated through the mess hall. Elara suppressed another giggle, the drone's endless enthusiasm a strange comfort against her recent turmoil.

She leaned back into her seat, her tummy still grumbling, and watched as Cooky returned to the galley, then reached in front of her to pick up one of the pastries. She chomped down on the doughy substance, the cream held within spurting out over her chin in a sticky glob. The surprising combination of sweet and savory washed over her, easing the trauma from the past few days.

I still have a lot of work to do, but we got him, the saboteur. The single red blinking light on her AR mocked her, nagged her with a sudden urgency. She gulped down the creamy, doughy bite and pressed her body up, against the complaints of her sore, quivering legs. "Guess I'd better get back to work."

She trudged her way back out to the corridor, hearing voices from outside in the darkness. She hid herself behind the jam of the hatch and peered out through the opening.

The captain leaned against the bulkhead, her hand brushed Varek's as he handed her a data-pad.

"The crew's stretched thin," she whispered, her voice tired but warm, a faint tremor in her words.

Varek's eyes, though attempting a casual air, held a deep, worried concern.

"I need you tonight," her voice caught in her throat, "more than just for medical checks."

Varek's fingers tightened around hers briefly before he pulled back, glancing down the hall. "After watch," he murmured, his tone laced with promise. He leaned in and gave the captain a passionate kiss, then pulled away and retreated into the med bay, the hatch sliding shut behind him.

The captain lingered. Her hand absently touched her lips, then briefly, almost unconsciously, pressed against her chest as if to quell a hidden ache.

There's such a deep connection between the two of them, Elara mused. *It's a powerful bond.* A stark contrast to her own loneliness that had been building up within her heart, and a flicker of longing ignited.

"Shouldn't you be resting, dear?" the captain's steely eyes danced along the darkened corridor.

Elara lurched forward from her hiding spot, and she smirked, "Shouldn't I say the same about you?"

The captain laughed, "Yes, well, perhaps we should both be locked in the sick bay, strapped to gurneys to make sure neither one of us goes off to do something stupid." She leaned against the bulkhead, a thin smile across her face.

Elara glanced at the blinking red light on her AR, then back at the captain. "There's one more explosive device out there. I'm afraid that if I don't go and disarm it soon, it'll go off and destroy the ship," her voice trembled.

The captain looked at her, "Hmm, where do we need to go?"

"We?" Elara's eyes went wide.

The captain nodded, "You might need help, I'm coming with you," her throat pressed against a wheeze that threatened to thrust her into another coughing fit, but she resisted the urge.

Elara looked down. *She's so frail, I can't risk her for something so foolish.* "The last bomb is actually…" she paused, not wanting the captain to know how dangerous the task really was, "…it's outside the ship, near the propulsion."

The captain hesitated, her eyes darting left and right as if silently calculating the odds of success, then she smiled and her eyes met Elara's once more. "Sounds like quite the adventure, let's go." Her voice was strong, steady.

Elara couldn't dispute her command, and nodded, "Aye, ma'am."

The two women made their way to the airlock. The sound of their clomping boots against the floor plating echoed through the silence.

Lockers lined the long walls that stood around the small changing room outside the outer hatch to the airlock. The space was cold. Elara sat down on one of the stainless steel benches in front of the numerous lockers.

The captain sat down beside her, she had pulled off her teal jumpsuit, revealing her athletic frame. Her delicate underwear clung tightly to her adult body.

Elara yanked open the nearest locker, expecting a standard suit rack and a stale whiff of deodorizer. Instead, a bundle of maroon cloth tumbled out and hit the bench with a dull, metallic clunk.

Imperial fatigues. Same color as Sylen's. But the inside wasn't fabric—it was machinery.

She turned the thing over. Joint braces with servo assist. Heel inserts that could add a few centimeters of height. Thermal mesh threaded through the lining that could flatten or distort a heat signature. Even a flexible strip of circuitry along the spine that looked like it could modulate gait.

It wasn't just a uniform. It was a skin.

Someone had gone to a lot of trouble to look like a Dominion marine. Her throat tightened. *Sylen, or a frame job?* The AR clock in the corner of her vision ticked down two seconds. *Not the time.* She shoved the modified fatigues back into the locker and slammed it shut. "One problem at a time," she muttered, opening the next locker for a suit her size.

A spacesuit hung inside, and she reached in and pulled it out.

"You'll want to remove your outer clothes before donning your suit," the captain said with a wry smile as she tugged the spacesuit over her long, slender legs. "The added layers make movement more difficult in these things."

Elara reached up to unlatch the bib on her overalls, the greasy denim fabric tumbling off her shoulders to fall around her waist. Her eyes darted over to the captain's figure, and she gulped at the sight of her feminine form, then glanced down at her own shapeless body. She frowned. *I wish I had as many curves as the captain. Heck, even Zora has more curves than me, I'm just a stick.*

"You know," the captain's sing-song voice emerged, "I once had a twin sister, her name was Lira."

Elara's breath stuck in her throat. *Lira.* A weight fell on her chest, it was so small, yet so heavy. *That was Mom's name.* The name that had been whispered in her best, safest memories, the ones she carried like something precious, something fragile.

A faint, agonizing spark of recognition, pure and immediate, fired in her mind. *Impossible. My Lira, my mom, she's gone, lost in the black smoke of that explosion so, so long ago. Probability zero. The universe doesn't just hand out loved ones, especially not here. It's a cruel coincidence, nothing more.*

She looked at the captain, forcing her face into a blank mask, "Lira?" Elara repeated the name, tasting the familiar ache of it, yet she let herself dismiss the possibility. *It must be a common name.*

"I… I knew someone with that name once," her voice trailed off, her eyes distant.

The captain nodded, "When we were young, I told her I wanted to join the fleet." She smiled at Elara. "She was the sweetest sister I could have ever hoped for."

Elara cast her eyes down. *Yes, she was sweet.* Her heart ached.

The captain continued, "She studied all the videos and technical manuals so she could tutor me, to make sure I was ready for the tests." She laughed, "I probably would have failed if it wasn't for her."

Elara kicked off her utility boots and let her overalls fall down to her ankles. She was a little embarrassed by the state of her ill-fitting and tattered underwear. She looked up into the captain's eyes. "What happened to your sister?" She scrambled to pull her spacesuit over her body to hide her indecency.

The captain hesitated and took a deep breath, "The gene-splicers said that she had a spontaneous mutation in utero, a genetic anomaly that would have been fatal. The protocol was to terminate the failing twin to save the healthy one." She paused, an unseen weight pressing down on her. "Our father, a brilliant gene-splicer in his own right, had developed a plan that he thought could save both of us. My DNA was perfect, and he ventured that through a kind of cellular override, some of my own epigenetic markers could be shifted to her, a kind of biological life support. It saved her, but the process created a new, systematic instability in my own DNA. It's like my own system is constantly running with an internal error message. I've been sick all my life, a living testament to a procedure that was never meant to be done."

Elara glanced up at the captain, her face was tired. "Is that why you keep coughing blood?"

The captain nodded. "I saved her life, but when I was born, I was sickly. The doctors couldn't explain it, but they said that I would never be strong. I've been living on borrowed time, on borrowed strength, always pushing, always concealing the toll it was taking on me. For Lira's sake, for my own aspiration. Lira had always encouraged me, she helped me to build up my strength, and helped me pass the physical trials." She looked into Elara's eyes. "As you know, even those lucky enough to be born in New Geneva must strive to always excel or else find themselves in the Dredges. Lira made sure that I excelled so I wouldn't have to rot in poverty."

She closed her eyes and exhaled, "When I was given command of the Prometheus, I got word that Lira had fallen in love with a Syndicate exile, a scientist who had gone on the run. She had to break ties with our family to keep us safe." She wrenched her hands. "Evidently, the Syndicate caught up with them. I was about to engage the Dominion fleet in the battle of Veridia when I got news that Lira and her husband had been killed in an explosion." She hung her head low," I had heard that they had a little girl. The genetic anomaly that I had taken from Lira had prevented me from ever having children of my own. I retired from the fleet to try and track down my niece."

Elara held her breath, it was almost as if her lungs had forgotten how to work for a second. *Explosion? Niece?* The math lined up almost too perfectly. *My mother's name, the war, the timing, the way the captain's eyes crease at the corners like Mom's.*

Elara calculated the odds in her head, then acquiesced to the reality, *No. Probability zero,* her rational brain snapped back. *The universe doesn't just hand you family on a silver platter, not in the Dredges. It hands you coincidences and corpses and calls it fate. Impossible, no way… that the captain… is my aunt… is there?*

The captain continued, "My heart broke to think of her alone all those years, but I never found her."

She wanted to ask her. *What would I even say? "Are you my aunt?"* The words burned to be spoken. *But there's no time, gotta disarm that last bomb before it goes off.* She glanced at the clock in her AR, *00:26, two days twenty-three hours and thirty-seven minutes have passed since Sylen accidentally tipped me off about his trap. There's only twenty-three minutes left until…* She hurried to finish donning her spacesuit. *Not enough time.*

The captain smiled, "We'd better go find and disarm that explosive, huh, Engineer?"

Elara nodded with silent determination. *I'll be sure to ask after we get back onboard.*

As the two women completed dressing in their space suits, they began to check one another's fit. The captain paused and pulled on a clasp on Elara's left arm, "These suits are designed to be wearable with access to your cybernetics while outside the ship." She pulled the sleeve free from Elara's mechanical shoulder and past the actuators of her wrist. Then she activated a seal on the suit's shoulder, with a hiss, the opening restricted against the rusted metal of the cybernetic arm.

The captain adjusted Elara's suit. It was a little too big for her, but by pulling at a strap here and a buckle there, it soon fit like a glove.

Elara gazed into the captain's eyes, "Thanks, Captain." She

smiled at the woman who suddenly felt far more familiar to her than she had the entire time she had been on her crew.

The captain plopped her helmet over her head and activated the neck seals, then helped Elara don her own. Both women were ready for their spacewalk.

"Ready, Elara?" The captain glanced back at her, her voice mimicking the same timbre that reverberated from Elara's memories of her mother.

Elara smiled to herself, *I know it's impossible, but what an impossible coincidence it would be if it were true.* She nodded, "Aye, ma'am."

Without hesitation, the captain led Elara through the outer hatch of the airlock. They each clipped a hard-case tool pack to their belts before stepping into the lock, the latches snapping into place with heavy, reassuring clicks. Wrenches, diagnostics, patch kits—enough to jury-rig a half-dead propulsion manifold if they got lucky. Within seconds, after letting the outer hatch close behind them, she pulled the release handle that sat beside the control panel.

A sudden rush of air pressed against their frames, which gently pulled at them, toward the opening outer hatch.

Elara's breath hitched, the sensation of being in an airlock as all the air evacuated wasn't something that could be easily described. Her heart pounded in her chest, her blood pressure spiked, and for a fleeting moment, Elara was genuinely terrified.

Once the airlock had completely depressurized, however, and the outer hatch hung open before her, her body's reactions stabilized. The entirety of the galaxy was laid out before her, with only a curved piece of plexiglass between her and infinity.

Her breath caught in her throat. The view was spectacular. Space unfurled like a velvet curtain, stars glittering like shattered glass across an endless void.

The captain tugged on Elara's right arm and pressed a button on her suit's control panel. She felt the *thunk* of her magnetic boots slam against the metal flooring. "These will help to keep you from getting knocked off into deep space," the captain's voice crackled over Elara's helmet's headset.

I hadn't thought of that, Elara froze, her eyes wide as she gripped the material of her space suit to try and hold onto something solid. "I don't want to go adrift," her voice quivered.

Pulse chimed in, "Yeah, make sure you don't, kid, we'll never figure out that microchip if we're both lost in space."

The two women slowly approached the outer hatch and climbed out onto the hull, having to adjust their centers to come parallel with the outer surface of the ship.

The *Aurora's* hull stretched before Elara's feet, its blue racing stripes chipped, pockmarked by years of cosmic dust.

Her magnetic boots thunked against the metal, sending shivers up to her knees. The suit's air tasted like cold steel, stinging her throat. She had hoped that the air quality from the suit would be better than that of the ship's limping life support. *I'll have to get that fixed when I get back onboard.*

The HUD on her helmet flickered with green readouts. 'Oxygen 98%, heart rate 120.' The heated air from the environmental control unit covered her like a warm blanket, a cozy seventy-five degrees Fahrenheit.

Beyond the ship, a nebula swirled, faint purples and blues, like a dream she'd never touch.

The captain's voice erupted over the helmet's comms, "Once we're in the Phoenix Reaches, you'll be surrounded with nebulae like that." A smile crackled over the radio waves. "It'll be truly breathtaking."

"Can't wait," Elara whispered.

The location of the explosive device was far aft, near the propulsion, and the two women made their way with slow, methodical movements, down the long, sleek fuselage.

They arrived at the correct panel to access the propulsion unit. The clock display on Elara's AR read '0039', she gulped down a mouthful of air, "Ten minutes."

"Plenty of time," Pulse interjected, "unless it goes off early."

"Shut up, gearhead," Elara blurted out, her voice echoing in the captain's helmet.

"Okay, Engineer, I'll zip it," the captain side-eyed Elara.

"Sorry, Captain," Elara whispered. A hypersonic destabilizer slid out of her cybernetic arm. "I wasn't talking to you."

The captain nodded, "I was about to say, I think you have way more gears than I do. Of course, it looks like they're all in your arm, not your head." She chuckled. "Is there anything that arm can't do?"

Elara blushed. She connected a magnetic tether to the panel as she began to cut it free from the hull using the hypersonic destabilizer. The panel floated away from the hull of the ship, clinging along the tether that prevented it from floating off into space.

Elara and the captain knelt down against the hull beside the open panel. The blinking red light on the explosive device gave away its hiding spot.

Elara reached for her tool belt, pulling at the Velcro to open a pouch. Her mechanical fingers swept the inside of the pouch and gripped onto the handle of a pair of wire cutters. However, as she pulled them out from the pouch, they slipped from the grip of her fingers and floated out in front of her. She lunged her hand out to try and take hold of the red handles, but the wire cutters. danced about, out of reach. She stretched her arm out to try one final attempt, pulling her magnetic boots to allow her to stand on her tip toes. Then she began to slip from the hull.

The captain took hold of Elara and pulled her back down. "Woah, careful there, Elara, you almost drifted off."

Elara's heart pounded, she could see the heart rate monitor on her HUD climb up past 140 beats per minute. "Thanks, Captain," she gulped down air, "but I lost my wire cutters. We don't have time to go back inside to grab a new pair."

The captain's fingers pulled another pair of wire cutters out from a pouch on her own belt, "Good thing I came along to help, huh, Engineer?"

Elara's fingers wrapped around the wire cutter's red, rubber-lined handles held in the captain's grip. She gasped, "Captain, I could hug you," She turned toward the open hatch. Then she felt it, reverberating along the hull plating toward her and the captain. A dull "whump" erupted and vibrated through the hull as a blinding flare spat orange sparks and jagged shrapnel.

Oh no, too late. The clock on her AR read '00:45.' *Wait, it went off early? Slag it, Pulse, should've kept your mouth shut!*

Elara's HUD flared red, warning klaxons blaring in her ears. A shard screeched past her, grazing her suit's oxygen tubing.

A cloud of plasma vapor glittered, freezing instantly in the void.

The *Aurora* shuddered, its hull groaning like a wounded beast as a thick cloud of shrapnel burst forth toward Elara, threatening to tear her to pieces.

The captain leapt forward, pushing Elara aside to shield her from the shrapnel as the explosion bulged from the hull, and the metal pieces pierced through her.

The explosion's flare blinded Elara, and her ears rang as the captain's body went limp, eviscerated from the shrapnel. A primal scream tore through Elara's throat, unheard in the vacuum.

"Mira," the name squeezed her heart, the image of her parents' explosion replaying with agonizing clarity. *Not again. Not another one.*

Elara had been pushed loose from the hull, the *Aurora* drifting out from under her feet. 'TETHER FAILURE,' her HUD displayed in large, unfriendly, red letters.

"Kid, you're adrift!" Pulse yapped.

The oxygen reading on the HUD displayed a rapidly depleting number. The oxygen hose lashed and whipped out in front of her like a viper, releasing her air supply into deep space.

I'm slagged. Her breath was shallow, with shock and terror rushing through her blood. The shape of the ship shrank in the reflection of her visor. Elara's life replayed before her eyes.

Her parents, their deaths, her life in the Dredges. All of it laid out before her in a flash. She tried to take hold of the passing memories, but they flew by her with an elusive malevolence that acted to torment her in her last moments of life.

'OXYGEN 20%,' flashed in big red letters over her HUD. Her fingers fumbled for the oxygen hose, its hiss sparking a memory.

Her father's hands, calloused, guided hers over a bottle rocket in their workshop. *"Gas out, motion forward,"* he'd grinned, her eyes fixated on the bottle that stuttered along.

Pain squeezed her chest, "I'm trying, Dad," she wordlessly choked as she reached for the air hose. Her fingers twitched and fumbled against the writhing hose, and she fought to position it, pointing back behind her. She lurched to the right.

"More to the left," she imagined her father's hands guiding her, but now, distinctly, it was Pulse's familiar mechanical voice that hummed in her head, guiding her with the same steady, encouraging tone she associated with the memory of her father.

She followed Pulse's instructions, her fingers wrapped around the end of the hose. She pressed on the material, and the expelled gasses slowly pushed her forward, toward the ship.

Her body slammed against the hull, and before she could bounce free, she reactivated her magnetic boots, allowing her to cling to the metal surface of the ship once more.

The captain, where is she? Elara frantically scanned the surface of the hull for Mira. Her body hung, suspended in the vacuum, one foot still stuck to the hull. Streaks of frozen blood crystals glittered in the cold vacuum.

Elara rushed to take hold of the captain in her arms. She had run out of oxygen and only had minutes left to get to the airlock before she passed out.

Step by step, she dragged the captain's lifeless body along the ship's hull. Her mind reeled against the inevitability, the constant thought screaming in her mind, *She's not dead, she's not dead.*

Each agonizing step along the hull brought a fresh ache to the weary muscles of her legs. The air in her lungs clung to her held breath, she was afraid to exhale, she needed every last molecule of oxygen that she had trapped within her.

By the time she reached the open hatch to the airlock, her vision was blurred, the edges completely black. She set the captain's lifeless body on the floor and crawled to the control panel against the screaming protestations of her body.

Her arm stretched up to the controls, and as the cold grip took her, her fingertips tapped against the digital button that read 'close hatch.'

The hatch slid closed, and the hiss of air urged Elara to hold on, her body relenting against the grip of oblivion that held her. Her mechanical fingers flicked against the seals on her helmet, and air rushed in.

Elara jolted awake against the sudden realization that her captain was still in trouble. She gulped down air with a profound, hungry gluttony.

The captain's body lay lifeless along the deck plating where Elara had left her.

She slid up to her, exhausted, her legs refusing to move, and pulled herself up to the captain, her body collapsing against her. pulled at the captain's helmet, yanking it off. The sterile hum buzzed, mocking her pounding heart.

"Captain," Elara panted, her breath shallow and ragged, "wake up, please."

The captain's face was pale and blood-streaked, but it wasn't hers, it was Elara's mother's, aged by years and scars.

"Captain, please." Her voice cracked, her hands trembling as she cupped the captain's cheek, tears stinging her blurred vision.

The captain's eyes flickered, soft like her mom's. "Elara... my niece, I've found you at last," her breath popped in her throat, her steely blue eyes pale, gaze distant, detached, as though she was looking past Elara.

"I know, ma'am." Elara smiled down at the captain, her fingers combing through the silver hair.

"Your mother… Lira, my… twin," she rasped, blood bubbling between her pale lips.

Elara nodded, "I know, captain…" Even though she didn't feel worthy of this gentleness, she clung to it anyway.

Looking down at the captain's body, the blood that had frozen to maintain the pressure seal in the captain's suit while she was out in the vacuum of space had melted and was soaking into Elara's own space suit. Everything was red. "You'll be okay…" she began to whisper to herself, repeating the words over and over, "you'll be okay…"

The captain's voice continued, oblivious to Elara's pleading, "She was frail… gave her my strength… so she could have you." Her eyes were fixed on something in the distance, and she smiled her usual wry smile, her teeth stained red.

The reality of the captain's words hit Elara like a physical blow. It stripped away every layer of formality, every hint of military rank. *Not the captain. No, not a stranger—this woman dying in my arms, she's family.* Her mind reeled back to the photograph in the captain's cabin, the two girls, so familiar, so much like herself. *Mom, and this woman…*

"Aunt Mira?" Elara choked, her arms clinging to Mira's limp body.

"You're… her legacy… the key…" Mira's voice was soft, barely audible, a waft of air against Elara's cheek. Her hand fell, limp and cold, her once vibrant eyes now dull and gray, gaze empty.

Elara's sob tore free, "No," her voice was raw and ragged, "not you too," she whispered as she collapsed over Mira's still form. *Elara, the orphan, who grew up on the rough streets of the Dredges. She laughed at the irony, I finally found my family, my aunt. And the universe chose to take her away from me in one cruel instant, before I could even get to know her.*

Tears poured down her cheeks. "Mira, wake up," her voice cracked. "I can't lose you, not like this."

Chapter Twenty-Six

The air in the brig was cold and stale. Elara was putting off her work toward a more permanent repair on the life support system. *Sixteen hours of oxygen left in the storage tanks,* she chastised herself, *and I'm standing in the brig instead of a junction box. But after the captain's… Mira's death…* she couldn't force her brain to track voltage and load ratings.

A more pressing matter had arisen. After having taken Sylen to the Brig, Kael had gone to disarm the explosive device that Sylen had been caught with. At first, he had assumed that Elara or the Captain had disarmed it, or even Zora. By the morning, however, after learning of Mira's demise, he discovered that no one had disarmed the device, no one except Sylen.

Kael had already made his decision, and Zora agreed. With Varek opposed and Pulse silently objecting in her ear, the final call, the tiebreaker, fell squarely on Elara.

Sylen had been waiting patiently for his final judgment. Elara stood before the locked plexiglass hatch that separated her from him.

Exhaustion had overtaken her, she hadn't slept since the night she had overheard the saboteur mention his trap. Up until the moment she stood before him, she had been convinced that Sylen was guilty, without a shadow of a doubt. Having discovered that he had not only disarmed the bomb he had been caught with but also many of the others that she, Kael, and Zora had not been able to get to, she was torn.

The fact of the matter was Varek and Pulse had both voted against letting Sylen go. However, since no one but her knew that Pulse even existed, the worst-case scenario meant her call wasn't just input, it was the pivot. Whatever she said next would decide if Sylen walked out of here or rotted in a cell.

Sylen's words carried an odd softness that disarmed Elara, "I'd been tracking those explosives since the night you broke your ribs."

Elara winced at the reminder. She hadn't given herself ample rest. *Foolish girl, traipsing all 'bout the ship, chasing down those bombs when someone else could've done it.* Someone else *had* been chasing them down, and it was the very person she had condemned for the act. She smacked herself in her forehead, *Sylen was a red herring, how could I be so stupid?*

Elara's mind drifted to the evidence that had been collected so far. The greasy Imperial Marine patch, the .50 caliber casing, the Imperial Dominion code that had been stolen from Mira and used in the saboteur's transmissions, and the fact that Sylen was immune to the effects of the failed life support due to his cybernetic lungs. *All these clues pointed at Sylen. All of it is circumstantial. I was so blinded by my hatred of the Dominion, my bigotry, I couldn't see past my own nose.* Her mind reeled against the evidence in the man's favor, the disarmed bombs, *is it enough to exonerate him?* Then her memory snapped back to the airlock, *The exoskeletal fatigues that were hidden in the locker... Thermal masking to alter the wearer's heat signature... lifts to make the wearer taller... even actuators and spinal supports to enhance the wearer's gait...* Her memory flashed back to the form of the saboteur as she chased him through the ship, how he moved, how his thermal signature matched Sylen's. *No, not Sylen... someone shorter, someone smarter... but who?*

Shame crept through her chest. She wanted to hide, but all eyes were on her. There was nowhere to go.

Her mind was heavy, still reeling from Mira's death. The words slipped out before she could second-guess them. "Let him out."

With a few taps on the keypad, Kael had input the security code, and the hatch that restrained Sylen slid open.

Sylen stood up; his imposing stature towered over Elara, but he didn't seem menacing to her. "Thank you, Elara," he softly murmured. He hadn't noticed that something had slipped out of his pocket as he stood.

The piece of thick paper flitted to the floor and slid under the bed. Elara scooped it up. "What's this?" She unfolded the paper. A beautiful, young, golden-haired woman in an elegant, pastel-blue dress and sparkling tiara posed with a subtle yet cute smile.

Sylen patted his pocket, then looked at the picture in Elara's hands. "Oh," he murmured, blushing, "that's my little sister Lillibet. Elizabeth." His head dropped slightly, almost defeated. He paused, his eyes darting from the picture to Elara's eyes. An air of reluctance permeated the space between them.

Go on… Elara nodded to him.

He cleared his throat and smiled, averting his eyes. "She was taken when I was younger, before I had gone off to join the Imperial Marines." His voice quivered, and he paused a moment to regain composure.

Elara could feel him holding back. *Come on, you can tell us.* She smiled at him, a reassuring, friendly smile that she hoped would disarm him.

He looked into Elara's eyes again and gently wrapped his massive fingers around her hands, easing the picture from her grasp. "I can't talk about it. I have to keep her safe."

"Just what we need, more secrecy in this crew," Pulse muttered, "make him spill."

Elara drew his gaze, her heart beating hard in her chest. She could feel her sweaty hand under his strong, metallic fingers. Her breath was shallow as she licked her lips, "You want us to trust you, right?"

He nodded, his eyes clinging to Elara's gaze.

"I want you to trust me," she glanced at Kael and Zora, "to trust us, your crew." She pulled his hands close to her chest and leaned in, holding his gaze, "Who took her?"

Sylen's composure shattered for the briefest moment. His eyes dropped, averting them to glance at the picture of Lillibet. His massive frame shrunk inward. "Elizabeth was taken by Prime Minister Malak," his voice was low, barely audible, "she was to be King Alaric's bride." He closed his eyes and exhaled, a deep, shuddering sound. The words cut a raw wound, an air of guilt cloaked him, a physical weight on his shoulders.

Is that self-loathing? His voice and eyes radiated it. *For all his outward stoicism, his massive frame can't contain his emotions, he's laid them all out for us to see.*

Surprised, Elara whispered, "Wait a minute, your sister is… the Queen of the Dominion?" She paused, calculating the meaning, "Why can't you talk about that? Heck, my aunt was the captain, if I'da known when I first got on board, I'da been tossin' out her name left and right, tryin' to throw my weight 'round."

Sylen let out an unusual chuckle, "Yet you didn't know and still you strutted about like you owned the ship."

The look on Sylen's face, a lighthearted scribble, disarmed Elara. She shot air out of her nostrils and gagged on her laughter.

The moment passed, and Sylen's grin grew pale. The gravity of the moment returned, his voice grim and troubled, "She's in danger because of something…" he averted his eyes and stared not at the picture of Lillibet but through it, "something I did." He ran his mechanical fingers through his short, dark-brown hair and sighed. His hand rested over his face, a makeshift barrier to hide his shame as he mumbled, "I was sworn not to talk about it, or else she'd suffer."

Zora stepped forward, gently pressing Elara aside. Her voice was low, mouselike. "You can't…" her voice squeaked. "I know from my own experience." She darted her violet eyes to Elara.

Elara nodded, *You're doing great,* an encouraging smile etched across her lips.

Zora sighed, then closed her eyes. She took a shaky step closer to Sylen. Her hands trembled, not from the cold of the brig but from vivid memories that were cold as plasma.

"You don't understand. Not really," her voice was quiet, raspy, and dangerously intense. Elara had seen her like this once. Then years of silence finally broke. "When they have someone you love, they don't just hold them… they hold the leash on you." Her eyes were intense and powerful, "That's the trap. That's how they break you."

She gripped her own arms, her eyes fixed on something distant, something beyond the length of her vision. "You talk about your sister as though she's some kind of bargaining chip. I know how that feels. My whole life…" her voice went to a low whisper, almost inaudible, "even the whole of the future itself…" she stared deep into infinity, her voice caught in her throat, "it's all just one big bargaining chip."

She focused her eyes back onto Sylen's, a cute smile spurting across her face, "They told me I could stop the pain if I just followed orders. If I just praised the Great One with all my heart," she flung her arms out to the side in a mocking gesture, her eyes shut tight, a wicked grin tearing her cheeks.

Her gaze snapped back to Sylen, full of a frantic urgency, "Listen to me, Sylen. You think following their orders keeps her safe? It doesn't. It just makes you a better servant, a slave. It shows them the exact point where your spine bends. And once they know that point, they'll push it again and again, until you've given up everything you are."

She leaned in, her voice dropping to a whisper, "You have one advantage that I never had in those camps and your sister doesn't have right now." She spread her arms out to Elara and Kael, "You have us. You are free, standing on a ship that is ours, that is still moving. They have to use proxies and threats. They can't just reach out and grab you."

Elara nodded, prodding her to continue, "You can trust us."

Zora finished, her chest heaving. "Don't let them have you. Don't let them win control over your sister's fate by first winning control over yours."

Elara recalled the words he'd offered at the end of the barrel of the gun held in her own hands, and she sighed to herself, the guilt still fresh. She glanced back up to Sylen, into his eyes.

"The orders came straight from the Prime Minister himself." He averted his gaze; he couldn't look anyone in the eyes as he continued. "It was supposed to be a simple mission: we go in, we secure Veridia for the Empire." He shook his head, "It was anything but easy, they had no military presence, no equipment, no intention of being ruled over by the crown."

Elara's eyes grew wide, and her breath caught in her throat, the only words that she could eek out was a feeble, "Understandable." *The Veridian Massacre, the last battle of the war,* her mind flashed back to the holo-vids that had been broadcast by the AP propaganda media. *The blood, the carnage.*

She glanced up at him, her eyes wet, and a profound hate bubbled up in her gut, *how can anyone forgive such a monstrous act?*

Her thoughts turned inward, Mira's voice echoing there, *"Think, then act."* She sighed, *Sylen may be a monster, but Mira knew what he'd done. Yet she still accepted him.*

She recalled the picture of Mira on the bridge of the Vanguard, *her final command, taken in battle by the Phoenix above Veridia, the same battle. How many crew did she say were lost?*

Elara hesitated, the thoughts weighing heavy on her heart. *I could blame him for all the pain in the galaxy, but what good would that do? He knows what was done, he has to live with himself every day.*

She had made up her mind, *Sylen deserves to be heard out, I only hope that I can forgive him like Mira had.*

Sylen's eyes pierced into Elara's gaze, "I had no choice, it was my duty, Lillibet's life was on the line." He paused and glanced at the picture still held in his mechanical fingers, "she would have been assassinated if I failed my mission."

Elara's gaze focused on the smile on Elizabeth's face in the picture, and she sighed. *How could you choose between what was moral and what was best for your family? Would I have reacted differently if it had been my own? I don't know.* "That's awful," she muttered, a controlled response.

"I was commanded to bring the colony into the fold under any means," he took a breath, his massive shoulders heaving as his lungs inflated. "When I hesitated, when I recognized my part in the injustice, the murder being caused, that's when he did it."

He pulled his maroon fatigues off his shoulder, exposing the rippling muscles of his chest. The flesh was gray and scarred, as though parts of his body had been forcibly removed, "That's where the delivery system for the combat enhancers were pumped through my adrenal system at the push of a remote switch." He paused, his breath caught in his throat, "My brother, her brother, saw my conscious turn against the plans, against his orders. He pressed the button that activated the true killing power of the Imperial Marines. We all became heartless, mindless monsters, bent on one task and one task alone… the annihilation of anyone who stood in our way." His voice cracked under the strain, "I slaughtered hundreds of defenseless colonists, all for the glory of the crown. Men and women, even the children, fell against our mono-bladed swords and heavy machine-gun fire.

They all died, and for what reason?" He hid his face in his hands.

"When the dust settled, my brother, the Admiral himself, his fleet led by the Phoenix, his flagship, were gone."

"I and many of my platoon were horrified at what we had done. We all fled. I ripped the control unit out of my own chest, a futile effort to regain control, but it was too late.

"How can I live with what I've done, Elara?" He took her by the shoulders and shot his gaze at her with pleading, desperate eyes. "How?" He let her go and slumped to the floor, defeated by his own past. "You should have pulled the trigger on me, it's the least I deserve for my crimes."

Zora knelt down beside his crumpled body, her fingers slowly brushing through the strands of his hair. "Shhh," she whispered.

He's... a monster, a tool of tyranny... but he's broken. Her internal bigotry, her hatred for the Dominion, began to crack, challenged by the undeniable humanity born before her. *He was forced into it, like how we were forced to steal and beg and hustle in the Dredges. At least I had a choice, I didn't have someone pushing a button to drive me into it. Is he so different?*

The internal battle, the struggle to reconcile her deeply ingrained bigotry with the man heaped before her on the floor, forced her to see clearer.

Just like the AP council, whose policies always ended up routing wealth and opportunity to the top, regardless of the lives they crushed under their boots below. She glanced at Zora, the image of the Elders and the inquisitors filling her mind, their rigid, unyielding fanaticism demanding human suffering to maintain their dogma. She paused, looking down at Sylen, not just at the parts that were broken but at the framework that had shattered him. The true evil wasn't the people; it was the systems that twisted them. The Imperial crown, the AP council, the Enclave Elders—different uniforms, same monster. They lived in the machinery, not just the men.

Her fingers toyed with the shape of her locket from under the fabric of her shirt, *the mechanism needs to be dismantled, is that what my father meant when he said what's inside the locket would reunite the factions?* She glanced at Kael, who had been unusually silent the whole time. *What's going on in that head of yours, Kael?* He leaned against the bulkhead, his gaze was distant, like he was staring through the ship, disconnected.

She smiled at him, and his hazel eyes twitched, then met hers. He let out a half smile but remained aloof.

Has Mira's death affected him so much? Is he unsure of his ability to lead the crew? He's the captain now. It was an unceremonious field promotion—the captain died, the first mate took her place, it was the natural order aboard a ship such as the *Aurora. Yet there's something in his eyes that's reluctant to take command.*

Elara returned her gaze to Sylen, his eyes darting up to meet hers, "Sylen," she whispered, "to tell you the truth, I'm glad I didn't pull that trigger." She sighed, darting her gaze to the side. "God, I wanted to. Veridia, the war, everything in me said Dominion soldier equals monster. Pull the trigger, end of story." She continued, "I can't erase Veridia. But I can choose not to repeat the same blind hatred that put me in that server room with a gun in my hand. Please forgive me for not trusting you."

Sylen stood up, and Zora helped support his massive weight. His eyes burrowed into Elara's. "You're not the one who needs forgiveness; I would have deserved it." He let out a low chuckle,

"Besides, the safety was still on that pistol," he cracked a smile. "Someone should really teach you how to use firearms."

Elara stifled a giggle, "Yeah I guess you're right." She was a little embarrassed, she hadn't even thought to check the safety at the time. She was glad it was on.

Sylen's face drew more somber, more serious, "If anyone should beg for forgiveness, it's me."

Elara shook her head, smiling, "It's not up to me to forgive you, you have to forgive yourself." She picked the photo up from the floor, took one more glance at Elizabeth's sweet smile, folded the paper, and tucked it into the breast pocket of his fatigues. "We're here to help you, no matter what you decide to do." She glanced back at Kael, a silent plea for his confirmation.

He nodded back at her, his gaze barely focused on their interaction.

Elara glanced over at Zora for her confirmation.

Zora nodded, then smiled at Sylen, "You can count on us."

Sylen smiled, and after looking to Kael and then Zora, he locked eyes with Elara once more. "I know, but there's no helping Lillibet now, especially with the King's... failing health."

"I don't get it," Elara shook her head, "if the king dies, doesn't she just take over until your nephew, the crowned prince, comes of age?"

Sylen shook his head, "No, it's not that simple. Prince Arion hasn't been coronated as the crown prince yet... he's still too young, and my sister is of lower nobility. Both his uncle, Lord Protector Valdemar, and his brother Prince Avrid the Brash-Hawk have much stronger claims to the crown."

Elara had heard the rumors of the impending civil war, the

Lord Protector versus the Brash-Hawk. It was all the Holo-vids that screamed on the monitors in the Dredges could talk about, *"It's only a matter of time,"* she recalled the words that had passed her lips when she had heard the propaganda.

Sylen stood there, tight like a drum, helpless against an insurrection that threatened his friends and family back home. They all knew that the AP counsel would be more than happy to take advantage of the civil strife and invade the IP. And Mira's death and impending funeral. It was all too much for Elara to take. A solid lump formed in her throat, and her voice caught as she tried to speak, "If there's anything we can do for you, big guy," she put her hand on his shoulder, the cold metal of his cybernetic arm contrasting with the vulnerability he had displayed before her and the rest of the crew.

Sylen looked back at Elara, "It's my cross to bear, little one," he sighed, then adjusted his fatigues, straightening out the wrinkles and standing tall. He looked at Zora, "How has D'Artagnan been since I've been locked away?" Sylen smiled.

Zora shrank behind her hair, her previous assertive flair long gone. She whispered, "He's been a good kitty."

Sylen's eyes lit up, a rare softness crossing his face as he looked at her, "Glad he's not eating your shoes," he said, voice gruff but warm.

He really loves that cat, Elara thought, smiling.

Sylen's gaze lingered on Zora, and Elara smiled to herself. *Her quiet strength, her fragile beauty. It always seems to disarm him.*

"To think that this heap of muscle is that rat's owner," Pulse almost sneezed at the thought, "I don't get it."

Elara chuckled to herself, *I can't believe I misjudged Sylen so badly.*

Her eyes went soft as she turned to Sylen. She wanted to say the words in her heart, *I hate myself for being so impulsive, for letting my anger take over, I'm sorry.*

Before she could form the words, a loud klaxon erupted from the intercom, *"Proximity alert, proximity alert,"* the robotic voice sounded over the speakers, *"Imperial Dominion drones detected, approaching the outer hatch of the cargo bay."*

The hair on Elara's neck shot up. She glanced about the room, *Sylen, Kael, Zora, Me...* "Where's Varek?" her voice was strained, ragged, she already knew the answer deep down inside her.

Sylen glanced around the room, "Wasn't he right here? He was here to vote for me to stay locked up, wasn't he?"

Zora nodded and looked at Kael.

Kael's eyes shot up, focused, "We need to get to the cargo bay to find out what's going on."

Elara nodded and followed the crew out the hatch, thinking, *The Omega strategy.*

Chapter Twenty-Seven

THE CARGO BAY'S ATMOSPHERE felt suffocating, its silence broken only by the low, predatory hum of six Dominion drones advancing across the deck. Their mechanical movements carried the quiet promise of violence—a stillness so sharp it pressed against Elara's lungs. A heavy, muted silence filled the space, broken only by the low, sinister whirring of six Dominion military drones. They lurched along the deck as the enormous external hatch latched shut behind them. Their mechanical servos were a quiet promise of violence. This wasn't peace. It was the calm before the storm, a stillness so absolute it felt like the air was slowly squeezed from the room.

Varek stood before the drones with a wild, fractured smile, his breath shallow and erratic as his façade of camaraderie finally crumbled, poised to greet his so-called crew, the very people he'd pretended to be part of for so long. He stood hunched in front of the military drones, his back heaving with labored breaths.

Elara stood forward from the rest of the crew. "You were the saboteur." She brushed a strand of purple highlights out of her eyes. "How could you!"

Varek paced in jagged lines between the drones, his voice splitting between calm and deranged. "Easily. You were so fixated on Sylen, you never noticed me right under your little button nose. Plotting and scheming." His breath drew in raggedly, "I might have gotten away with it, had I cared to learn that that secluded corner of the ship was where you'd chosen your stateroom. You'd have never heard my communique, never known the bombs were planted on the ship."

"I don't get it, though," Elara interrupted Varek's mad tirade, "why would you destroy life support if you knew you'd be affected too?"

Varek's smile widened, his bloodshot eyes popping, "You fool, do you think you're the only one who has cybernetic gadgets at their disposal?" He held his gaunt fingers up in the air, a mocking attempt at quotation marks. "Open your eyes, girl. Clearly, I'm a super spy sent from the Syndicate to cripple your ship," his voice returned to his standard carefree, silken cadence.

Surely he's not being serious about being a super spy, Elara glanced over at Kael, rolling her eyes at him, and he returned her glare with a smirk.

"Neotech has access to tech that boggles the mind," his voice cracked, his tenor stirring into something more erratic. "Perks of my loyalty," he chuckled to himself, then turned to start pacing again.

His voice drew low, his attention turned inward. "Of course, they could always remotely shut off the cybernetic lungs in my chest at the push of a button," he halted and stared through the bulkhead of the ship, "in fact, they could shut down any number of the neural and cybernetic enhancements they gave me to make me their perfect little corporate puppet."

His manic gaze returned as his body careened back around to face Elara. "Can't you see, girl?" He lumbered in long, clomping steps toward Elara. "I had no choice; I had to destroy you all, destroy Mira..." He halted mid-step, his hands quivering in the air, poised to grip Elara by the throat, then collapsed to the floor. "... The only woman to love me."

His voice calmed, his steady eyes piercing Elara's as he craned his neck to catch her gaze, "But you, girl. You!" His voice penetrated the stillness of the room, the sound echoing off the bulkhead. The reverberating effect momentarily disarmed him, and he stood shocked, his mouth agape, then continued, his eyes sunken, weary, and old, "Why did you have to take her out there?" his voice was ragged and uncontrolled, "Mira was all I had left. And you let her—"

He leapt back up to his feet and lunged at Elara. Kael positioned himself between them, taking his arm in his hands, "Hold it, Varek."

Varek pushed Kael aside, ignoring his authority. He stuck his long thin finger in Elara's face, "You let her die! It was you, not me. Not me..." he halted at Elara's glare.

She pushed his pitiful finger aside with her cybernetic fingers, "You dare blame me for this?" She stepped forward, pressing her mechanical fingers against his gaunt, sunken shoulders. He reeled back at her forceful approach. "You're the maniac who planted explosives all over the ship," her assertive, commanding voice sent shockwaves through his frail frame, "You killed her, Varek. You!"

Varek retreated to the safety of his drones. His fingers fiddled in his pocket and produced a small control pad, his body convulsing. A terrible horror fell over his visage, and his eyes trembled as he shot a pleading glance back at Elara. "I had no choice," he relaxed, his casual, flirty personality peeking out from behind his madness. "They have too much dirt on me to let me go."

Elara halted mid-step, her eyebrow cocked, "Who has dirt on you? Are you trying to make us believe you were being blackmailed?"

Varek nodded, his demeanor calming, and the madness faded. His breath was shallow, his voice strained, "All I had to do was stop the *Aurora* from reaching the Phoenix Reaches and make it look like the Dominion was responsible." He lowered his head into his hands, "but sweet Mira didn't have to die in the process," he shot his gaze back up to meet Elara's. "I could have gotten the both of us off the ship before…" He stood up straight, gulping hard, and gestured at the military drones that stood behind him, his voice calm, collected, "…before all this."

"But why," Elara muttered as she side-eyed Varek, "why go through with it?"

A sadistic, sick laugh rumbled from Varek, enough to make her skin crawl. "All I had to do was make it look like the Dominion was trying to stop the *Aurora* from fulfilling their mission, and the Allied Planets would have no other choice but to declare war on the Dominion."

He inhaled a ragged breath, "I would finally be free from their grip, out from under Chairman Mateo's thumb."

Chairman Mateo? Elara's mind reeled at the impossibility, *the CEO of Neotech, all the way to the top of the corporate ladder, the leader of the Syndicate himself?*

"I would finally be free to pursue my own ambitions without their interference. It was all for me, in the end." He stood, poised to press the button labelled 'Omega Strategy' on the control pad, but he paused, and his voice broke into a soft chuckle as he shook his head, "You know, Torren would have hated all this."

Elara's mind didn't just race, it seized. *The name Torren,* it hit her with the sickening finality of a system overload. *Lira,* it was coincidence enough. *Now Torren too?* It was an impossibility. *My father's name.* The second, critical impossibly specific data point connecting her lost life directly to this ship, to Mira, and now to this smiling, maniac saboteur.

Her knees buckled, and she grabbed for something to stabilize herself. Sylen rushed to her side and propped her up. Her knuckles went white. Her entire mental architecture, built on logic and probabilities, began to career. *The odds… they aren't just small… they're zero.* The known laws of the universe could never hope to account for the impossibility.

No. It's a hallucination. Her analytical mind desperately tried to filter the input, to find the flaw in the circuit. She closed her eyes tight, *I'll open my eyes and I'll be back in the Dredges, all this will be nothing but a dream. Only my own slagged-up mind could imagine this whole scenario.*

She squinted her eyes back open, unprepared for what she might see. The disbelief reeled shockwaves through her frame, the sudden awareness shocked her as she darted her eyes about. *No… This is all real.*

She stared at Varek, unable to breathe, seeing not a villain but a ghost. A ghost who had just named one of the two people she had spent her life trying simultaneously to remember their faces and forget their fiery deaths, the ones she constantly grieved.

Varek continued, his voice shallow, lost in his memories, "He could have stopped this whole thing decades ago, but," he paused, his head hung low, the control pad dangling from his thin fingers, "but alas, my hubris," he laughed loudly at himself, "my greed prevented me from seeing his vision, and in hindsight, I regret nothing but the loose ends." His voice lacked true remorse for the lives he'd ruined, only a bitter acknowledgement of his own thwarted ambitions.

He looked up into Elara's eyes and pointed to her, "That microchip you wear around your neck," he sidestepped, creeping slowly to Elara.

Elara darted about the cargo bay, she caught the eyes of her crew, *Kael, Zora, Sylen...* the shame of her secret, her own deception, bore down on her shoulders.

Varek's fingers curled and wrapped around the silver chain around Elara's neck, and with a jerk, he pulled her toward him, their faces inches apart, his dark, sinister eyes glaring into hers, "I'd have recognized it anywhere. I helped to invent that little marvel of technology stored on that chip."

Elara glared back at him, her skin hot, the fury of his lies bursting in her gut. She gasped, "Liar, my father invented it, before I was born!"

"Wait a minute, kid," Pulse interrupted. Code cascaded over her AR, a rudimentary hack attempt to access some mundane system within the cargo bay.

The cargo bay's holo projector hissed and spat as the ambient light within the cargo bay began to bend. A point of intense, crystalline, violet light coalesced.

As the form materialized, its structure became violently unstable. It was the frantic, shifting image of a man. The figure was composed of flickering, high-resolution pixels, but they didn't hold their integrity. The digital flesh pulsed and twitched as though trying to throw off its constraints.

One moment the hologram was a solid, three-dimensional structure, the next it was a blurred, spectral sheet of data, revealing the underlying matrix of code.

Pulse wasn't rendering himself, he was fighting to maintain the illusion of existence. His eyes, the brightest point of the violet light, burned with a new, terrifying confusion. This wasn't the same presence that Elara knew. This was the raw, horrified psyche of a man who had suddenly awakened from his digital prison, locked away for decades.

The light wavered, and a new, desperate sound resonated from the cargo bay's intercom speakers, cutting through the air. "Varek," the voice was the familiar, sarcastic tone Elara had lived with in her head. It held the shaky, ragged texture of a man trying to remember how to speak, "I-I know you."

Varek stood back, a glare of shock spreading across his face as he glared at the holographic construct, "Torren?" his voice had changed, no longer ragged, worn, but softer, more relaxed. "Doctor Vayle, I-I thought you were in exile."

The projection examined its new form, "Exile?" Pulse muttered. "Yes, I went to Earth after..." he paused, "Neural imprint integrity at seventy-four percent," the hologram added absently, as if reading some invisible HUD only he could see. "Primary cognitive pattern: Torren Vayle. Secondary interface designation: 'Pulse.'"

Elara's heart lurched. He wasn't just an AI wearing her father's voice. He *was* her father—digitized, fractured, but undeniably Torren.

His digitally reconstructed eyes blinked blankly as he placed the final pieces of the puzzle together in his mind, "After you refused to allow me to release the plans for the warp drive to the public." His voice had become more human, warmer, *real*.

He pointed his holographic finger and accusatory eyes at Varek, "You wanted to keep it for yourself. For profit," he spat the words like bile.

"Not for myself," Varek interrupted. "For the both of us—we would have been able to climb out of that forgotten corporate basement and make our way to the Sepentary Apex."

The Sepentary Apex, the 7777th floor, the highest point in the city of Silicon, Elara exhaled, *where the board of directors rule over the Syndicate.*

"Ah, yes," Pulse's violet projection began to pace, "The never-ending climb to the top, is that what would have made you happy, Varek?"

"You're slagged right it would have, Torren." Varek tried to remain calm, but his tenor echoed against the cargo bay's bulkhead. "It's *everyone's* dream to make their way into the board of directors, even into the seat of the chairman of the board himself—you were no different."

"Perhaps," Pulse reflected, "but if we released the warp drive to the public, we could have unified humanity instead of all this cold war and tension…"

The electronic eyes of the drones flashed on, their bright red lights burning to life. The actuators in their long, spindly armatures whirred and clanked against the metal floor plating as they slowly inched forward.

Varek whirred around, "No… you can't activate… not yet." He held up the control pad and repeatedly pressed the stop button in feverish vain, "Why won't these things stand down?"

"Targets acquired," the lead drone sounded with a mechanical voice.

Machine-gun fire whizzed through the air, ricocheting off the bulkheads and cargo containers. Bedlam had erupted as flecks of high-velocity shards of metal rained through the cargo bay toward the crew.

Sylen leapt into action, pushing Elara down behind a stack of plastisteel crates, his heavy muscular frame shielding her from the shrapnel and gunfire, "Lillibet, look out!" A burst of the automatic fire sliced through the actuators of Sylen's left cybernetic shoulder, and his body slumped against Elara, his breath heavy and hot against her skin.

"I'm Elara," she whispered to Sylen, her warm breath soaking into the nape of his neck.

Sylen craned his right arm to lift himself off her, "I know," his breath was heavy, "are you alright?"

Elara nodded, "but you're not, you got hit in the shoulder." She pressed her hand against his limp frame and propped him up against the stack of crates in the seated position. "Here, let me take care of that." She began to tend to the ruptured cybernetics with practiced ease, quickly glancing across the cargo bay.

On the other side, Kael had pulled out his sidearm, a Frontier Special 9-11. "You guys okay over there?" He stood against the stack of crates and fired a barrage of pitiful gunshots toward the drones; the fire ricocheted off the back bulkhead.

Sylen's damaged arm dangled, useless, and Elara answered, "Sylen's been hit, his left arm is out of commission." She had produced the relevant tools and was already busy with the repair. "I'll have it back up in a jiff."

Varek had taken cover from the drones. "No, no, no," he panicked, "what are you doing?" He continued to press the grayed-out 'Stop' button on the control pad, to no effect. "There's some kind of override encrypting the controls." He gasped at the horror that he had inflicted on the crew. "The Omega Strategy," he spat. "They've hard-locked my access. This isn't my code—somebody higher up the chain is flying these things now."

"Pulse!" Elara belted as she slammed a new capacitor in line with the actuators in Sylen's shoulder, "What's going on between you and Varek?"

"I've had a corrupted memory node," Pulse erupted from the intercom speakers, "I've been trying to access it since your father installed me into your neural link four years ago."

Kael's sidearm clicked, "Empty. Zora, what's in that crate," he pointed back to a crate labelled 'munitions.'

Zora peeled the plastisteel lid off, her eyes going wide, "It's some kind of heavy weapon," she gasped.

Sylen gulped down air as the actuators in his shoulder sprang to life. "That's the mini-railgun, slide it over here."

Kael helped pull the crate to the edge of their cover behind the stack of crates that protected them from the continual gunfire. With every inch of strength the two could muster, Zora and Kael pushed the crate across the gap between them and Sylen. However, their attempt slid short by a yard.

There's no way he'll be able to reach it, Elara mused, she licked her dry lips. Her muscles tightened, *Time to do something stupid, girl.*

Sylen could see Elara's idea well in advance, and his body lurched to grab hold of her to prevent her from the foolish act she was about to perform, but before he could restrain her, she had leapt from out of the safety of their cover into the kill lane of the drones.

Elara bolted and slid behind the crate, catching herself on the corner to prevent her body from sliding past. The bullets slammed into the side of the crate that she clung to.

Sylen leapt after her, pulling a plasma grenade from his bandoleer and lobbing the projectile out as his frame skittered along the distance between him and Elara. His voice was low, trembling in his throat, "I can't lose anyone else." The plasma grenade bounced off the carapace of the nearest drone, then rolled along the floor before exploding in a fiery burst that engulfed the area between the drones and the crew.

Sylen pulled himself onto his feet and yanked Elara and the crate back behind the safety of their stack of crates. "You alright?" Sylen pulled Elara up to inspect her.

Elara looked down at herself and nodded. "I'm fine." *No, I'm not, I belong in the nuthouse, what the hell was I thinking?* Her hands were shaking and her eyes darted about as her gut bubbled with the fear of mortality. She was momentarily catatonic.

Sylen smiled down at her, "You should've been an Imperial Marine. With that kind of recklessness, there's no way the AP would've ever hoped to stop the ID," he chuckled.

His words were playful, but Elara could feel the seriousness, the concern in his voice. She snapped out of her catatonia with a nervous chuckle of her own, "As if I'da joined the Imperial Marines. If I'da joined the teal berets, we could'a beat the Dominion before the war ever started."

Sylen smiled at her, "You're probably right, you're absolutely insane." He pulled the mini-railgun out of the crate and snapped a cartridge into the receiver, smirking as he hefted the weapon in his mechanical arms. Despite its absolutely massive size, in his hands, the weapon appeared manageable, average-sized.

"Varek," Kael belted out from behind the safety of his crates. He may have been a syndicate saboteur all this time, but he was still part of the crew, and Kael offered the command, "Shut them down, now!"

Continually pressing the dead button on the control pad, he replied, "I can't, they're not responding to commands."

"Hack into their systems," Pulse coaxed Varek.

Varek poked his head over the tops of the crates that had been providing him cover. His long fingers pulled a data-pad out of his pack, and he began to wire it directly to the control pad, "I need a few minutes. Sylen, can you draw your fire on my mark so I can plug directly into the lead drone?"

Sylen raised the heavy railgun into the air to signal Varek, "You got it." He set the railgun to spray a wide arc, then held his breath, bracing his massive frame against the stack of crates. He waited for the signal.

Varek tapped on the data-pad, attempting his hack. "Wait, that's not going to work," he muttered to himself, "the Rigella algorithm is a bust."

"Try the Haegmann algorithm," Pulse approached Varek, the drone's machine gun fire passing harmlessly through his holographic frame, "If I remember right, the Syndicate still hasn't found a countermeasure for that hack."

With deft tapping on the data-pad, Varek inputted the hack. "Bingo, old friend." He looked up at the drones, but their machine gun fire bursts had failed to cease, still spraying through the cargo hold. Varek gulped in air, closed his eyes, then let the breath out in a burst, "Now, Sylen!"

At the signal, Sylen leapt out from behind the crates. The mini-railgun sprayed the cargo hold in a wide spread. He had gotten the drones' attention, drawing their fire.

With his opening visible, Varek dashed out from cover and slid behind the lead drone.

His long fingers shot up to plug in a data cable into the central processor. "This should do it." He pressed 'execute' on the data-pad.

The screen of the control pad flashed red, the Syndicate logo flickering once before being overwritten by a cascade of angular, alien characters. "What kind of fresh hell is this?" Varek hissed. "This isn't Neotech encryption. Omega's override is chained to something off-grid." Sweat began to form on his forehead, "Elara, I need you over here!"

Elara looked up at Sylen, her eyes fraught with concern. "Cover me?" her breath caught as she inhaled.

Sylen nodded, then pulled the railgun up to his shoulder to brace it. His massive frame bounced on his thick, metallic legs, and he took a long, deep breath, his eyes closed. For a moment, he stood there, silently psyching himself up, then his steely gaze fixed on his target, and he jolted out from the safety of the crates, running across the cargo bay, spraying the mini-railgun in controlled, vibrant bursts.

"Now, kid!" Pulse erupted in her head.

Elara's legs pumped under her frame hard, harder than she had thought possible. The machine gun fire peppered throughout the bay and ricocheted and whizzed through the air.

She slid along the metal floor plating, the frayed fabric of her overalls heating from the friction. She braced to twist, to dig her cybernetic hand into the deck and stop.

Her left arm locked. Fingers froze mid-grip, elbow rigid, the entire limb seizing like someone had poured molten slag into the joints.

"Kid," Pulse snapped in her head, sharp and panicked, "that's not me. I'm reading an external injection on your motor pathways coming in through the neural-link port you opened to the ship. You never locked it back down."

The dead weight of the limb dragged her sideways. A ricochet screamed off a nearby crate and slammed into the exposed gears of her frozen forearm. Rusted metal shrieked. Wires spat sparks that lashed against her skin like tiny whips. The arm took the full force of the hit, shielding her chest, but the impact shattered the actuator housing.

The limb went completely dead, a heavy, useless mass of twisted metal that hauled her to a stop right next to Varek. She stood in a crouched position, "Agh, I'm here, now what?" she winced against the loss of her limb.

Varek looked up at her, his gaze steely and cold, his tenor practiced and calm, "Your locket," he held out his hand, waiting for her to hand it to him, "hurry!"

Elara stared at his outstretched hand, then down at the tarnished silver locket, warm against her chest. *Give it to him?* The thought sent a jolt of ice through her veins. *My father's legacy, my last link to him. The key to everything I believe in. And Varek? The saboteur. The man who betrayed my father. The man responsible for Mira's death.* Her fingers curled around the locket, clutching it tight with the impulse to refuse, to lash out at him for his audacity. She screamed out in her mind, *"No!"* her inner monster raged, *"Don't you dare!"*

But the whirring of the drones was relentless, the crackle of machine gun fire echoing through the cargo bay. *Where's Sylen, is he wounded? He's out there, drawing fire, a shield for me.* She glanced back at Kael and Zora. *They're so exposed, so vulnerable. My crew… no, more than just a crew. They're my family.*

Mira's voice, clear as a bell, echoed, not in anger but in a calm wisdom, *"Take a moment, think, then act."* Then her father's voice, Pulse's voice, *"The galaxy is on the brink. Unify the factions."* This wasn't about Varek. It was about the ship. It was about the crew. It was about everything her parents died for.

Handing over her father's legacy, his hopes, her heart, to the man who had caused so much pain felt like a final, devastating act of self-betrayal. *I can't trust him, but I have to choose. I have to give him everything.*

With a trembling hand, she unclasped the locket. Her eyes met Varek's, not in anger but in a grim, desperate resolve. She pushed the locket into his open hands, "Fix this!" she shouted, her voice low and fierce, a raw cry of hope and a terrifying leap of faith.

The sound of a grenade launched through the air drew Elara's attention back to where she once stood, behind the crates. The flash was brief, the shattered plastisteel crates and scorch marks against the floor plating sent a surge of finality through her heart.

If Sylen hadn't gotten me out of there, that would've been me splattered across the deck. A wave of profound gratitude mixed with the ever-present ache of the loss of her parents washed over her.

Varek closed his hands over the locket and lifted it up to his eyes, "This locket is a relic," his voice was matter of fact as he examined the back plane of the object, "a relic of an ancient race." he slid the back cover of the locket open, revealing the complex circuitry of a microcomputer.

A small data-port jutted out from the maze of circuitry, it was an odd little connection point that Elara had failed to recognize. *Is there anything known to man that can plug into there?*

Varek pulled out a cable from his pack and jammed one end into the data-port on the locket, "Your father and I had to make this little baby when we were using it to help us develop the warp drive design." He smiled, "It's kind of like a mega-computer in its own right, this thing holds enough computing power to solve the universe's greatest mysteries." He plugged the other end of the cable into his data-pad.

The moment he pressed the 'execute' button, strange alien runes ignited along the locket's inner ring; fourteen smooth, looping sigils, twelve tiny constellations picked out in sharp lines, and a fan of cross-hatching numeric marks. The symbols flared in a pale violet, then lifted off the metal, hanging in the air like a halo of cold fire.

The control pad's red error screen flickered, then washed over to green as a torrent of new, indecipherable code cascaded down.

"That should do the trick," Varek murmured.

Across the bay, the drones jerked. Their optics flickered from blood-red to a dull, empty gray. One by one, their barrels sagged and their servos went slack. In seconds, the six Dominion war machines stood frozen mid-step, like puppets with their strings cut.

Chapter Twenty-Eight

The cargo bay fell silent as a strange weight settled on Elara's consciousness. The walls and floor seemed to fall away, revealing a deeper, stranger layer of reality.

The gray, dead landscape of a barren planet shimmered into existence. The soil under her feet thrummed, vibrating into her bones. The thick atmosphere hung low above her head, refracting the red and purple nebulae that loomed overhead.

The Phoenix reaches, her mind knew. *It's beautiful,* but her skepticism snapped back hard. *A vision, yes… but from where, and why?* No part of her wanted to accept some cosmic revelation at face value.

She couldn't see them, but she felt their presence, she knew her crew was there with her, *Kael, Zora, Sylen, even Varek.* A wordless, telepathic echo reverberated in her skull, and she could read their awe, their confusion, their thoughts.

A deep, resonant hum rumbled through the dirt, vibrating with a low, hypnotic rhythm. It was a sensation that travelled up her legs and rattled through her bones.

The hum drew Elara closer, it grew more insistent, a chant without words, building in a low, agonizing crescendo that pushed against her eardrums, vibrating faster. The hum provoked her, a forced march into a yawning cavern, deep into the dirt. The taste of dust and ozone hung in the air, growing colder.

An imposing obelisk, impossibly black and incredibly smooth, loomed above her. Its surface was marred only by the runes that glowed with a soft, violet light, runes that mimicked those that had emanated from her locket.

She and the crew stood before the towering object, within the stretching shadow cast by it. Elara turned to face them, her eyes fixed on Zora's.

Long, pallid arms, too thin, too wrong, snatched Zora from the edge of the vision. They took her by the arms, by the feet, by her torso, and pulled at her… dragging her into darkness… into the shadows. It was a purpose Elara failed to understand.

Elara reached out, the word, "Noooo," engulfed into the void. Her fingers failed to save her friend, and she watched, helpless, as Zora was swallowed up into darkness.

The hum pulsed, an invisible heartbeat echoed off the cavern walls, the purple light glowed and pulsated in rhythm with the hum, intensifying, growing brighter and brighter, until it was a blinding flood, consuming the entire cavern.

Elara's mind fractured, the thoughts of a trillion voices penetrating her soul, echoing their pain and strife. For a brief moment, she knew the secret of the universe, the purpose for suffering, the universal inevitability of it.

It was palpable, *An inherent feature of humanity, no… not just humanity—existence itself. The universe is full of so much evil, so much cruelty, there's no way to overcome it… no, there is…*

Her mother and father stood before her, alongside Mira, their voices merged, mimicking the ancient chant that had drawn her to the obelisk, but she understood their words, *"Act against the vile nature that lurks in your heart, Elara. The perfection of the universe comes from within, not from gods, empires, or cosmic forces. Only from people choosing, every day not to feed the monster inside themselves."*

Of course, it's so simple, why hasn't anyone thought of it that way? She paused, unblinking. *No, they have… from hundreds of religions and philosophies of humanity's past alone… That's the universal truth… isn't it?*

She breathed against the burning light that pierced her retinae. Then, as swiftly as the light had appeared, it was gone, replaced by blackness.

Nothing, she thought. *No, there's something out there.* Her eyes adjusted to the darkness, tiny pinpricks of light penetrated the inky black, but not in the center. *No, a large, imposing structure, blocking the starfield.*

She approached the surface. A colossal structure constructed of corroded metal loomed under her feet. *So big… What is it? It was constructed, engineered, but by what hands? Human? Precursor? Something worse?* Her skepticism prickled at the neatness of the imagery.

"Find me, Elara…" an ethereal voice penetrated her mind.

The whisper resonated within her, not a sound but a feeling. *That voice… so familiar, so intimate. Where do I recognize it from?* The voice was distant, incorporeal, a distant echo… *Mom's voice.* Her breath hitched in the back of her throat. The echo was warped by distance and time. *Is it a memory?* The echo frayed and danced at the edges of her vision, *a ghost's plea?*

Then all faded, the blackness dispersed, the light receded, and the cavern dissolved. She was back in the cargo bay.

She stood there, surrounded by her crew, all stunned in silence. The familiar sounds of the *Aurora* returned, but they seemed distant, ethereal, as if heard from underwater.

Elara's heart raced, and a wave of nausea toyed with her gut. The air, once thin, now felt heavy and wrong. She saw the pale, shaken faces of her crewmates and knew they had shared her vision. A cold dread settled over her. *Was that a vision of the future? Our destiny? Or did the drones lob a gas grenade when I wasn't looking?* She dismissed the thought and focused her attention back to the present.

Varek fell back onto the floor, his muscles convulsing. His hand opened, and the locket slid from his grasp tapping against the toe of Elara's boot.

Elara blinked as she snapped out of the fog in her mind. She knelt down and picked up her locket, then she started laughing. Sweat soaked her forehead.

She darted her gaze about the cargo bay and caught the blank stares of her crew. Kael and Zora sat against the floor plating blinking their eyes. *Where's Sylen?*

Varek smiled up at Elara, "We did it, kid," he was panting as he sat up and slapped Elara on the back.

Elara leaned back against the cold metal floor plating. Her head rolled to the side, her chest heaved, and she couldn't catch her breath. Something in the corner of her eye caught her attention, *What is that? It's red.* Elara lay there, failing to process what was before her. *That's where Sylen ran to.* Her frame shot upright, then froze when she saw the blood pooled across the deck. A beat of dead, awful silence passed before instinct overtook her, and she ran. "No, no, no!" her voice strained against the silence. She reached the stack of crates on the other end of the cargo bay.

Blood had pooled around the limp body, already congealing. Elara stared down, and the sheer volume of the gore… the violence, the overwhelming redness that clung to him… it was too much.

Her senses snapped. The brilliant scarlet didn't fade; it simply and suddenly died. It morphed before her eyes into a thick, dull-gray substance.

"Sylen!" she cried, scrambling down to her knees. She knelt beside him, blindly plunging her overalls into the viscous, monochromatic sludge, dismissing it as mere moisture as her focus zeroed in on the terrifying, expressionless pallor of his face.

Varek knelt down beside her and began to examine Sylen. His fingers felt around his throat; he paused and silently counted. "He still has a pulse. It's faint, but I should be able to stabilize him."

He pulled a canister from his pack labeled "Versa-Fiber," a spray adhesive used to seal up open wounds.

He took Elara's fingers, pressed them up against Sylen's throat, and a faint flutter pulsed under her fingers. Varek whispered, "Do you feel that?"

Elara nodded, her eyes wide. *Save him,* she tried to say, but her voice wouldn't come out.

"Let me know if it changes at all." His eyes caught Elara's, and he nodded.

She nodded back. She could feel the sweat on his skin, its smell permeating her senses. Her heart began to beat faster, and she licked her lips to moisten them, then leaned in close, his blood soaking into her clothes. She could feel his breath against her neck, it was icy cold.

Varek ripped a hole into Sylen's fatigues just above his rib cage, blood still oozing from the open wound. He pulled a handheld spectral analyzer from his pack and started to scan the wound, "Good," he said, "all the metal passed through."

Elara's eyes met the dull, lifeless eyes of Sylen. They fluttered and looked back at her. His lips moved but produced no sound.

Elara leaned in closer, straining to hear. The effort only brought her face inches from his, and in that moment, seeing the dim light of recognition in his eyes, a light she had thought was gone forever, the world narrowed.

Varek's concentrated breathing vanished. It was just her and Sylen. She saw his chest stutter, his breath falter, and panic broke through. She leaned down to give him air; clumsy, instinctive, half-remembered CPR from street first-aid vids. But when his lips moved against hers, weak but deliberate, the shock nearly stole her breath. His lips were cold, slack, and tasted of metal and blood. A horrifying reality struck her.

The faint pulse under her fingertips that she thought was slowly slipping away, quickened, then strengthened.

She almost pulled away, until she felt his lips press back against hers. Her head suddenly became light and airy. She was lending him her breath, her lips began to quiver at the touch, then she broke the contact, a strand of her saliva stretched out between their lips, then snapped back. She was breathless, her eyes squeezed shut. She paused to regain composure.

He's so weak, so still. Her heart continued to pound in her chest, her cheeks flushing with a profound heat that radiated from her. She could feel Sylen's breath warm up against her skin.

Varek, oblivious to Elara's stolen kiss, had applied the Versa-Fiber over his wounds. He took her by the hand, snapping her out of her lustful intoxication, "Elara, I'll take over now." He slid Elara's fingers off Sylen's throat and pressed his own in their place. He closed his eyes and counted in a hushed mumble to himself, his eyes snapping open in surprise, "Huh, his pulse is much stronger now." He gave Elara a wry smile, "Whatever you did, kid… trying to breathe for him or whatever that was… it worked. His pulse just jumped."

Elara sat there, touching her lips, a soft pressure lingered. Her breath was soft and low.

He called over to Kael and Zora, "He's going to need some blood, take him to sick bay and hook him up to a bag of type-O syntha-blood, I'll be there momentarily."

Kael and Zora exchanged a look, half disbelief, half judgment, and Elara's cheeks burned as she realized they had seen her panic-born attempt at saving Sylen. A deep red blush flushed her skin, and she tucked herself behind her hands until they carried Sylen's body away.

When she glanced up, she was alone with Varek. She gave him a mean glare and balled her right hand into a fist, drawing her arm back. Varek could see the punch from a mile away but took it across the chin. "What the hell was all that back there?" Elara belted at him.

Varek muttered, more to himself than Elara, "Something strange, alien in nature, had control of those drones. They overrode the control circuitry." He was distracted and matter-of-fact.

She glanced down at the control pad discarded on the floor…
then she saw it.

Amongst the usual lines of code that had flooded the control
pad's screen, she saw a script made from a completely unknown
script, bold crimson lettering that was jagged, angular, and
impossibly complex. The script seemed to write against the
digital interface. They pulsed with an eerie, rhythmic beat that
felt dissonant, a mocking beat that contrasted with the ancient
hum she had just felt in the vision.

A cold wave of recognition washed over her. Not a memory, a
kind of certainty. *The Serpent's Eye. That alien conspiracy book. The
tall man with the mournful, brown eyes standing over the junk stall…*
The plot to destroy the ship was exactly the kind of cynical,
deep-seated manipulation she had always scoffed at.

Are they real? Elara's mind stuttered, *Aliens?* The thought made
her laugh; thin, hysterical, brittle. She wanted to dismiss it as
junk-stall conspiracy fodder… but the script wasn't human. And
the vision's hum still vibrated in her bones.

Her laughter, however, was thin and brittle. The script was
somehow alien in nature, that much she was certain, however…
the crude depiction… compared to the sublime power she had
felt in the vision… *That power, that hum, that gargantuan structure…
that was human.* The crushing realization struck her. *Are we just
pawns, caught in some inhuman intergalactic war? Penance for the sins
of my species?*

As her mind reeled, a dull, agonizing ache pulsed through her
left arm. She glanced down at her cybernetic arm.

Its usual ticking was replaced by a gruesome, unmoving

stillness. Twisted wires poked out from a jagged hole, and a crucial gear was shattered in two, exposed like a broken tooth.

It was dead beyond repair, and grief stabbed deeper than she expected. That arm hadn't been scrap. It was her mother's last gift, her survival in metal form. Losing it felt like losing her all over again. A wave of despair washed over her, a strange grief for a piece of machinery. *it's been with me for so long.*

Varek rubbed the lingering pain on his jaw, but his eyes were drawn to her destroyed arm, "That looks… severe," he murmured, his voice surprisingly gentle, all traces of his previous madness gone. "I might have a suitable replacement in the lab. Better than that scrap, even. Consider it… a start of making amends."

Elara looked at him, her anger momentarily abated in the face of this offer. *A new arm?* The thought was jarring yet intriguing.

Varek rubbed his chin, then began to laugh, "Torren, your daughter has quite the punch."

Elara's mind seized on Varek's words, *"Daughter,"* a label that echoed, not from a friend but from the man who had threatened the ship and her crew.

She looked at the hologram that Pulse had constructed for himself. The shape of the light that coalesced before her was so familiar yet different. Her father had looked older, not like the ghost of this young man who stood before her in the form of a hologram. However, the resemblance was unmistakable. It was her father.

She glanced over to Varek, the lab partner who had just shattered her paradigm with a simple laugh.

The world didn't spin, it froze.

Elara wanted to scream, to collapse, to hide somewhere no one could find her.

Instead, a chilling certainty took hold. The pieces of a thousand small, odd moments with Pulse snapped into place. The strangely personal advice, the uncanny understanding of her fears, the way he would sometimes speak like a man burdened by wisdom. She remembered how Pulse had stopped her from shooting Sylen, how it had been her father's voice, then Pulse's. She assimilated the startling reality… *Somehow, Pulse… he's my father.*

Her voice let out an eek of a sound, "Daughter? Pulse, what does he mean?"

The holographic projection strode up to Elara, "Your father is dead, that much is true," Pulse's voice was low, "however, before he was exiled, he created me, I'm not a mere computer program like all the other AI out there, I'm a neural recording of your father from back when he was a Syndicate scientist."

"A neural recording," she repeated, the words tasting sterile and wrong on her tongue. Her voice was flat, hollowed out. She raised a hand, not to strike but as though to ward off the sheer volume of the revelation. Her eyes, wide and fixed on the holographic form, burned with a desperate, frantic search for the lines that defined the program from the man.

"You… you were there," she whispered, the realization like a physical blow. "All this time. Inside my head. The voice. The thoughts." Her gaze swept over to Varek, cold and sharp, "And you knew. You kept him a secret, even from himself."

She took a shaky breath, her one hand clenched into a fist at her side. The urge to strike Varek again was replaced with the desire to touch her father's face. She lifted her fingers, stretching them slowly toward the shimmering projection. The face was so different from her father's, despite the stark resemblance. It was the voice that she knew, almost better than her own.

"You're not Pulse," she said, the reality finally settling into her gut. It wasn't an accusation but a stunned recognition. "You're Torren." The name, her father's name, sounded impossibly alien yet deeply intimate as it left her lips. Her whole body tensed as if braced for the weight of four years of compressed history, grief, and companionship to finally settle upon her shoulders.

"It took me until just now to realize it." The hologram tried to touch Elara's outstretched hand, but his projection phased through the solid matter. "But yes. For all intents and purposes, I am the very essence of what made your father who he was when he created me." He paused, then continued, "I'm not Torren anymore; I'm not really your father, either. I've spent all these years as Pulse," the holo-projection looked down at the floor. "Perhaps, it's best if you just keep thinking of me as that, how it used to be."

Varek stood up, his thin finger pointed at Elara's locket. "That microchip you wear around your neck in that silver locket. It's the design for an experimental warp drive that your father and I developed. I can help you decrypt it." He pointed at the holographic projection of Pulse. "And Torren here isn't only the key to decrypting the chip but also the warp drive's operating system."

Elara stood there, her mind twisted around the concept. *All this time, Pulse was...* Her mind shot back in time. She could see him standing before her, his strong hands over hers as she tried to steady a soldering iron.

"Keep it steady," her father's voice had permeated her mind, his tone and demeanor a mocking reflection of the Pulse she had grown to know.

"I'm trying, Daddy." Her hand had shaken, then, with borrowed resolve from her father, she had applied the small bead of metal to the circuit board before her with an unknown agility she had never known she possessed, *"I did it!"*

His smile began to fade from her memory. *"You sure did, kid."* His voice was replaced by the mechanical voice of Pulse, "You sure did."

Chapter Twenty-Nine

The med bay wasn't just cold, it was frigid, a plastisteel fortress of thin, hostile light that felt actively opposed to fragile life.

Sylen lay motionless on the gurney, an anomaly in the sterile metal room. His skin was a washed-out gray that seemed to mock the faint promise of his pulse. The only sign that the fight hadn't already ended was the slow, almost imperceptible flutter of his chest. His stuttering breath seemed to catch and hold the entire attention of the room. Elara leaned closer, terrified that if she blinked, that minute, desperate heaving would finally cease.

Her fingers curled between Sylen's as she sat silently by his side. The gentle pressure that had passed between their lips still lingered. *The only reason he's here is because he drew the fire from those drones.* Her thoughts fractured under the weight of the memory.

Her mind's aversion to the color red had still not ceased, leaving her utterly unaware of the damage. Elara's overalls, from legs to bib, were soaked in what she only saw as a thick, dull gray. The massive, rusty discoloration of the dried blood was completely hidden from her sight.

Her thoughts were broken as the hatch to the med bay slid open, and her hand jumped, letting go of Sylen's as she twisted her head toward the open hatch.

Varek lingered in the hatchway, a data-pad dangling loosely from his hand. His posture was hesitant, every movement slow and deliberate. The soft tap of his boots echoed against the med bay floor. "I figured you'd be here," he hummed gently. "I wanted to talk to you about…" he hesitated, "well, you know."

Elara nodded. "We have a lot to talk about." Her gaze hung on Sylen.

Varek positioned himself on his swivel chair and rolled beside her, "Yes well…" he buried his head in his hands, letting his silver hair tangle in his fingers, then he lifted his head in a desperate jerk, "it all escalated so quickly."

Elara stared at the plastic tubing that fed Sylen. The crucial, life-saving substance within it, the color of blood and life, was still filtered out by her mind into a dull, thick gray. The stubborn persistence of the blockage was a mirror to her soul, a refusal to acknowledge the full extent of the gory, intimate reality she faced.

Her shoulders slumped in a moment of utter exhaustion, before a flash of cold fury hit. She straightened and drilled Varek with her glare. "I can't believe I thought it was him," she hissed, her voice a low, perilous murmur. "When it was you all along."

Varek's frown deepened. "It was by design." His voice was low as he attempted to explain," The board of directors wanted the Allied Planets to think that the Imperial Dominion was involved. To force a war. To control both sides. To make a profit," he winced at the word 'profit,' like it formed a visceral reaction, as if bile had risen into the back of his throat. A bile that he could no longer stomach.

All this time. Pro-war, anti-war. A political ploy for control, for profit. Elara's mind reeled with the scale of the deceit.

"I wish I could take it back, but—" Varek's voice snapped like a cable, cut short by a choked gasp. He violently suppressed the emotion, then spun away from Elara to face the wall. She watched the tremor run through his frame as he whispered, "Mira, I wish you were still here."

The words were an indictment and a confession all at once, and Elara's mind immediately began the cold calculation, *is that raw agony in his plea? True regret for the havoc he's caused? Or is it only the unbearable weight of his own personal loss. Does his love for Mira outweigh his guilt toward the crew?*

Elara had heard enough, and her body shot up like a turbo-rotor's spring, a rigid command ringing out, "Hold it right there." Her voice was calm, controlled, but the strain was visible in the cords of her neck, masking the fury she buried. "Mira's death is all your fault, you know."

Varek slid his fingers through his silver hair, the familiar gesture of a man trying to smooth over a mistake. His hair, despite the distress, snapped back into its perfect coif. "I know," he sighed, a pitiful, defeated sound. His broad back still faced Elara, "I don't know if I'll be able to forgive myself."

"Why?" the calm in Elara's voice broke. "Why did Mira have to die?" Her fist plunged into her hip, the sting that radiated was a small thing compared to the pain in her heart. Her voice dropped to a low whisper, "Tell me, Varek, why did you do it?" The plea was no longer rhetorical, it was her heart trying to make sense of the madness.

Varek sighed. He pulled a handkerchief from his pocket and cleaned his face before turning back toward Elara. The distress of his emotional outburst remained. He took his seat on the swivel chair once more, dropping his swollen eyes, then lifted them up to lock with Elara's. They were filled with softness and compassion.

"Your father, Torren, he was like a brother to me." His voice hitched as he drew in a ragged, jittery breath, "I remember how we would laugh over cheap coffee as we worked in the lab throughout the night. He was always dreaming of the stars. I thought he was naive."

He let out his breath, and it quivered as it passed through his thin lips in a long, hesitant sigh, "I should have listened to him." He shook his head. "I should have never sold him out, should have never let my own desire for greatness get in the way of what was truly important." He paused. "And then Mira…" his voice cracked.

Elara watched his delicate dance, practiced and perfect. A strange feeling of pity threatened to overtake the cold anger that twisted in her gut. *His regret,* she decided, *seemed more theatrical than genuine. He's focused more on his own fractured life. Opportunities lost, rather than the devastation he's wrought.* The performance was familiar, *a man trying to save face, not a soul truly broken by the lives he's destroyed.*

The rage flared again, a searing heat, the same heat that made her almost shoot Sylen, almost made her refuse Varek's demand for her locket. She knew that desperate, self-justifying pull, that blinding rage. She had been able to tamp it down before, to push past it.

Her father's whispered instructions penetrated her psyche, *"Reunite the factions."*

I need his knowledge. I don't forgive him.

A flicker of hard-won pride warmed her chest. She had made her choice, and it had saved them.

Varek sat for a moment, letting his breath in and out slowly in controlled, fluttering sounds. He looked back up to Elara, his steely blue eyes clinging to hers. "When we were developing the warp drive prototype, your father and I, we had to perform some—" he gulped hard and licked his dry lips, "some illegal genetic procedures."

Elara's eyes went wide, "My father wouldn't," she gasped. A cold dread twisted in her stomach. *My father?* A man she idealized. *He did something… unethical? Immoral?* The suggestion of it felt like a wicked betrayal. She watched Varek's face, searching for any sign of deception, but his gaze was direct, unsettlingly earnest. *No. He's telling the truth.*

Varek nodded. "We had to," his voice was quiet. "Our projections were clear. The human body would tear itself apart in the warp field. So, we rewrote the genetic code of our test subjects."

There was a direct and profound reason genetic engineering was only performed in utero. The procedures that spliced the DNA sequences within adult subjects would always render their genetic structures unstable. A fatal result always followed.

His eyes quivered as they bore into Elara's, not blinking, not pulling away. He pursed his lips, "But when our test subjects died, your father was ready to give up. I refused to let our research go to waste, and I developed a new plan."

Elara shook her head, the motion more a dazed tick than a gesture of denial. *My father?* The words felt foreign, wrong. Her throat tightened, the ideal of the man shattering like glass. *The man who whispered of a better future was also capable of… this?*

Varek continued, pointing at Elara's neural link port under her ear, "That's when I came up with the tech to record neural imprints. Your father didn't trust me to be the subject, so he imprinted his own brainwaves and created Pulse." He slapped his thigh, and a burst of excitement shot through the room, "That little AI of yours proved to be the solution to the problem all along. As it turns out, the problem was never in entering the warp field. It was stabilizing it, and Pulse was meant to do just that."

Varek stood up and walked to the other side of the room. "Torren couldn't take the guilt, and when I hesitated to release the design to the public, he ran. And when the authorities came to the lab, I was left there to answer for our crimes."

His vision danced through the small porthole in the bulkhead, "Neotech had the lab bugged all along, and when they lost the design, they wanted to get something out of their investment. I was forced, by punishment of the law, into becoming their spy. I reported directly to the board. My missions had primarily been focused on industrial espionage and sabotage. I would pose as a scientist for a rival corporation poised to corner the market with something big that could shatter the galactic market. And I would either steal the tech or destroy it.

"I was planted on the crew of the *Aurora* as one final job. I was going to be free from their grip once I fulfilled their plan." He let his breath out from his lungs in a long breath.

A subtle change in the pressure, a faint stale scent of air made

Elara turn around. Zora stood huddled in the open hatch, looking small and withdrawn. "S-sorry to intrude," she whispered, her voice soft and low, "I'll come back later."

"Nonsense," Varek slid toward the hatch, "I was just about to go catch some z's," he faked an exaggerated yawn and stretched as he slid past Zora into the corridor.

"I-I just wanted to check in on him." Her eyes pointed to the floor.

Elara looked at her friend, the vision of watching her being dragged into the shadows fresh in her mind, "Zora…"

Zora held up her hand to stop Elara, "I know, I saw it too." she frowned. "But if you don't…" she glanced over at Sylen, her face engulfed in shadow, "They'll get the obelisk."

Elara nodded, "I know, but…"

Zora held her finger to Elara's lips, "We can't let that happen." She let out a long sigh, as though she had finally let the weight of her inquisition rest on her shoulders. "For the first time in my life, I don't know who the Great One is." She hesitated, watching her words carefully, a silent pull still held within her heart, the sudden snap of it almost visceral. "But now I know he's…" her voice withdrew, dropped to a ragged whisper, "bad."

The truth of Zora's words sent a shock through Elara's frame. She recalled her previous visions, the cosmic horror that inhaled Zora's fragmented soul, the strange man's words about truth, and the vision of Zora being dragged into the shadows. *These aren't just visions of what may happen… they're visions of what must…* she choked on the thought, *what must happen.*

The cold shudder within Elara's frame was interrupted by a soft meow that announced D'Artagnan. He nudged his way past

Zora's legs and trotted directly toward Sylen's gurney. The fluffy Siamese kitten leapt lightly onto the edge of the bed, settling himself carefully by Sylen's side, purring loudly and nuzzling himself against the massive man's bandaged torso. He licked at Sylen's mechanical fingers.

Zora's countenance lifted, a soft smile touching her lips. She followed the kitten, her hand instinctively reaching out to gently stroke D'Artagnan's fur as he comforted Sylen. The tips of her pale, scarred fingers slid along the bare flesh of Sylen's massive chest, and it heaved up and down as he slowly breathed.

Sylen's eyes fluttered open. His jaw softened, a faint smile teasing his lips. "Careful," his voice was soft and relaxed, "don't let D'Artagnan see you fussing." A broad smile pierced the growth of brown stubble that covered his face.

Zora's cheeks flushed a delicate pink. She lingered by Sylen, and a quiet warmth penetrated the space of the med bay. Elara's eyes danced between Zora and Sylen, trying to catch the two.

Zora raised her hand, her movements slow and deliberate, before it froze mid-air. *She wants to touch him,* Elara thought, recognizing the hesitation. A soft, warm smile played on Zora's lips. She retracted her hand, settling it on the thick fur of the kitten.

Then her gaze lifted, snapping away from Sylen, fixing on Elara.

It was a deep, knowing look. Her eyes, usually so guarded, were wide and desperate, a wordless agonizing plea. She slowly and silently mouthed to Elara, "What happens to him... if they don't take me back?"

Elara silently mouthed back to her, "What happens to him if

they do?"

Zora's eyes closed briefly in a shudder of final, profound resignation. When she reopened them, the desperate light was gone, replaced by a terrible calm. She returned her attention to the kitten, her smile fixed, but brittle.

Zora's shoulders, usually hunched and protective, softened slightly as she leaned into Sylen's presence. She hung there, stuck between the comfort of her own inhibition and her visceral need to display her utter devotion to the man. It was more than shyness, it was a visible struggle to overcome her instinct to retreat. The metamorphosis into something brave and assertive remained unfinished, halted by her own hesitation. She was like a butterfly that had perished, trapped within the walls of its own cocoon.

A subtle, almost holy longing radiated from Zora, palpable even across the room, and Elara watched, suddenly feeling like a voyeur. A third wheel.

That longing twisted the knife in Elara's gut. The sharp, cold memory of the cargo bay, of pressing her lips to Sylen, stealing a kiss when she thought he was dying, rushed back, leaving a profound residue of searing shame.

He was dying, and I took a kiss. And both Zora and Kael had seen it. She recalled the disapproving looks on their faces, the tension in her gut. *Their sideways glances, the silent 'tuts' from their lips,* her cheeks burned, *I selfishly violated their trust.*

But looking at Zora, the guilt faded away, replaced by a painful, immediate clarity. *Zora and Sylen. They look incredibly cute together.* The massive, stoic man and the fragile, quiet woman, connected by the warm weight of a purring cat. The connection felt fragile, new, a delicate bond that Elara realized she couldn't bear to crush.

Her own complicated, warring feelings for both Sylen and Kael loomed. It was a dangerous storm that threatened to shatter her home, her new family, the fragile peace they had built on board the *Aurora*.

Any wrong move could break the crew apart. The thought was a cruel dread. If *I pursue him, if my complicated affections fractured this newfound family,* her mind reeled, *I'd be truly alone again, the ultimate price.*

Elara had made her peace with it. She consciously relinquished the kiss and the dangerous desires that followed it, mentally stepping back from the gurney.

I can't risk this fragile family, not for a moment of desperate selfishness. Zora deserves him more than I do. The intense warmth radiating from the pair made the rest of the med bay feel impossibly cold, amplifying her sense of isolation.

She glanced down at her overalls, the invisible gray gore a sickening reminder of her selfish urgency. However, as she started to rise, preparing to slip away, her eyes registered a flicker. It was a sensation, not a color, a mental static that cleared in a single, painful instant.

The world snapped.

Where a moment before there had been a uniform, dull gray, her overalls were suddenly, violently saturated in thick, drying crimson. It was a massive, hideous stain, a geography of dried gore running from the knees to the bib, crusting the threads where she had knelt beside Sylen. The sheer, shocking volume of the blood hit her with the force of a physical blow.

She froze, acutely aware of the horror she was covered in, the absolute casualness with which she had treated the wound.

She had dismissed this… this sickening, sticky evidence of near death… as mere sludge. Her cheeks burned with a sudden, overwhelming wave of embarrassment and self-revulsion. She was literally painted in the trauma she had mentally avoided.

Slowly, quietly, she rose, desperate to escape the med bay and the eyes of Zora and Sylen. She turned her back on the picture of warmth, her blood-soaked figure merging seamlessly with the silence of the corridor outside as she stepped through the hatch. She didn't look back, the sound of the med bay hatch hissing shut the sound of a door closing on her own desires.

Chapter Thirty

The captain's stateroom hatch hissed shut behind Elara, but Kael, the new captain, didn't flinch. She found him elbows-deep in a closet unit, tossing meticulously folded uniforms with a speed that bordered on frantic, yet making scarcely a sound.

He was moving through the private space of the dead with the desperate, quiet intensity of a man searching for a misplaced treasure. His eyes were wide and strangely detached, flicking over the fabric without truly seeing it, the turmoil of his reflection far outweighing the task at hand.

The weight of command was palpable on him. It wasn't an honor or even just a burden; it was a foreign gravity that bent his posture. His usual quiet assurance, normally a fixed point in any storm, had dissolved, leaving behind a shaken man going through a ritual he was wholly unprepared for.

Kael suddenly whirled around, his movement sharp and mechanical, betraying the tension he tried to suppress. His gaze met Elara, then immediately dropped to the grotesque, crimson-saturated overalls. He didn't even register her face, only the evidence that remained of her shameful act of stealing a kiss from the dying Sylen.

"Elara," his voice was flat, perfectly level, and devoid of any emotional recognition. "You should get changed into something a little more…" his blush mocked the crimson stains that he averted his eyes against, "…appropriate for the funeral." He glanced away, back to the closet, and pulled out a stiff teal jumpsuit from the stack of folded uniforms he had been working his way through. He handed the jumpsuit back to her, "Here, this one should fit."

He couldn't look at her. She remembered the last time she had seen him, pulling Sylen's limp body out of the cargo bay on his stretcher. She could still see the disapproving glare that penetrated her after she had stolen that kiss. She knelt down and took the teal jumpsuit from Kael's grasp, the thin material flopped in her hand.

A guttural, stuttering sound blew out of Kael's lips, but he hesitated, the silent chastisement palpable between them was not to come, not from his mouth. He shook his head and uttered an almost imperceptible whisper. "None of my business."

The chill of his detachment shot down Elara's spine, a ghostly shiver. *Here I am, standing drenched in the visceral reality of Sylen's trauma. No wonder Kael's treating me like some contaminated object in need of decontamination. I would've been better off walking in here bare-bottom naked. At least he'd look at me.*

Kael's clinical tone had stripped away the last vestiges of her newfound belonging. Her shoulders tightened as she felt the sudden, uncomfortable surge of heat in her cheeks, raw shame replacing her recent guilt. She wasn't an officer, or a friend, or even a crewmate. Just a stowaway, out of place in a room meant for the dead.

The air was so heavy with unspoken accusations that Elara felt she might suffocate. Kael, finally abandoning the hopeless task of the closet, sank back against the bulkhead. The movement was one of pure surrender, and with the weight of a sack of gears dropping to the floor, his internal guard fell.

"I hate this room," he mumbled, fingers dragging through his light brown hair, then pausing at the base of his neck as if grounding himself against an unseen weight.

"I don't know what I'm looking for. Mira had everything in its place, except her dress uniform... it's a ghost now, like everything else."

He lifted his eyes, finally meeting hers, and the raw exhaustion was far more damning than any glare. "I'm not her, Elara. I'm not the captain," his voice cracked on the final word. He leaned forward and rested his forehead on his fists.

"You know what I wanted? I wanted a little scout vessel. A Federated Colonies Ranger ship. Three people, maximum. Just enough deck space for my own little crew, my own rules, out on the fringes, charting anomalies. That was the dream. Independence." His eyes were worn and his voice low and drawn, "And now, what have I got? I got command of a freighter big enough to swallow the moon, a crew I'm responsible for, and a target painted on my back."

He gave a short, bitter laugh. "I knew who you were from the moment I saw you lurking along the causeway like a little mouse at the spaceport, you know. I kept my mouth shut. The captain told me I was wasting my time, that I should trust you." He rubbed his eyes roughly, the admission hung between them like a fragile, crystalline bomb. "She saw a future for this crew. All I see is the edge of the void."

Elara sighed, eyes searching the room for somewhere, anywhere, to shed the weight of Sylen's drying blood. The denim felt stiff, wrong, like it didn't belong to her anymore.

"Kael," she said quietly, fingers hooking under the straps of her overalls, "turn around. Please don't… look."

He didn't argue. He just nodded once and stepped closer to the bulkhead, planting himself facing the wall, hands clasped behind his back like he was on inspection. His shoulders were rigid, his gaze fixed on some imaginary point in the plastisteel.

Elara unlatched the bib. The fabric peeled away with a wet, tearing sound as the crusted blood released from the cloth. Cold air prickled against her skin as she stripped down to her ill-fitting underwear. *Changing in a dead woman's room,* she thought, shivering. *It feels wrong. Like trespassing on a grave.*

She pulled the stiff teal jumpsuit up over her legs and hips, the material unfamiliar and thin after years of heavy denim, then tugged the zipper up to her throat. The blood-stiffened overalls lay in a sad heap at her feet.

The intimate tension, thick enough to choke on, finally became too overwhelming for Elara. She didn't cry or speak. She snorted, the sound so sudden and ridiculous that it fractured the heavy silence. A nervous, messy laugh, a startled, uncontrolled chortle, erupted from her chest. She folded over, hands pressed to her midriff, trying to stifle the absurd noise.

Kael, completely disarmed by the collapse of her composure, let out his own startled chuckle. He was instantly overtaken by the same release, and the forced professionalism was shattered. He joined her, leaning into his laughter, it was as raw and strained as his earlier confession.

For a brief, necessary moment, the new captain and the shamed stowaway were just two people, dissolving into the absurdity of the situation.

The shared, breathless laughter died down, leaving the stateroom quieter and heavier than before, and an acute wave of embarrassment landed on Elara's shoulders. The memory of Sylen's blood on her overalls, and the stolen kiss flooded back. She could feel Kael's own shame at how he had openly doubted his leadership capabilities.

Elara quickly averted her gaze, standing up to smooth out the teal jumpsuit over her hips. The thin fabric rested lightly over her skin, leaving her with the uncanny feeling of nakedness, despite being clothed. She partly missed the feeling of the thick, heavy denim and wondered if she could ever get used to wearing something so thin, so delicate.

Kael pulled himself up to his feet, his face instantly regaining its clinical mask, but his eyes briefly met hers. Then lingered on her lips.

He saw it all. My kiss with Sylen. My nakedness. My soul. Her heart fluttered under her chest. She touched her chest. *You can see me, can't you? My shame, my desperation to feel connected?* She recalled watching Mira with Varek in their quiet, secluded embrace, *I want that, can't you see?*

His eyes drifted down to the floor, *No I guess not… duty it is, I guess. No room for that nonsense.*

In that moment of clarity, a profound recognition struck her. *Sylen. It was always primal, fierce, forbidden.* A raw, dangerous impulse against the Imperial she was raised to hate through propaganda.

But Kael… Kael's different. He saw my shame and covered it with a sterile uniform. He had acknowledged her past with a quiet admission of his own failures. *The pressure of holding this crew together. The crushing mantle of command. It's already too much for him to bear.*

They turned away from one another. It wasn't a denial of their attraction, nor a denial of their feelings, it was a wordless agreement on their priorities. Sure, Zora and Sylen were free to build on their connection of quiet devotion and mutual comfort, but Elara and Kael were bound by shared leadership, mutual understanding of sacrifice, and the heavy weight of the future. *He and I are the ones left standing to fix the broken pieces of the Aurora, that's how it's always been. Wanting him and needing him to lead are two very different things,* she realized, jaw tightening. *I only have room for one.*

"Help me find that uniform, Captain," Elara said, the title deliberate.

Kael's gaze flicked to hers, then away. "Please don't call me that," he muttered. "I've half a mind to name you my first mate if you keep it up." A faint, humorless smile tugged at his mouth. "Just Kael. For now. Besides, it's no use. I've scoured this room. The uniform's nowhere."

Elara's eyes darted to the locked chest under the captain's desk, "have you looked in there?"

Kael knelt down beside the massive lockbox and pulled a key out of his pocket. "I found this when I was searching the closet. The captain had it hidden under her…" he blushed, not wanting to reference Mira's underthings, "er, unmentionables."

Elara knelt down beside Kael, taking the key from his grasp in her fingers, "Perfect, let's see if it opens the lock."

Elara could remember seeing the lockbox taunt her from under the captain's desk the first time she had been in Mira's stateroom to learn of *Aurora's* orders. She remembered the curiosity, the sheer desire to pop that lock open to see what secrets Mira had hidden. The urge was stronger than ever, now having the key in her grasp.

She held her breath as she fit the key into the padlock. With a twist, the heavy brass fitting snapped open, and the lock hung loosely on the hasp. She pulled the lock aside and lifted the lid to the chest, her heart beating hard in her chest.

On the top of the chest rested the captain's dress uniform. Bright white synthetic fiber with pale teal accents along the arms and legs. A full rack of medals, gleaming and polished, rested on top, and underneath, a pair of patent leather dress shoes, polished to a mirror shine.

"This is perfect for Mira's funeral," Elara beamed at Kael, lifting the uniform up out of the chest. She paused. Underneath sat stacks of envelopes addressed to Mira, from… *Mom?* She held her breath as she lifted the first letter out of the chest.

She glanced up at Kael, a silent plea to let her have the space in peace. He had gotten what he needed from the captain's room, so he nodded and departed out the hatch, leaving Elara alone, free to read the sacred texts delivered from her mother to her aunt.

Her eyes flitted down at the letter, the words dancing before her, a secret world she was never meant to find.

May 13th, 2415

My dearest sister, Mira,

I can't believe how long it's been since I've seen you. How many years have gone by? My little pumpkin has been growing so fast. Torren just laughs and says she'll be captain of her own star cruiser by the age of twelve. God, I love that man; he's so strong and brilliant.

I know you told me he was too quiet for me, but he's my rock. Even with all this political noise swirling around us. The Anti-War Party meeting last night was tense. They think this awful war will be over soon. You'll be home, safely away from all that awful space combat against the Imperial Dominion.

The Enforcers have been circling the block again. It's becoming harder and harder to simply exist here in the Dredges without feeling like we're being watched. I tell myself it's just paranoia, but the fear is starting to taste metallic in my mouth, like blood.

Here's the funny thing—when Elara gets cross, she's starting to do that little jaw-clenching thing you used to do! She's got your restless curiosity, my dear twin. I try to keep her secluded, but she's determined to explore everything.

Please write back soon. Tell me about the void. Elara gobbles up every word you say about space. Especially the plans for that freighter you want to name Percius. I still think Aurora would make a much prettier name. Tell me about anything that isn't here.

Love, Lira

Elara's eyes welled up at her mother's words. She remembered how her mother used to call her her little pumpkin when she was small, especially when she wore an orange onesie that made her look rolly-poly like a little pumpkin. She smiled to herself at the memory. *I was just like Mira, huh.* She tucked the letter back into the envelope, then sifted through the pile, her fingers tracing over one in particular, and she opened it.

November 23rd, 2418

Mira,

This is not a drill. Stop asking me to come visit. It's too dangerous. Torren has been different. Quiet, haunted, paranoid even. He finally broke last week. It's not the enforcers we should be worried about; it's always been the Syndicate.

You remember what he did, that work before we met? They haven't forgotten about the design he snuck away with, right under their noses. God, he still feels guilty about leaving poor Varek holding the bag.

They're actively looking for us. Torren says it's a matter of months, maybe a couple more years if we're lucky, before they find us. When they do, they won't just deport us back to Silicon to do God knows what to us. They want the plans back, and they want us dead.

The life we built here—it's a phantom. A beautiful, impossible lie. We're packing up and heading deeper into isolation. I don't know when I can write again.

Love, Lira

Varek was telling me the truth about that, Elara stared through the bulkhead, unblinking. *The Syndicate had been after them? It was never the Enforcers?* Her mind drifted back to the night her parents had been taken from her in that fiery explosion.

The fear in their eyes, the whispered words they shared with one another. One phrase had always stuck out wrong in her gut, *"Neotech, they've finally found us,"* she remembered the words that slipped out from her father's lips before he died.

She felt numb, and her fingers danced among the loose envelopes of their own volition, until she was staring down at her mother's last words to her aunt.

February 18th, 2421

Mira,

Listen to me. If you are reading this, it means that we've run out of time. You were the only one I could trust, the only one far enough out in the black.

I've put Elara's full identification package with the emergency drop-ship manifest. I know you're still planning to acquire that old Imperial freighter once the war is over. I still think you should call it the Aurora. I think that would be the safest place in the black for her. The manifest is coded to that vessel.

You have to take her. The moment you get the signal, you have to. Don't hesitate. Don't look back. I know you never wanted to be tied down, but she needs your strength and your silence, away from this terrible place, this terrible war, and the shadows Torren brought with him.

I beg you, Mira. Protect my daughter. Raise her for me. Give her the other half of the Navigator's Coin when she's old enough to understand. Tell her I loved her more than the light itself.

If anything happens to us, tell Elara that she carried both our hearts. Look after my little pumpkin, please.

Love, Lira

The welling tears in her eyes threatened to burst free, and she glanced down into the chest. She had sifted through the mass of the letters, she'd have time to read through the rest later, after the funeral, after she got the ship back in order.

No time now, but later.

Her eyes fixed on two golden coins, each with a golden chain dangling from them.

She pulled the halves out of the chest and held them up to her eyes. One coin was slightly larger, its center carved with a shallow groove, just wide enough to accept the smaller piece. The outer rim was etched with strange alien runes—eerily similar to the symbols she'd seen glowing on the obelisk in the vision, and the ones that had risen from her locket.

The smaller coin was ringed with twelve tiny constellations, none of them matching any star charts she knew. It, too, had a narrow groove running through its center.

She slid the smaller coin into the groove of the larger one. They clicked together with an unnervingly precise *snap*. For a heartbeat, the room seemed to tilt—not enough to knock her over, just a brief, dizzy shift, like gravity had twitched.

A faint hum buzzed against her fingertips. The etched runes along the outer edge glowed softly, cycling through muted violet and blue before fading back to dull gold.

Turning the joined coin, she noticed a third, empty channel along the inner disk, a groove with nothing to fill it. *Of course,* she thought bitterly. *Nothing about my life is ever complete.*

She shuffled through the chest for another piece, but time clawed at her spine. No more delays. Mira's funeral wasn't going to wait for her to solve another mystery.

Elara slipped the chains over her neck. The cold weight of the joined Navigator's Coin bumped gently against the silver locket at her chest. *Mother. Father. Mira,* she thought, fingers brushing the metal. *You're all here with me now. Right where you belong.*

She stuffed the letters back into the chest and closed the lid, then, hefting it up, she trudged out through the hatch.

Chapter Thirty-One

Elara's new uniform felt stiff and formal, the teal fabric a jarring contrast to the thick, bloodstained denim she had shed. It was the color of the Allied Planets, Mira's color, her color now.

A twinge of longing streaked across her left arm, a phantom sensation from her past. She instinctively glided the tips of her fingers along the surface of her new limb. Gone was the familiar, clunky scrap metal, the exposed wires and ticking gears that had been a part of her for so long. In its place, a sleek, gleaming arm, a smooth alloy of brushed silver, seamlessly joined at the shoulder.

Varek had worked tirelessly since the firefight, programming and assembling the new limb in the brief windows between tending Sylen's recovery checks. He hadn't rebuilt it all at once, just enough to make it functional; there was still more he planned to refine later. The arm was now silent, its servos gliding with an almost organic grace. It was more than a replacement, it was a testament to his strange offer of atonement, a jarring symbol of her own new beginning.

The arm felt simultaneously natural and alien. She still longed for the familiar rattle of her old limb, but beneath that grief hummed a faint spark of excitement. This new arm held capabilities she didn't yet understand. Though, she mourned the loss of her old appendage, as it had been a physical reminder of her mother.

Her fingers brushed against the teal fabric that loosely clung to her chest, the familiar impression of her father's locket accompanied by the twin navigator's coin halves that clinked against one another. The feeling of home, a sensation that she had barely remembered from her years lost in the Dredges, fluttered in her heart. The *Aurora* was her home.

Mira's body lay lifeless on the airlock floor, still encased within the vacuum-proof suit that she had died in. Elara couldn't bear the sight of the pale, lifeless figure. The thought of her captain, her aunt, floating in the endless void was overwhelming. However, it was tradition to send your deceased crew off to explore the stars in their eternal afterlife.

Zora entered the airlock holding the fleet dress uniform that Kael had asked her to dress Mira in, the insignia of an Allied Planets Commodore gleamed under the airlock lights. "Elara," she whispered, her voice fragile, "we should dress her."

In a silent ritual, the two girls pulled Mira's limp, pale hands through the uniform blouse and her feet through the legs of the trousers. Elara's eyes were blurred and wet as she struggled to align the silver buttons on the blazer, fighting for the composure Mira deserved.

She felt Zora's fingers tremble beside her own, a fragile echo of shared grief, but Zora held Mira's collar a heartbeat longer than she normally would, a small show of courage Elara didn't miss. She remembered the night she and Zora had spent in the infirmary with Mira. They had both been afraid that she would die. The only difference was that Elara had only at that moment realized the finality of the scene, Zora had been battling with those emotions for months, maybe even years. She recalled the tone in Zora's voice, the real her, the Zora that only her true loved ones could ever hope to see. She remembered how she had said, *"The captain, she's like a mother to me."*

The moisture that had pooled over her eyes finally broke, a stream washing down her cheek.

Once dressed, the two girls slid Mira's thin body into a teal vinyl bag and zipped it up to her chest. Elara placed the teal beret over her silver hair.

Sylen, Kael, and Varek stood outside the airlock, watching through the thick plexiglass.

Elara and Zora joined the men, then Kael stepped up to the window, his shoulders heaving under stifled breaths. He wiped a piece of cloth against his cheeks, then took a deep breath before turning to face the crew... his crew.

He paused for a long moment, his breath steadying. He held an elaborate wooden box in his hands and whispered a silent word to himself, inaudible, then cleared his throat and opened his eyes. "Thank you all for coming," Kael began quietly. "If anyone wishes to speak... step forward." He stepped aside to make room.

Zora stood rigid for a moment, then, with an uncanny urgency, she approached the spot where Kael had stood. She took his place before the crew, clutching a tightly folded piece of red and white canvas to her chest. Her violet eyes darted to Sylen, allowing her gaze to linger, and she drew in a deep breath as though she was drawing in his strength. Her courage began to stir behind her long, raven hair. She parted her lips and paused, then looked down, "When you found me, a refugee from the inquisitors, you took me under your wing." Her voice trembled. "You saw something in me... I wish I could be as brave as you. You make me want to be better."

She bit her lip, then held up the piece of canvas, letting it unfurl. A white signal flag with a red saltire stitched in, "The Victor signal flag," her voice rang unusually resonant, "to be held aloft whenever you are in need of assistance. We will always answer your call, Captain." She quickly refolded the flag and slid into the airlock, dropped to one knee, and slipped the flag into the vinyl bag, then stood up and slid back to join her crew, stepping to the back, hiding behind her long hair.

Sylen stood tall before the crew, the dagger from the captain's bookshelves held in his strong mechanical hands. Its various gemstones gleamed under the soft lighting.

Elara remembered the cold implement from her vision, how it was used to mar Zora, *an Inquisitor's blade.*

"Mira, I wanted to thank you for taking a chance on me." His voice went low, his gaze dropped. "You know why I had to leave the Dominion, and that kind of horror is unforgivable."

He glanced up, his eyes caught Zora's, and a small, fragile hope lingered in his voice. "Well, that is... you forgave me. Perhaps one day I might even be able to forgive myself."

He glanced down at the dagger held in his mechanical fingers, his eyes cast down. "This dagger..." his voice hitched. "I still remember how we faced off against that inquisitor who was hunting Zora." He paused and looked up into Zora's eyes, she was caught by surprise, as if unaware of the memory that Sylen was sharing.

"Heh," he drew the dagger from the sheath, his eyes resting on the cracked blade, "That's where he struck me, where the blade got jammed between titanium ribs." He smiled.

"If it weren't for you, Captain, that scrag inquisitor would have had me. I was merely the distraction, but you, Mira? The tip of the spear."

He slid the dagger back into its sheath, then held it up above his head with both hands, nearly punching the ceiling with the sheathed blade. He jumped slightly, then lowered the blade to eye level. "To protect you on your journey."

He lumbered into the airlock, squatted beside the captain, then stuffed the dagger into the vinyl bag. He towered back to his feet, then lumbered back through the airlock's inner hatch, falling into line with the crew beside Zora. He offered her a smile, and she glanced up, returning the gesture.

Varek strutted to the front. He glanced at the crew, a shockwave shooting through his frame, his shoulders slumped, his breath shallow. He turned to look through the window at Mira's still body. "Mira, my love. I know it's not much of a secret that you and I were..." He cleared his throat. "I don't know if you'll ever forgive me for what I did to you, to your ship." He turned and glanced at the crew, then his eyes settled on Elara, a pleading look trembling in his eyes, "How can I forgive myself?"

Elara shook her head and mouthed the words, *"I don't know."*

Varek lowered his head and took a deep breath. A moment of silence passed, then he shot his usual, casual glare back to the crew, "We were thick as thieves, Mira and I. She hated my taste in music." He laughed, a hollow sound. "I guess we didn't have all that much in common, but..." he turned to face Mira through the plexiglass, "I love you."

His fingers slid along the bulkhead, "I swear I will make amends in all your hearts. I promise to help you decrypt that microchip and fulfill Torren's dream."

Elara could tell he was speaking directly to her.

"You always told me to stay the course, Mira. That's what I'll do. I'll watch over your crew and see this through. Someone needs to give this ragtag motley crew of kids some adult supervision," his voice dropped into a low rumbling chuckle that trailed off.

The words resonated deep into Elara's soul. *Somehow, I believe him.*

He turned back to the plexiglass window, his fingers touching the transparent surface. He lingered there for a moment, a silent sob heaving his shoulders before he withdrew to the back of the crew, his glossy eyes averted.

Kael looked over to Elara to urge her to the front. She mouthed the words, "Captain goes before first mate."

He silently chuckled at her inside joke, then took his place before the crew, standing stiffly, almost too formal. "Captain Mira Thalren…" He relaxed his stance and dropped all formality.

"I don't know if I can live up to you as a captain. I hope I can. I hope I can be worthy of the trust you placed in me."

He gave a quick glance up at Elara, a silent plea in his eyes. *He wants me to believe in him,* she realized, the idea resonating in her gut with a strange ache. She nodded back and offered a reassuring smile. *I can see your strength, Kael, your commitment. It cuts through your self-doubt.* His gaze lingered on her, the vulnerability in his hazel eyes a testament to their sacred bond of duty they had forged.

He held up the box and opened it. The polished brass reflected the light of the outer locker room outside the airlock. "A compass, so you will always know your way home." He closed the box and walked into the airlock. He knelt down beside Mira, slid the box into the vinyl bag, then slowly stood back up and stepped out from the airlock, rejoining the crew and standing next to Elara.

Elara took Kael's place, a depth gauge from an ancient submarine in her hands. The grease had been wiped off to reveal its tarnished brushed steel surface.

"Mira, you were a great captain." She paused, looking down at her boots. "Actually, you were the only captain I knew, but you were pretty great." She clutched the combined mass of the locket and the two halves of the navigator's coin under the material of her jumpsuit, holding it all tight.

"I came to this ship running from the shadows of my past." She looked back at Mira through the plexiglass, then returned her gaze to the crew, "I've been alone for a long time, and I carried so much anger at my mother for sacrificing herself for me, for leaving me."

She paused again, looking down at her feet for a moment, *No… that was a lie.* She cleared her throat. "I was a pickpocket on the streets of the Dredges. I wasn't alone… I had three friends who were my responsibility… and I failed them."

She had promised herself that she wouldn't cry, but she knew that some promises were impossible to keep, her cheeks were soaked.

"Poor Milo…" she smiled past her tears, "he was six, he carried this stupid little doll around everywhere, it never left his side." She looked up to the ceiling, she couldn't meet the gaze of any of her crewmates, she was too vulnerable. She laughed, "He had a cute little makeshift bandoleer with a pocket just for his Olly Polly, that's what he called the doll." Her voice stuttered and quivered, she was losing it. She tried and failed to regain her composure, continuing on, her voice spasming, "When… I came… home to get them… they were gone… all that was left… was Olly Polly. He was tossed aside… a rag abandoned… by the only one who mattered to him. Milo, forgive me." She couldn't go on any longer, she struggled to regain her composure for a long moment, wiping away her tears, unable to speak her heart, feeling stupid and lost.

She began to calm herself, her fingers instinctively sliding down her shoulder, along the sleek metallic finish of her new cybernetic arm. Gone was the familiar sensation of the rust that had comforted her in the past.

She took a deep breath, changing the subject, "For years, all I felt was the weight of what I'd lost. But with you guys… with Mira…" Her voice caught, but she pushed it back and continued, "My father had always called the space elevator a ladder to freedom… I haven't felt truly free until now, here among my crew."

Tears streamed down her cheeks, but her voice caught a quiet confidence. "For the first time in four years, I'm glad you saved me, Mom. I would never have met Mira, my aunt, or her wonderful crew—"

A low murmur interrupted her, erupting from the crew.

That one will cost me, Elara thought. *I just dropped a truth that can't be unspoken. But this isn't the moment to survive it. This moment belongs to her.* A sea of confusion and questions reverberated against the bulkheads. Elara closed her eyes and hung her head, letting the commotion die out.

She swallowed, drawing strength from her crew... her newfound family. "Mira taught me so much. She taught me that anger... that impulsiveness... can lead you down a dark path. I almost learned that lesson the hard way," she held her up a finger gun and pretended to shoot at Sylen.

Sylen played along, jutting his tongue out, crossing his eyes, and pretending to get shot. Elara let him play out his mimicry. Then her voice fell low, soft, "She taught me to choose what was right, even if it's hard. Because of that, because of her, we're all still here."

She held up the brushed steel depth gauge in her hands, "A gauge, to mark the depth, Mira. To remember the incredible pressure you had to withstand to keep us all alive. You never broke, and neither will we." She trotted into the airlock and knelt beside Mira's body, sliding the depth gauge into the vinyl sack and zipping it closed. She then stood up and trotted back out to rejoin her crew.

Varek stepped up to the control panel, his hand hovering over the controls. He pressed the control to shut the inner hatch. It slid closed silently, as if the ship itself offered its own reverence.

Kael called out to his crew, "Stand to," then raised the boatswain's whistle to his lips and blew once, sharp and final.

Varek's hand paused for a moment, then he took a deep breath and pressed the button. The outside door to the airlock slid open.

The sudden, silent vacuum pulled Mira's body out into space.

She was gone.

All that remained was the promise they had just made her.

Epilogue

Sylen stood at the tactical panel, running a final diagnostic loop on the aging railgun system He had told the captain, Mira that is, before they had left New Geneva that the entire system needed to be replaced. She had only smiled with her usual confident flair and told him, *"I know you can make do, Sylen. You always do."* He'd been refitting the entire system since they left the spaceport, and it still wasn't ready.

The brutal pirate clan known as the Blood Reavers had laid claim on the Phoenix Reaches, it was common knowledge. There was no way they would be fully prepared if the bullets started to fly. There was no doubt in Sylen's mind that the crew was stepping into the rift.

Kael had made it clear that their orders would take utmost precedent. They had one narrow window to reach the target sector before the Dominion forces did, and he was determined to lay claim on that small strip of useless space for the slagged AP that had sent them on this fool's errand.

Elara had managed to make a more permanent repair of the life support system. Instead of running out of the stale, dizzying oxygen in the next couple hours, her repair job had brought on the conditioners to make what little air they had left as sharp and clean as the precision snap of a newly calibrated magneto rifle lock. However, the scrubbers were still on limp mode, leaving the crew with maybe a day or two of breathable air.

At least our last breath will taste sweet.

She'd wanted to finish the repairs properly, but no, Kael had demanded that she get to work on the propulsion systems that had been damaged by Varek's explosion. She had managed to get the propulsion up and running, but despite her protestations, Kael demanded that they get a move on, the nav computer had made the calculations, and they were ready for the jump.

Captain Kael, he said we were ready… ready my ass. We're slag against the Blood Reavers. Half a life support system, a jury-rigged propulsion system, and the railguns? Sylen was doing his best. After being laid up in the infirmary for the past few days, he barely got the system up and running but hadn't had a second to run any diagnostics yet.

He leaned in to check the railgun's diagnostic. As he straightened, a shadow flickered at the edge of his enhanced vision. It was too quick to be anything, but Sylen snapped his head to the port-side bulkhead.

Nothing, Just the dull gleam of the plastisteel.

He started to return his gaze back to the panel but then saw another faint shadow dart into the floor plating near the base of the tactical station. He kicked his heavy boot out instinctively, expecting to feel resistance, but his foot met only cold, empty metal.

Just the ship settling, he told himself, but the cold prickle down his spine said otherwise. He'd seen those flickers since the vision.

They were brief, wrong, gone the moment he turned toward them, yet they left behind the unnerving feeling of being tracked by something that didn't cast a physical reflection.

The intercom squelched to life, and Elara's voice crackled, clean and resonant with resolve, *"Engineering reporting in. Jump drive ready for execution."*

She's just like Lillibet, so much fire. God, I miss her. Perhaps after we're done with all this Phoenix Reaches nonsense, I can take some time to go see her.

A smile pulled at his lips, his mind returning to Elara. He remembered the way she had stood there in the server room, her arm twitching, her brow furrowed. He laughed at himself, *I know it was a dire moment, I wonder what would've happened if I'd told her the safety was on. Would she have switched it off and ended me? I would've deserved it if she had. The tremendous strain she's endured. It didn't break her, it tempered her. If only I had so much strength.*

A phantom tugged at his lips, a memory that he was barely conscious of. *When I was dying there in the cargo bay . . .* he touched his lips with the tips of his titanium fingers. *Something strange . . . God, I wish I could remember, but I feel like I should be dead . . . like something stronger pulled me back from the brink. Heh, why am I thinking about this now?*

"Understood," Kael, the new captain, replied. Sylen watched the young man from across the bridge.

A familiar tension knotted in Kael's shoulders. *Mira's command chair,* he stifled a chuckle, *it almost swallows him despite his outward attempts to remain calm.*

Kael's gaze flickered with a nervous energy, a silent plea for reassurance that Sylen recognized. *He's trying to fill her boots. Good luck, kid,* he grunted to himself. *It'll take nerves of steel to get us out of a confrontation with space pirates, given the best conditions, let alone with the* Aurora *limping like a battered heavy artillery battery being dragged onto the final line of defense.*

Kael turned to Zora. "Sensors report."

Zora looked back at him, her violet eyes darting with concern. *She can feel something's off,* Sylen knew that she had a knack for sensing when things were about to go awry.

She hesitated. The entire crew was put into a tremendous amount of strain to make sure the *Aurora* would make the next jump. She took a breath, the final decision set, "I don't know about this, Captain," she finally raised her voice, but only just enough. She returned her gaze to the console, then back to Kael. "The long-range sensors aren't picking up any contacts, but I have a bad feeling about this."

Sylen detected a slight tremble in her fingers as they hovered over the console, the way her shoulders hunched inward, as if physically retreating from the spotlight. *Way to go, girl, tell him.* Her instincts, Sylen knew, were rarely wrong, sharp as a honed blade. "*That's it, Zora, trust your instincts,*" the words that he had spoken to her countless times before echoed in his mind.

Zora shook her head, her gaze acquiescing to the sterile data on the console. She closed her eyes and exhaled a sharp breath, "Coast's clear, Captain," her voice was shaky, unsure. "My readings don't show any contacts at the destination."

"Understood." Kael whistled, clearing his throat. He wasn't listening to her, not really, he only heard what he wanted to hear. He turned his attention back to Sylen, "Make sure the weapon systems are charged up and ready," he paused, "in case the nebulae are scrambling the long-range sensors." He took a deep breath and hesitated a moment, then leaned in, "Just keep us on our toes, okay Sylen?"

Sylen nodded and let the air out of his lungs in a loud grunt, "Aye, sir." *Can't you see it, Captain? The crew is on edge, we're not ready for this. Just give Elara the chance to get the ship fully repaired, and let me make sure the railgun is operating properly.* And yet he knew why Kael wouldn't wait. Every wasted hour brought the Dominion closer. Waiting wasn't safe. It was surrender. *Give us a fighting chance.* He ran his mechanical hand over his face and let the thick fingers settle into his brown hair. He let out a low, rumbling sigh.

His gaze swept over the bridge, assessing the nervous energy. *Elara's quiet determination, Zora's lingering fear, even Varek,* who sat wordlessly at the science station, *his face a mask of strange focus. This is the crew, a disparate collection of damaged souls. And I? The monster of Ares Prime? I'm the worst of them all, and somehow I've found a place among them.*

A fleeting, painful image of Lillibet, smiling in the photograph, flashed through his mind, a sharp pang of guilt settled in his gut. *I'll protect them at all costs. Penance for my sins.*

Kael pressed a control on his console, "Jump in ten, nine, eight…" he began the countdown.

The act was unnecessary, but it was a ritual Captain Mira had maintained. *"It's reminiscent of humanity's first attempts to penetrate the veil of space,"* she had told Sylen. He smiled, *the urge for adventure, for exploration is no less powerful now than it was four centuries ago.*

Kael continued the count, "Three… two… one… mark—"

His words were cut off. The seconds stretched, thick with anticipation. A deep, familiar thrum reverberated beneath Sylen's feet. It was a vibration that had always signaled Mira's command, her control. This time, however, it was filled with Kael's subtle uncertainty, his inexperience.

The air crackled with kinetic energy. The jump vibrated through Sylen's cybernetic limbs, and then… All sound ceased, the bridge was the kind of quiet one would hear the night before a bloody skirmish. The starfield outside the bridge's viewport turned blinding white with stars… a single, brief tear in reality.

Then… the moment was gone.

The starfield returned to view, but it was choked with dozens of ships, painted in crimson.

The klaxon blared from the intercom, *"Proximity alert! Proximity alert! Unidentified craft detected!"* the robotic voice shrieked.

A massive battleship slid into view, its angular bulk eclipsing the other pirate ships like a predator. Sylen's breath hitched, the action startling his conditioned reflexes. *The primary weapon ports, the angled prow… The Phoenix!*

He knew that silhouette better than his own face. It hadn't been since the Veridia massacre, since his brother, Dread Admiral Torvax, thought he had won the war. *He's alive. He's here.*

The realization hit with the force of an armored shell. *The man who ruined our family. Who let the Prime Minister shackle Lillibet to a gilded throne, he's staring right through his viewport.* The hatred was a dizzying wave, quickly followed by the cold dread of absolute certainty. *We're not just facing pirates. We're facing the man who destroyed me. Only, this time… there's no escape.*

"Kael!" Zora spun in her seat, her voice tight with panic. "There are twenty frigates, seven destroyers, three cruisers, and one battleship. The battleship is hailing us on a Dominion channel, sir."

The war hadn't ended. It had only just remembered his name.

The End of Volume One, to be continued in Volume Two: Reach of the Phoenix.

Acknowledgements

This book was powered by an alarming amount of caffeine and the hospitality of several local Beaverton landmarks. My gratitude goes to the crews at the **Einstein Bros. and Starbucks on Nimbus** for the early morning fuel, and to the team at **Insomnia Coffee Co. in Murray Hill** for providing the perfect atmosphere to tackle the harder chapters.

A special nod to the crew at the **Cedar Hills Starbucks**—and specifically to the cute barista: may your glasses ever be whipped-cream free. Let's just say I enjoy working there for two reasons, and the plethora of electrical outlets is only the second.

Building the **Galactic Powderkeg Universe** required a crew that could handle high-pressure environments and even higher creative stakes.

My deepest thanks to the 'Engineers of Sound' who built the sonic foundation of *Aurora's Edge*: **Liliia Kysil**, for providing the hauntingly beautiful vocals, and **Nathanial Wolkstein**, for the violin work that gave the trailer its grit and soul. To **Kamarpro_Studios**, thank you for rendering the backgrounds with more atmosphere than the sector actually possesses.

On the visual and structural front, I owe a debt to

Reece-Alexander Norris-Paterson for a cover that commands attention, and to my editors, **Lucy Benedict** and **Marnie Macrae**. They were the final line of defense against my more questionable impulses, tightening the bolts on this story until it was space-worthy.

To the illustrators who populated the world for our campaign—**Charli Hinson, Christian Gomez, Niki Mitsuki, Shibushio, Alessandro Battini, Yurisa Adhi, Emily Davis,** and **Tallah Watkins**—thank you for visualizing what was previously only a series of complex equations in my head. And a very special shout-out to **Carolina Fitzgerald**; it turns out talent is the one thing in this universe that can't be engineered—it has to be inherited.

To my editors and the veterans who kept this project from red-lining: the hangar doors are open. To the readers, the artists, and the thinkers who see the universe not just for what it is, but for what it could be: you are the reason Chronos Press exists. Let's see what this thing can do.

About the Author

 **Dane Reavers** writes from a life spent inside the machines. A US Navy veteran, he served as an Electronics Technician aboard the USS Vandegrift, navigating the world from the ports of Bahrain to Hong Kong. After the Navy, he returned to his roots in Portland, Oregon, working everywhere from the Nike Air-sole factory to the cleanrooms of Intel.

With a BS in Electrical Engineering from Portland State University, he later designed the very power and signal distributions that keep modern industrial systems running. This lifetime of technical expertise is the backbone of *Aurora's Edge*, where he brings a "wrench-in-hand" authenticity to the grit and gears of deep space. A father of three, he continues to live and write in the Pacific Northwest, dedicated to stories of the people who keep the engines turning when everything else fails.